THUNDERCLOUDS
OVER
AMERICA

THUNDERCLOUDS OVER AMERICA

Frits Forrer

Holland's Glory   PO Box 488, Gulf Breeze, FL 32562

This is a work of fiction. Names, characters, places, and incidents either are the product of the author's imagination or are used fictitiously. Any resemblance to actual events or persons, living or dead, is entirely coincidental.

Copyright © 2010 by Frits Forrer

All rights reserved. No part of this book may be reproduced or transmitted in any form or by any means, electronic or mechanical, including photocopying, recording, or by any information storage and retrieval system, without permission in writing from the author.

This edition was prepared for printing by
Ghost River Images
5350 East Fourth Street
Tucson, Arizona 85711
ghostriverimages.com

Cover illustration by Betty Shoopman
bcshoop@bellsouth.net

Contact the author at:
fforrer@bellsouth.net   or
www.fritsforrer.net
850-916-7566

ISBN 978-0-9822207-2-6

Library of Congress Control Number: 2010904677

Printed in the United States of America

April, 2010

10 9 8 7 6 5 4 3 2 1

Contents

DECEMBER 11, 2009	9
SAILING ON THE HAARLEMMER MEER	15
HEZBOLLAH, TRIPOLI	21
LATVIA	26
THE BALTIC SEA	31
ABOARD THE *JOPPA*	37
PRISONER ABOARD THE ISRAELI FRIGATE.	42
FBI, SECAUCUS, N.J.	48
TRIPOLI, LEBANON	53
BETWEEN FOUR WALLS	59
FBI, N.J.	64
MEZZADE PRISON, ISRAEL.	70
FBI, N.J.	76
WASHINGTON, D.C.	81
BEIRUT, HEZBOLLAH HEADQUARTERS.	87
FBI, N.J.	93
FBI, N.J.	99
FBI, N.J.	105
FBI, N.J.	111
TETERBORO AIRPORT, N.J.	116
NORTH BERGEN POLICE HEADQUARTERS.	122
FBI, N.J.	128
HAZMIEN HOTEL	133
NORTH BERGEN, NJ. POLICE HEADQUARTERS	138
LANGLEY AIR FORCE BASE, VIRGINIA.	144
FBI, N.J.	148
FBI, N.J.	154
FBI, N.J.	158
FBI, N.J.	164
FBI, N.J.	169
MANHATTAN	175
CALDWELL H.S. STADIUM.	181
FBI, N.J.	186
FBI, N.J.	192
THE HAZMIEN HOTEL	197
NORTH BERGEN FORMER POLICE STATION.	202
NORTH BERGEN, FORMER POLICE STATION	208
FBI, N.J.	214
NORTH BERGEN POLICE STATION.	220
FBI, N.J.	226
FBI, N.J.	232
FBI, N.J.	238
QUEENS BOROUGH CEMETERY	243
LOWER MANHATTAN	249

RITZ-CARLTON 255
QUEENS BOROUGH CEMETERY. 261
TWIN TOWERS MEMORIAL 266
BEIRUT, HEZBOLLAH HEADQUARTERS. 271
QUEENS BOROUGH CEMETERY. 277
CALDWELL, N.J., BONGERS HOME 281

EPILOGUE 287

AUTHOR'S NOTE

This is a work of FICTION, pure and simple. Exciting, but simple.

Many thanks to my number one spelling genius, my Katy.

Also, thanks to the dedicated members of the West Florida Literary Federation that make up the *"Writers Anonymous"*: Joe Hefti, Jim Webster, Andrea Walker, Judy Fawley, Diane Skelton, Jeanie Zokar, Lynn Huber, Dr. Joe and Marilyn Howard. My *English* improved daily under their watchful eyes.

The critique from my buddies in the *Belles & Beaux* was very helpful and inspiring. True buddies: Kay, Selma, Fred, true buddies indeed.

Special thanks to Pauline Bensman, Debbi Campanella and Marci Douglas for their outstanding critiques.

Again, many thanks,

Frits

Dedicated to

KYLE, RUSSELL and JOHN,
serving in the
Air Force, Marines and Navy.
Thank you, men!

Chapter One

DECEMBER 11, 2009
TRIPOLI, LEBANON

"Parlez moi d'amour." Yousef was singing in the shower. *"Redite moi des choses tendres!"* His voice resonated through the empty house. He had every right to be overjoyed. His new love was exquisite, his upcoming assignment was exciting and all his dreams seemed to be falling into place.

From his bathroom window he could see for miles across the blue Mediterranean and the gentle waves reminded him of earlier days and earlier romances. It seemed hard to believe that it was just two years ago when had he sailed the lakes of Holland with the love of his life. His first true love really or at least true infatuation.

He continued reminiscing as he dried himself while strolling into the bedroom. The waves outside his window were different, longer, rolling endlessly, south to south-east. On the Haarlemmermeer, they were choppy, shorter, and more playful. "Like my life," he thought.

"Playful, choppy."

At that time he was an engineering student at the University of Delft, in the Netherlands, two years from graduation. The school had an outstanding reputation and the staff was most cooperative when it came to translating the lecture into English or French. English came naturally to him because of all the American and British top-hits of his era. Years ago Beirut had been called '*The Paris of the East*' with all the casinos and nightclubs and the radio in his parents' home near Tripoli resounding with Elvis and Beatles music.

French was actually his second language. His mother was a native of Morocco and insisted speaking that melodious tongue in her home, rather than that *"abrasive Arabic,"* as she called it.

As a result he had no problems with the courses at the ancient and revered school and he fit in rather well with the many other foreign students. Girls and parties were aplenty and that suited him fine. An Italian girl had become his regular bed partner, but his main interest had become a Dutch girl, named Ankie. Blonde and blue-eyed, she shared some of his advanced math classes and was always willing to help with the translations from Dutch into English. French was not her forté.

Over coffee in one of the many cafés, they revealed their pasts, their likes and dislikes and their personalities. She steadfastly refused his cigarettes and hash, but would gladly drink a beer. Yousef was just the opposite; no alcohol, but soft drugs and cigarettes had become part of his existence. She also steadfastly refused to accompany him to some of the swinging parties that sprung up every weekend in the medieval town.

The more she turned him down, the more interested he became. He wasn't used to having women resist his handsome good looks and his sexy smile. While he kept up his sexual activities at night, he sought out Ankie more and more and lunches and dinners became very frequent. In his Arabian mind, he could easily justify his infidelities, because after all, sex was at least as necessary as eating, drinking and exercise.

When one day he asked her, "What do you do for excitement?" she answered, "Sailing!"

"Sailing? That's it? What's so phenomenal about sailing?"

"It's a good workout, it takes skill, and it's fun. Lots of fun."

"Would you take me some time?"

"Sure!"

The train trip on Saturday morning took only a half hour and the ensuing bus connection twenty minutes. They were outside the little village of Halfweg, literally half way between Amsterdam and Haarlem. A five-minute walk landed them at a neat-looking farmhouse that had rows and rows of greenhouses behind it. It seemed like there were miles of them.

"Is this your dad's business? What grows in there?"

"What grows in there? Where have you been? This is Holland. Flowers! Flowers everywhere!" She exclaimed, "We grow roses in some and gladiolas in the others. Thousands of them."

"Is that why you're majoring in math? So you can count them all?"

"Haha! That's funny. No, I take math so I can count all the money rolling in. Hahaha."

She laughed at her own joke. "Let's see who's at home and if anyone wants to go sailing with us."

Only her mother was home and she greeted Yousef with polite reservation. She ignored his hand and nodded, "How do you do?" Her English was heavily accented. She frowned when Ankie directed the young stranger to her bedroom to change into his shorts.

"What are you doing with that man?" she asked her daughter when Yousef was out of earshot.

"What am I doing with that man?" Her voice echoed her surprise. "Doing with him? I'm gonna show him how to sail. He's never done that."

"Why this foreigner? Aren't there any Dutch boys at your school?" They had switched to Dutch while alone in the room, but reverted back to English when the young Lebanese reappeared.

"Is nobody else home?" Ankie addressed her mother.

"They're all working, but they'll be here for supper, that's for sure."

"Okay, we'll be back by then. Come on, Joe! We're about to sail the stormy seas! See ya, Ma." She gave her mother a fleeting kiss and led her friend out of the house, through the backyard to a long dock that berthed several boats.

11

Ankie had travelled in shorts and sneakers and seemed ready to tackle any seaworthy craft, but the boat she jumped onto was the smallest of the trio that was tied up along the wooden pier. It was barely sixteen feet long.

"Stand there and undo the lines when I holler." She bent over and bailed water out of the bottom with a rusted coffee can until it showed less than an inch of water.

"It hasn't rained much of late apparently. Okay, untie the lines and hop aboard."

His first sailing adventure reminded him more of Venice than Holland. Ankie produced a long pole and expertly pushed them away from the slip and through the narrow channel until they drifted onto the lake. After attaching a line to the top end, the pole was positioned in a hole in the center seat and a keel was dropped through a contraption in the middle of the vessel. As far as Yousef was concerned, it was barely big enough to be a rowboat and certainly not big enough to be a sailboat.

A triangular sail, attached to the vertical mast and controlled by a line on the far end, had them speeding along at a whopping three kilometers an hour, about two mph. He laughed uproariously at the gymnastics she performed in order to keep the raft from tipping over. She ducked underneath the sail as it swung from port to starboard while manipulating the rudder with her left hand and controlling the sail with the other.

Apparently Ankie didn't appreciate his humor as much as he did, and with a swift toss of the sail, while pushing the rudder in the opposite direction, she pitched him overboard into the choppy waters of the Haarlemmer Meer.

Now it was her turn to laugh. Within seconds, she was twenty feet away from her victim and while he was screaming and waving in the cold water, she turned the boat in a big circle and headed back toward the soaked engineering student. Curling the sail around the mast, the vessel slowed, but became less maneuverable, and she passed within ten feet from him. Up went the sail again, back into the wind, cutting and tacking until she nearly ran over him, so he could grab the sideboard and hoist himself back in.

"How do you like sailing?" She giggled.

"If the water wasn't so damn cold, I might enjoy it." He stripped off his jacket and shirt and tied them onto the mast with their sleeves. "They'll dry in a minute, I hope."

"They will, they will." She was still laughing.

Not chancing to stand up and get pitched again, Yousef crawled to the back of the boat and grabbed Ankie in a bear hug. "Willing to go overboard too?"

"Who will rescue us?" She held on tightly to the rudder handle but kept on laughing. "You should have seen yourself diving overboard. I wish I had a camera."

The young Lebanese didn't relax his grip on her and nuzzled his face onto her throat and groaned softly . . . "You smell so nice." . . . groan . . . "Dutch flowers? . . . Right?"

Ankie enjoyed the wet embrace and forgot all about sailing. She dropped the line that controlled the sail and pulled his head up to her face, so she could brush his lips. They had been friends for four months, but had never kissed. The gentle brush turned into a passionate embrace and not until he tried to slip his hand into her bra did she stop him.

She came up for air and breathed, "No, no, no, no!" and pulled away. "Let's sail some more."

"Let's not!" He pulled her close again, but she was adamant.

"No, no! Come on, get back in the bow, and I'll steer for home before the wind dies and strands us in the middle of the lake."

She knew what she was doing, because the sail barely fluttered anymore and the waves became just a light chop. His clothes were still too wet, so in his bare chest, he admired her navigational skills, because he had no notion where they were or where her house was. Everything looked the same in all directions. A distant church tower, an occasional house, lots of reeds along the coastline and softly babbling waves under the bow. That was it, no matter where he looked.

Ankie started to sing softly, "*Hoe zachtjes glijdt ons bootje al op het spieglend meer. De riempjes net en proper, gaan lustig op en neer."*

"What are you singing?"

"About us. About a little boat slowly gliding along on a peaceful lake, just like we're doing. Isn't that romantic?"

"I'd find it more romantic if I were holding onto you again."

"Patience, boy. Patience."

2

SAILING ON THE HAARLEMMER MEER

Yousef was getting more and more impressed by Ankie's handling of the sail, the rudder, the pole and the docking. Her movements were so smooth, her body so supple and graceful, that he thought to himself, "This is a different kind of woman, so self-assured, so capable. I could probably spend the rest of my life with someone like that."

It wouldn't happen though.

He had barely changed back into his slacks and a sweater when the men came in from the field. Her three brothers and their father, Hendrik.

"*Wat is hier aan de hand?*" ("What the hell is going on here?") Those were the first words out of Hendrik's mouth.

"*Dit is mijn vriend Yousef.*" ("This is my friend Yousef.") Ankie switched to English as she stepped in front of her fellow student. "I invited him to come sailing with me."

"Well, he's not welcome here, and get him the hell out of the house."

"But why, Pop? Why? What has he done?"

"What has he done? What are they doing? They're murdering

women and children, even their own kind. They murdered our politician Pim Fontein and our filmmaker Van Gogh, because they spoke up against the way they treat their women, and you bother to bring him into this house and worse than that, take him sailing. You're lucky you didn't get raped or killed or both. These bastards . . ."

"Papa! Yousef is a nice man . . ."

"A nice man? My ass! They're a bunch of religious fanatics, that'll kill you faster than they can say Allah. Get him out of here and . . ."

Yousef raised his hand and tried to step in front of the girl, but she stopped him. "I think you owe him an apology. You don't even know this man. You don't even know if he's Muslim . . ."

"I can tell 'em from a mile away, and most of the time I can even smell 'em. We're gonna run them out of the country, just like they're doing in Denmark. We don't want any more foreigners in Holland who won't fit in with our culture and customs, who insist on treating their women as inferior human beings and kill people who speak up against them. Holland has always been the most generous and hospitable country in the world. We took in the Jews during the Spanish Inquisition. We welcomed the Pilgrims from England and the Huguenots from France when they were persecuted, and they all became citizens and mingled with our population without murdering anybody or pushing their warped opinions on us. These Muslims are trying to take over, and they don't care who they hurt or who they murder. Well, I'm gonna set an example and run this dark-skinned bastard out of our house and if you ever associate with him again, I'll take you out of that fancy school and put you to work on the farm and . . ."

"You can't do that Pop . . ."

"Oh, no? Right now, as we speak, they're probably raping a young girl and then declare that she has disgraced herself in the face of Allah. and she gets conned into blowing herself up in a busy market place, killing innocent women and children under the pretense of redeeming herself with Allah. What a bunch of crap. Innocent women and children . . ." He pointed at his wife. "Not fighting against other soldiers . . . No, women . . . The cowardly bastards."

He took a step forward and pointed his finger at the Lebanese. "Get out of here before I get a pitchfork and give you some of your own medicine."

Two of his boys stepped in front of their father and the taller one said. "I'll drive him to the station . . ."

"Like hell you will. Let him walk. Maybe he can hitch a ride on a camel . . ."

"Pop! . . ." But Ankie was pushed out of his way and the mother stepped in front of her husband. "Papa, calm down. He'll leave and we'll eat."

"Come on." The big brother waved at Yousef. "I'll get you back to the station."

"You do and you won't get back in this house. No one here is gonna support those criminal bastards . . ."

Yousef moved around Ankie and edged his way to the door, while she reached for him. "I'm so sorry . . ."

"You better be sorry." Her dad cut back in. "Get out! Get going and never talk to my daughter again . . ." The door closed behind the student.

"Pop, he may not even know how to get out of here . . ."

"Good. I hope he drowns."

"Hendrik! Hendrik! Is this a Christian way of treating somebody?" Mama nearly screamed at him.

"It sure as hell is my way of treating a murdering criminal, and he's lucky he got outta here alive."

"Ankie, come on, let's set the table."

For Yousef, it was a sobering experience. As he walked along the dike toward the lights of town, his mind raced in different directions.

Until today, he had been very fond of the Dutch people. They all seemed so gentle and friendly, but he had read about the undercurrent, a groundswell of resentment, especially when a most popular politician was murdered. He didn't agree with all the Turks, Moroccans and Algerians who set up their own communities and continued in their own customs, wearing headpieces and veils. They even insisted that young girls should be able to wear them in schools or in the pictures for driver's licenses and passports. They, obviously, were not trying to fit in.

When he reached the outskirts of the little village, he looked for a bus stop, so he could make it back to Halfweg and catch a train. A passing policeman on a bike steered him in the right direction, and two hours later he was back in his flat in Delft. He realized that old Hendrik's attitude was indicative of the feelings of a lot of Dutchmen and would possibly get worse.

So he packed his bag and called the airlines. He made up his mind never to return to Holland and to hate every *non-believer* from here on in. That was the beginning of his true conversion to Islam. Until that day, his folks had not been very deeply religious and Yousef himself never had any cause to visit a mosque very often. That all changed on that pleasant afternoon in Holland. Not only did he study the Quran on a daily basis, he became a fanatic, obsessed with Muslim's laws and teachings. He joined the *Hamas* organization and participated in raids in the Golan Heights, blowing up Jewish outposts and launching rockets into the Kibbutzim across the Israeli border.

On one of his missions in Beirut, he encountered a beautiful woman who fast became the only love interest in his life. Lavana was French of Moroccan descent. Because of her European looks, Yousef strongly suspected that her real father was actually French, rather than Moroccan, but she never hinted at that. According to her story, her parents had migrated to France from Tangier in the 1960's, and there was no hint that her mother had ever been unfaithful.

The important thing was, she was twenty-four and beautiful. The fact that she was two years older than Yousef didn't bother either one of them, and their sex life was great. She was insatiable. She could do it morning, noon, and night, and he did his best to keep up with her.

Her body was perfect, and she worked out regularly, keeping it that way.

All these thoughts were running through his mind while he dressed and gathered up his papers for the trip into the town of Tripoli. The leadership of Hamas had summoned him to join in a meeting with Iraqi Saddam Hussein sympathizers who had escaped Iraq before the Americans could get to them.

According to rumors, these *"Freedom Fighters"*, as they called themselves, had years of experience in sabotage, murder and torture. Whatever mission they were planning, Yousef was anxious to get involved and he was flattered to have been invited to such an important event.

His father's old Citroen was still in mint condition and it took him into the ancient part of town in just twenty minutes. The problem was where to park it where no one would steal his tires or mirrors. A generous tip to a gas-station attendant ensured him protection and he continued on foot, repeating the directions in his mind until he reached an old four-story brick building that once had been painted white. Probably a century ago.

The massive wooden doors wouldn't budge when he tried the handle, but a brass knocker got someone's attention, and a small gate swung open in the left half of the ancient portal.

No one was in sight, so Yousef crossed the open courtyard and tried the knob on a standard size door. It opened noiselessly and within two steps he landed in a dark hallway. Ten more paces and he was in front of a curtain that easily swung aside and revealed a large room with pillows and low tables along three of the walls.

Six men in traditional Arab garb were sitting in a semi circle, sipping mint tea and smoking hash.

"Sit, brother, sit!" A large man in the center of the group pointed to a hassock in the middle of the oval and smiled broadly. "Welcome, Yousef. You know some of us here and let me introduce the rest. I am Ahmed Bin Behumed. Originally from Iran. Presently from Gaza.

To my right . . ." He continued introducing each one, while his piercing black eyes tried to penetrate Yousef's after each name he called out.

Yousef wondered if he was being scrutinized for any reactions of recognition, but his face remained a blank. He had never heard some of the names before, only the three members that he had worked with in the past.

Ahmed had a well-trimmed black beard and mustache, neatly cropped to elongate his brown face. His attitude and posture indicated that he was used to being in command, and Yousef knew instinctively that he had to respect and obey that man.

To what extent, he'd soon learn.

3

HEZBOLLAH, TRIPOLI

Of the three men in the room that Yousef had worked with before, Hassan Nasrallah was probably the most famous, or infamous, depending on one's viewpoint. He allegedly masterminded the assassination of Prime Minister Rafiq Hariri. Besides that, Yousef had worked with him in the Golan Heights, and he knew the man as being absolutely ruthless.

"Kill the Jews! Kill the Israelis! Drive them out of Palestine!" Were his regular shouts of encouragement as they lobbed grenades into the valley.

The other two he recognized as the organizers of Hezbollah in Lebanon. They had initiated the crusade against the Catholics, who had been a majority at one time. Also the attack on the American Marines had been credited to these fanatic terrorists.

He felt he was in great company, nearly the same as being invited to the Royal Palace in the Netherlands. He was anxious to find out why they needed him. He hadn't proven himself as yet, other than that he followed orders and was fearless under fire. He wondered if his faith was about to be tested.

A handclap produced a servant who refreshed the tea and poured the new visitor a steaming glass of mint brew. After the man withdrew, the meeting came to order. At least some sort of order.

Ahmed Bin Behemud took the lead. "Young man, we've been watching you and we hope that you will aspire to do great things for the glory of Allah. Before we go into your possible next assignment, we have some questions. Your mother? Was she raised in the Catholic religion?"

"No, she was raised as a Muslim, initially in Tangier and later in France." Yousef was puzzled by the question.

The older man didn't change his expression. "Did you attend Catholic services here in Lebanon?"

""Yes, I attended a Parochial school from the age of six to ten, when I transferred to a public school in Tripoli. Why?"

"I'll ask the questions." Ahmed appeared annoyed. "Was your father a Catholic?"

"No, he was raised as a devout Muslim in Persia at an early age, right above our border, and when he was twelve, his folks moved south to Lebanon, where he met my mother."

"Where are they now?"

"My parents? In Beirut on business." The young man being questioned couldn't understand what his parents had to do with all this.

"But where do they live?"

"Live? In the same house where I live, just north of town. We've lived there for nearly twenty years."

"Your father is a rug merchant?"

"Yes, he learned rug weaving from his dad and grandfather, but he likes dealing in tapestries better than fabricating them and . . ."

"He makes a good living?"

"He has always provided well. Our house sits right on a cliff overlooking the Mediterranean, and he has provided us with a good education and . . ."

"Are you an engineer? Did you get a degree?"

"Yes, I studied in Holland, but ended up getting my degree from Stevens Institute in the USA"

"How did you like America?"

"Mixed emotions. The studies were hard, the professors were tough. The town was ugly . . ."

"What town?"

"Hoboken, New Jersey, right across from Manhattan. The local people…"

"Were you there during 9/11?"

"No, that was before my time. But like I was saying, the people in the neighborhood of the school were mostly Puerto Rican and Black and a lot of the students were from India and they all had one thing in common; they lived in filth. Rundown apartment buildings, junk cars in the streets, garbage all over the place…"

"Where did you live?"

"In a flat in Weehawken, just north of Hoboken, and I could make it back and forth to the institute in twenty minutes, so that wasn't too bad."

"So you speak English and French. Any German or Dutch?" The bearded man kept interrupting him.

"Some Dutch, but German? None."

"Can you write in French and English?"

"Certainly." He straightened his posture as if he wanted to add additional pride to his statement.

"Are you willing and able to undertake an important mission for Allah and our cause?"

"Well . . ., of course." He put much emphasis on his last words. For a moment he felt that his dedication to Islam was being questioned. "What's the mission?"

"A fairly easy one, but very important. We understand you have a girlfriend, yes?"

"Yes, why do you ask?"

"Let me remind you: *I ASK THE QUESTIONS!*" The black eyes sparked with anger. "Tell us about the girlfriend."

"Like my mother, she's of Moroccan descent, but born and raised in France, where she received . . ."

"Do you sleep with her?"

Yousef froze. Was that really any of their business? He hesitated and chuckled, "I try to stay awake with her."

That evoked some chuckles from the other men in the room, but

Ahmed was not amused.

"Would she travel with you as if she were your wife?"

Again, the young Lebanese was thoroughly puzzled. Travel where? And what danger might she be exposed to? "Probably." He answered. "But she works. How long would we be traveling? She may lose her job."

"You should not question this council or our intentions, but I can assure you, she'll be well compensated for her time. So back to my question; will she travel with you?"

"Oh, I'm sure she will. Is it important that she come with me?"

"There you go again with your questions. Submit to Allah's will and our orders and the Kingdom of Paradise will be yours."

Yousef stiffened. It sounded like he might not come back alive. He wasn't quite ready for that. "Will she be in danger?"

The black eyes flashed and his voice became loud. "Will you serve Allah unquestioningly, or do we look for another volunteer?"

"No sir, I will do as Allah wills me."

"That's better. Here's your mission. You will travel as husband and wife. Your passports will be ready. You're working for a national building company, and you will purchase lumber in Latvia. You and your wife will arrive in the capitol, stay in an elegant hotel, and you will inspect the materials that have already been ordered. You will oversee the loading of the Russian ship when it arrives at the docks in Riga. Here's where your engineering degree comes in. We don't want the boat to capsize because of an overload. You see, the hull will be filled with Russian and Chinese missiles, guns and ammo. Your job is to cover that load with lumber in such a way that it will withstand an inspection by Israeli or American warships. You see, you'll bring the boat through the Baltic, the North Sea and the Mediterranean and on to Kahn Yunis next to Gaza, where it will be unloaded."

He smiled at the befuddled Yousef and continued. "And the nice thing about all this is,..." He stopped and laughed. "All this is financed by the nice new president of the United States and his congress. Isn't that nice?" He laughed out loud, and the other members of the team laughed right along with him.

"You're kidding?" The young man smiled, but his face was one big question mark.

"No! Isn't that funny? The American Jews are actually paying for the rockets that will kill the Israeli Jews." The whole group roared with laughter. The merriment was contagious. Yousef started to howl along with them.

"Seriously now. Your mission will be to oversee every aspect of the transactions and the shipment. If you're stopped at sea, you'll provide the proper papers, and you will convince the potential attackers that this is a legitimate business transaction. In whatever language they speak."

"So," Yousef hesitated. "Lavana and I will be making the sea voyage as well?"

"Lavana? Lovely name. Yes, and both of you will be well paid."

"When will we be going?"

"In about three weeks. First, you'll be traveling to meet the execs of the building company and learn all about lumber. Then you'll fly to Riga and one of the first things you'll do there is to buy a luxurious fur coat for Lavana because it's cold up there and you'll want to look successful. Don't forget to tell her to thank the New York Jews!" His companions laughed out loud. He thought he was so funny.

"Wow!" was all Yousef could think of, but he said, "Allah il Allah!"

4

LATVIA

Riga was indeed cold. Not freezing, but cold just the same. It reminded him of fall and winter in Holland. The temperature was just above freezing, but a driving rain seemed to permeate everything. They bought heavy lined raincoats instead of a fur coat. Also fur-lined boots.

The city itself was reminiscent of his student days in Delft, like the many medieval buildings that were well kept and attractive. Whenever the rain stopped and Yousef had time available, they'd stroll the ancient streets and enjoy their walks along the *Daugava River.*

The 380 room *REVAL HOTEL* had all amenities and an excellent restaurant. The food was different from the Mediterranean cuisine that they were used to, but generally exquisite. Much to the pleasure of Lavana, the exercise room was a well-equipped unisex salon and during the long hours that her soul mate was gone, she worked out and lingered by the indoor pool with a good book.

They had checked in as a married couple from Paris, in town as representatives of a Lebanese building concern on a shopping mission for good quality Baltic hardwood. Everyone spoke English, and the taxi drivers were cautious and efficient. Yousef got to all the shippers and suppliers without any problems, but he had to make sure that he didn't slip into Arabic accidentally and having to explain why a Parisian business man mastered that language as well.

Theoretically, he was a French wholesaler, contracted by the Palestinians to buy and deliver a load of lumber. All went well, the lumber was already being stocked at the harbor and the *Motor Vessel VLADIVOSTOK* was due in two days.

Just one thing went wrong. A major argument evolved between them and worst of all, it happened in bed. After some passionate lovemaking, Lavana was playing with Yousef and remarked, "I'm so glad that you're not circumcised. You give me so much more pleasure."

Yousef shot up in bed and screamed, "How do you know? How do you know the difference? Have you slept with Jews? Have you? How . . . ?"

"No, no, no!" She jumped up as well. "Never! Yousef, never!"

"Then how do you know?"

"Yousef, many men are circumcised and . . ."

"No! Only Jews. Frenchmen and Moroccans aren't, so how can you compare the pleasure I give you with other men unless they're Jews?"

"Oh, Yousef, listen to me, please . . ." But he had gotten out of bed and pulled his pants on. Lavana reached for her peignoir and followed him to the bathroom, but he locked the door before she got there. She banged on the door.

"Yousef, please, don't do that to me. Please open up."

"Go away. Find another Jew."

"No, no, no. You gotta believe me. I swear by Allah . . ."

"Go away. Leave me alone."

She walked back to the bed and sprawled across it, heaving with sobs.

He slept in the other bed, and in the morning he refused to have breakfast with her or listen to her. He left her crying while he rushed to the harbor to check the last of the deliveries.

Upon his return, he found her packed and ready to go. "Please give me my passport and I'll be out of your life."

"You can't do that!"

"Yes, I can. I'm not your wife, nor will I ever be your wife because I have no desire to be the oldest of your four future wives and live under your stupid Muslim rules. I'm a free French citizen and I'm leaving right now."

"Now wait a minute. Let's sit down and order up some lunch and talk about this. I have done some thinking . . ."

"I don't care and I'm leaving. Just give me my passport." She remained standing.

Yousef walked over to the table and sat down. "I can't do that and I won't do that. I have a mission to complete . . ."

"I don't give a damn about your mission and . . ."

"You can't get out of the country without your passport, so sit down and listen to me a moment."

She remained standing.

"I've been thinking, " he continued, "I realize that you were not a twenty-three year old virgin when we met, but the idea that you would have slept with a Jew was so repulsive to me and . . ."

"American gentiles, every John, Joe and Bill and Harry are also circumcised, I think it's their military law, I don't know, but that is not really any of your damn business. I didn't ask you any questions about your past sex life, and you have no right to question mine either. Right now I had a brief forecast of what life would be like if I lived with you permanently and I don't like it, so why don't you just give me my papers, and we'll forget we ever met." She was still standing by the door.

Yousef reached for the phone. "I'm ordering lunch, so please . . ." He made a beckoning motion with his left hand. "Join me and let's calmly talk about this."

Since there was little she could do about it, they had decided on a temporary truce, but at night, he climbed into the spare bed with his underwear on. Neither one could sleep and before long, she crawled in with him, stark naked.

"Just kiss me, Yousef."

"We have a lot to talk about yet . . ."

"Not now. Just kiss me."

The *VLADIVOSTOK* was a 280 foot trawler that had seen better days, but was plenty sea-worthy according to its papers. The captain, a burly bearded man spoke enough English to con Yousef out of an additional $500 for himself, so, if inspected, they wouldn't notice that his precious weapons cargo was being cleverly hidden.

"My name is Gregorio Yuridanski, but everybody calls me Yuri. So can you. Now understand, I run the ship. You just tell me our destination and that's all. Do not interfere or question anything I do, or we'll toss you overboard. Your woman and you will have the first mate's cabin, but I have to have 25% of the freight in advance and the rest upon delivery."

"But sir, the freight has already been arranged with your company in Saint Petersburg and . . ."

"We'll see. I radio. Keep loading."

The result was, some telegraphs went back and forth to Beirut and St. Pete and a cash delivery of five big ones was made to the captain. He seemed pleased and offered some vodka that Yousef refused and that proved to be a mistake. The drink was meant to be a peace offering, but the young Lebanese didn't see it that way and his beliefs kept him from touching alcohol at all. The captain felt insulted.

Why the elders had insisted on an engineering degree back in Tripoli was incomprehensible. With all the weight of the armor in the bottom of the ship, it was impossible to ever capsize the boat with all the wood above it. A kindergarten kid could have figured that out, Yousef felt, but he did his job overseeing the loading anyway. The important thing was that an inspection team could not possibly discover all the metal cargo beneath the lumber. It seemed real simple.

Departure was scheduled for the following morning, after the ship took on additional diesel fuel. "Cheaper here." the captain explained.

At eight o'clock, the young "Parisian" couple boarded and moved into the cramped quarters that were to be their home for the next ten days. The main advantage was, it had its own little bathroom and shower, but otherwise, there was barely room to turn around.

"I'm glad I bought some good books. I guess we won't get to see a lot of beautiful scenery, and we won't visit any exotic ports, will we?" Lavana already dreaded the trip and they hadn't even left port yet.

"It won't take that long. Let's just hope for pleasant weather. The North Sea can spook sometimes, but it can also be very gentle. Let's hope for the latter."

The departure through the Riga harbor was very scenic, and they both hung on the rail, enjoying the fact that the visibility was great and there was very little wind. The breeze came from the east, probably from the dry steppes of central Russia. Their heavy raincoats and some ski hats were all the protection they needed for the moment, but both of them were looking forward to the warmer climate of their homeland.

The Baltic Sea looked black, compared to the blue waters that they were used to, or maybe it was the solid overcast that created that effect. Anyway, the sea didn't look inviting at all. Yousef tried to visit the bridge and follow along with the navigation, but was firmly rebuffed.

"Only for ship personnel." The sign was very explicit. He wished he'd bought some maps, so he could figure out their progress, but it was too late for that now. He decided he might as well start reading some of Lavana's books.

It might be a long boring trip, and he still didn't know how much Lavana and he were to be paid for their efforts, if any.

5

THE BALTIC SEA

It didn't take long before they could distinguish the Swedish mountains to the North, and as darkness approached, the ship maneuvered through the narrow straights of the *Kattegat* that separates Denmark from the European mainland. Yousef could have kicked himself for not bringing an Atlas, because he was dying to plot their position between the two countries. Before long they were back in open water, and even though it was dark, he knew that Norway had to be out there to his right. With nothing left to see but water, he retired to his cabin and the beautiful girl, completely wrapped up in a book.

"Ready to eat again?"

"Is it that late already?" She sat up in bed.

"I guess they don't ring a bell when it's dinnertime, but my stomach is a good indicator. You coming?"

"Give me just a moment." Lavana disappeared into the miniature bathroom.

The chow hall was half empty, and the young couple introduced themselves to the sailors whom they hadn't met during lunch. The men all eyed Lavana with wide-eyed appreciation, because she was indeed a beauty. Most of the crew was Russian, but all of them seemed to have a workable command of the English language, and the conversation during dinner flowed easily. The food was excellent, although a bit spicy and to Yousef's surprise, they served vodka with the meal. Somehow he had figured that no booze was allowed on these freighters, but maybe Russia was an exception. Lavana would have liked some, but she was afraid that she might upset her boyfriend again, so she politely declined.

After dinner, Yousef stood at the railing for hours, but with no moon or stars, he had no notion which way they were heading and he finally turned in.

The chuck-chuck-chuck of the engine easily lulled him to sleep, while Lavana kept reading.

The morning revealed nothing but fog, sometimes light, sometimes dense. The ship had slowed some, but with the radar swinging around steadily, the chances of a collision were minimal. When the weather cleared a little from time to time, Yousef determined that the sun was directly behind them, meaning they were heading due west. Later, when the sun moved to port, or slightly behind and to their left, it meant that their course was steady, while he felt they should be turning south toward the channel between England and France. The captain was inside the wheelhouse, and the young Lebanese didn't have the nerve to disturb him with questions about his navigation.

He returned for coffee in the mess room and at that point, the engines slowed and finally idled. Puzzled, Yousef carried his mug up top and to his surprise a warship appeared from the fog and started to pull alongside.

"Inspection?" flashed through his mind. "Americans? British? Norwegian?" The ship flew no flag and showed no markings, no name and no numbers. It showed plenty of muscle though. Cannons and machineguns were aimed at the Russian freighter, and without any audible announcements, the foreign navy ship slipped closer on a parallel course.

Because of the fog and the no-wind condition, the sea was very calm and a lifeboat was launched from the frigate and was alongside the *VLADIVOSTOK* in fifteen minutes.

Yousef moved to the side of the ship and watched with amazement at the agility of the seamen who exited the craft and climbed a rope ladder that was thrown over the side by the Russians.

What did surprise him even more was the fact that three uniformed foreign seamen straddled the rail, walked right up to him, pistols drawn and swung him around and handcuffed him. He started to scream, but was told, *"TA GUELLE, TOI!"* (Shut up) in no uncertain terms and was nearly thrown overboard into the lifeboat, which crossed over to the warship with their new captive.

The attack had a ripple effect over half the globe.

• • •

BEIRUT. Lebanon. Hezbollah Headquarters.
"Vladivostok disappeared off the map."

SAINT PETERSBURG. Russia. Georganik Freight Co.
"Vladivostok, missing in the North Sea near Iceland."

PORTREE HARBOR, Skye Island, Scotland. The Harbor Master.
"Dock alongside the Aegean Sea at slip 4 south."

WASHINGTON, USA. Associated Press.
"Russian freighter, carrying lumber, reported missing off Norway. Search initiated by British Navy."

TEL AVIV, Israel. Mossad Headquarters.
"We got the ship. Moving to Skye for weapons transfer. We have mastermind, Josef Saban. Please identify."

• • •

Yousef had no idea that within hours of his capture, he was

making international news. Well, he really wasn't, but his kidnapping and the capture of the Russian ship had made the airwaves, because a radio operator transmitted the news the moment the ship was boarded and minutes before the captain knocked him out with his pistol butt. Apparently, the radio man was about the only man aboard who wasn't in on the swindle.

The young *"Frenchman"* was protesting loudly that his capture was illegal, against all international laws, and demanded immediate release.

Well, the only release he got was the removal of his handcuffs while he was seated in a small cabin without portholes.

"We have your name as Josef Saban, born in Paris. What's your real name?" The grey haired Israeli had a very thin face and very piercing eyes. His crew cut told Yousef he was dealing with a military investigator. The question was posed in Arabic and he nearly fell for it.

"English, please!" He answered without flinching. "English or French."

The thin man continued in Arabic and Yousef deducted that he was probably born in Palestine and therefore definitely bi-lingual.

"We know that you intended to bring weapons to Gaza and we need to know who financed this whole deal."

The Lebanese was tougher than the Israelis expected. In French he asked, *"Quesque vous voulez?"* (What do you want?)

Thin face continued in English, "You probably know how Saddam Hussein managed to get information out of his prisoners. Don't you? Well, not many survived, but he got his information anyway and you have the same option. You may live or die. Your choice. You may also die after suffering unbelievable torture and after all that you may still see Allah and the seventy-two virgins, but the pain you'll endure is beyond your comprehension. Beyond human comprehension, but we don't care. We want the information and we'll get it. One way or the other. So…" He took a long drag from his cigarette. "Who financed this deal? The Arabs?" He waited for a reaction. "We know that the Palestinians don't have this kinda money. Bin Laden?"

"*J'ne sais quoi.*" (I don't know.)

The interrogator turned around and shouted some orders. Yousef was grabbed by two sailors and cuffed again. This time much tighter. The metal dug into his skin and bones.

While he twisted his position to relieve some of the pain, an attractive blonde walked in, wearing a formfitting military uniform. She seated herself in front of him and started in a soft sexy voice; "*Monsieur Saban?*"

"*Oui,*" he answered in French.

"Would you like to see your wife again?"

"My wife?" It caught him off guard. He nearly said, "What wife?" But instead he asked, "Where is she?"

"She's in good hands, but she might not endure pain like you can, so your best bet is to cooperate with us and save both of you a lot of suffering. We know that your name is false and that your home address in Paris is phony, but we really don't know much else about you or this operation. You have choices. You may be reunited with your lady, or you may never see her again. One way or the other, we'll find out what we want to know, but it's your decision if you two will be treated gently or tortured beyond belief. So let's talk." She leaned forward. "Who financed this deal? Who paid for the weapons? We know that the Lebanese construction company paid for the lumber, but who paid for the weapons? Where did the money come from?"

"What weapons? I bought lumber, that's all."

"Mr. Saban, I see that we will have a very difficult time with you."

• • •

PORTREE HARBOR, Isle of Skye, Scotland. Harbor Master.

"*Dock at slip 5 and unload lumber, then move back to the Aegean Sea and unload iron ore? I don't understand. And then reload the lumber? Okay, if you say so. Proceed.*"

WASHINGTON, USA. Associated Press.

"Piracy in the North Atlantic? Too far from Somalia. Cloud cover stymied satellite searches. Icelandic navy ships have joined the search."

TEL AVIV. Mossad. The office of Meir Dagan.

"Reloading will be done on schedule. One day and the Vladivostok will be back on course. How did the press find out?"

6

ABOARD THE *JOPPA*

The interrogation continued endlessly. The lady in uniform introduced herself as *Major Leva Weisman*, but Yousef assumed that it was a fictitious name, so he wouldn't be able to identify her if he ever got out of his predicament. The thin-face crew-cut Israeli man never mentioned his name, but the detainee overheard others calling him *'Ari'*.

They took turns pressuring him, threatening him and attempting to bribe him, but Yousef stuck to his story.

"Josef," the major continued in French. "We have people in Paris right now, checking out your alleged address and that of your supposed girlfriend Lavana. We already know that you're not married and that this whole charade is just a front for Hezbollah in order to ship weapons into the Gaza strip. Well, it isn't working. The weapons are going to Tel Aviv, and we'll use the Chinese *Stingers* and the Russian *AK-47's* against any Muslim terrorists that threaten the State of Israel. So as you see, your mission has failed miserably and your partners in the Lebanon are going to be anxious to wring your scrawny neck." She paused, drank some coffee and continued. "So, Monsieur, you don't have much of a future ahead of you. You will never see your girlfriend again . . ."

"Did you kill her?" He sounded disturbed.

"No, why should we? She's invaluable as a spy for our cause..."

"Your cause?" He was flabbergasted.

"Yes, of course, OUR CAUSE!" She put the emphasis on the last two words. "You didn't really think she was working for Hezbollah, did you?" She chuckled and smiled broadly at the startled Lebanese. "She's one of our finest undercover agents. Her grandparents died a horrible death in Dachau, and her father was tortured as a little boy in France, but was rescued by the Franciscan Nuns of Toulouse. She's one of the most devout Hebrews you'll ever encounter."

Yousef straightened up in his chair. "I can't believe that. She's Jewish?"

"She sure is. Her mother is an evacuee from the ghetto of Chefchouen in Morocco. She's also a victim of the Islamic hatred for Jews. They're both very dedicated."

"Where is she now?"

"The mother?"

"No, Lavana."

"Oh, she's on her way to Israel, reporting directly to Mr. Dagan at Mossad Headquarters and getting prepared for her next mission."

"I can't believe it."

"You better believe it, and by the way, she said she'll miss you because you were a great lover."

"*Mon Dieu!*"

• • •

PORTREE HARBOR, SCOTLAND.

The harbor master was adamant. "None of this lumber will be reloaded until we have been paid for the transfer of crates from the *VLADIVOSTOK* to the *AGEAN SEA*. You are flying under the Russian Flag, and your company in Saint Petersburg better come across with the money or we'll hold your ship as well as the cargo."

Captain Yuri was in a real quandary because he couldn't afford to have the international news agencies blast this story across the airwaves and embarrass Mother Russia. He could just imagine the headlines: *"Russia Supplies Rockets to Terrorists in the Gaza Strip."*

They would scalp him by the time he reached Saint Petersburg again. That would be the end of his career, or worse. He could spend the rest of his life in Siberia. He decided to pay the harbor master himself and start looking for a way to convince the world that he had encountered problems at sea, rather than admitting that Israeli pirates had captured his vessel and stolen his precious cargo. The $500 he had conned out of Yousef was not enough to cover the Dock Master's bill, but with a company credit card and an ATM machine, he raised the rest. After three days he was finally on his way. He decided to turn north, around the tip of Scotland and then end up near the Azores, where his company would develop a big trumped-up ploy that pirates had detained him off the African Coast.

• • •

TEL AVIV. MOSSAD HEADQUARTERS.

Lani (Lavana) was sitting across the desk from Meir Dagan, Mossad's top executive.

"Lani, great job. Any particular problems?" He stopped while tea was being served. There were two more people in the room. Himey Greenbaum and Lev Levi, two of Dagan's most trusted and experienced agents.

"No, not really, although I had not expected to be involved in one of their actions this soon. I had only been in Lebanon for seven months and had known Yousef for only five.

It's rare that they involve women in some of their schemes, and I had thought it might take years before I'd get called on. But in their minds, this mission really needed a husband-and-wife team and guess what? We were it. I was really fortunate though, that Yousef grew up speaking French at home, because that made it easy for me. My Arabic never was tested."

"That's beautiful. We don't have to ask you anything about the cargo, because we already have it and so far, the press has not made any big deal out of a missing Russian freighter, so we don't expect any interference from the Americans as we get into the Mediterranean and on to Tel Aviv." He sipped his tea and continued. "Lani, did you get any inkling how the thieves in Beirut got hold of the money to pay the Russians? Did Yousef know?"

"I don't think that he had any idea about the money transactions. He just knew that the weapons were paid for and all he had to oversee was the lumber transaction and that was handled directly by the construction company in Lebanon. He does have papers in his possession of the actual transfer of money to Riga, to the lumber suppliers, but I don't think it gave any indication where they got the money. Originally, in Riga, I had plenty of time to scan and fax what I thought was important, but you already have those. Did any of them help?"

"Not necessarily, because none of them told how the Hezbollah got hold of the money that was transferred from the U.S. to the Palestinians. That's still our main question. The process of money transactions from the Americans, once it has been authorized by their president?"

He looked around the room. "How does it work within our country and whom can we ask. Lev! Get on that. Find out what the money trail is. How does it flow from point 'A' to point 'I', 'Israel'? How many stops does it make along the way? We have to figure that out. We're close to interrupting one money flow, from the Bin Ladens in Saudi to Osama in Pakistan. If we can change the flow of the oil dollars into our own coffers, we would put that Taliban terrorist out of business within a month. One of these days we're gonna do that. Right now, and this is embarrassing," he looked at his assistants, "right under our noses, Hezbollah has pulled a fast one that we have never been able pull off in forty years of trying. Like I said…, embarrassing."

Turning to Lani (Lavana), "Is there a chance we'll get that information out of your friend Yousef?"

"I don't know if he knows. He's just a newcomer to the group.

Two years maybe. He may never have been involved in the planning of the higher-ups."

"Would torturing do any good?"

"Not if he doesn't know anything."

"Could he be converted?"

Lani looked puzzled. "Converted to what? Islam to Hebrew? Christianity?"

Dagan leaned forward. "To our cause. He did attend Catholic schools; he studied in Holland and the States. Might he be dissuaded from being so fanatically Muslim?"

Lani hesitated. "He came through to me as positively devoted to Allah, the Prophet and the Quran."

"We have been questioning him now for three days, and he has not budged. He's an intelligent man. What are our chances of turning him into a double agent?"

"No way! If he ever gets back into Lebanon, they'll kill him for sure for having failed his mission. They'll never let him back into their confidence." She shook her head.

"Unless it's a suicide mission. Unless he escapes from our custody and brings them a lot of valuable security information. No?"

"How would we rig that?"

"Oh, honey, we can rig anything. How do you suppose we've survived these last sixty years? By playing possum, as they say in America? No dear, we'll concoct a scheme that the Hezbollah will fall for. Just one bad feature. We'll never be able to let you work with him anymore. Too much of a security risk."

"Why?" She pulled her eyebrows together.

"Too much of a security risk, honey. Too much of a risk." He turned to his assistant, "Himey, have them relax the custody of the Lebanese on our ship. My orders, okay?"

"Okay. Any additional orders?"

"Have him brought here."

7

PRISONER ABOARD THE ISRAELI FRIGATE.

"Yousef, relax. We're taking your handcuffs off, and you can tell us what you'd like to eat or drink." The female major seemed unexpectedly friendly.

Too friendly, the young Lebanese decided. He answered, "I'd like to sleep for about twelve hours."

"Okay. Give us about two minutes." She nodded at the sailor who had been taking notes, closed his notepad, got up and left. Thin-face moved behind the prisoner and undid the cuffs. Yousef massaged his wrists and even licked his left hand where the bone looked bare.

"Bastards," he said under his breath, but he followed the woman without a word when she signaled for him to follow her. He was led to a small cabin that had a sink, potty and two hammocks.

"Anything we can bring you?" Again, she sounded too friendly. It made him suspicious.

"Orange juice? Tea?"

"Okay." And she closed the door.

Within minutes a swabbie appeared and left a pitcher full of juice plus a glass.

Yousef checked the door, but it was obviously locked. He wondered if he had tried to escape, would they have shot him? Did they really need an excuse? Nobody in the world knew where he was, so why wouldn't they just kill him if they wanted to?

"The hell with them." He muttered as he drank directly from the pitcher and crawled into the lower of the hammocks and rolled over, clothes and all. The thud-thud-thud-thud of the engines lulled him to sleep quickly.

• • •

Ten hours later, shaved, he finished all the juice and knocked on the door. There might have been a guard on the other side, but it took five minutes before his interrogator appeared.

"Ha! You look spruced up." She still spoke French. "Are you ready for some fresh air?" Without waiting for an answer, she walked away, expecting him to follow. They climbed two sets of stairs and arrived on deck under a brilliantly blue sky.

"Where are we?" He remembered it was foggy and cold, the last time he was out in the open.

"Somewhere in the Atlantic. Are you hungry yet?"

"Come to think of it, I'm famished. What time is it anyway?"

She pointed at the sun. "Going on midday. You really needed the sleep. Come, let's get some food." Again she walked away as if she was confident he would follow. He looked around and decided that was his best option. There was no land or any other ship in sight.

In the officer's mess they were alone, with the exception of a steward who took his order and poured the coffee.

"What happens now? Are you finished torturing me?"

"Torturing? You call that torturing? Ever heard of Saddam Hussein? He taught the whole world what torture was. No, boy, we only questioned you and . . ."

"Look at my wrists . . ."

"That's just from keeping you restrained. That isn't even close. No we don't do torture on this ship. That may come later."

"Really? Later? What are you planning to do with me?"

"You may have to testify in world court about Hezbollah and their murdering leaders, you . . ."

"Never! I will never testify against the children of Allah and . . ." His knuckles turned white around the fork he was holding. "Never!"

"Life in prison is no joke, no matter what country is holding you. No girls, lousy food, awful accommodations. You wouldn't last twenty years in those conditions, you may consider suicide . . ."

"Never! Just kill myself without taking a bunch of infidels with me? Never!"

"Or, when you testify in the International Court in The Hague, tell the truth and you may be given amnesty in another country, America or Australia and Hezbollah will haunt you for the rest of your life, trying to murder or capture you."

"What have I done? What crime can they accuse me of?"

"Conspiracy in grand theft, millions of dollars. Intent to slaughter innocent women and children, transport of illegal weapons, et cetera. Enough to keep you locked up for life."

"And Lavana knew about all that?"

"Of course."

"That bitch!"

"She had a job to do and she did it well. Her race has been persecuted for centuries, and she's getting revenge."

"That bitch!" He stared at his scrambled eggs. "What choices do I have?"

"Cooperate."

"Cooperate with you people? I would never be able to set foot in my native country again, never see my parents any more . . ." For a moment it seemed he might start to sob.

"Let's get back to your cabin. We'll bring you some books. Do you prefer Arabic, French or English? A good spy novel? Ian Fleming? Tom Clancy? They always have positive endings."

"English, please."

• • •

As the sun was setting off the coast of *Madeira,* a helicopter appeared and hovered next to the *JOPPA.* Yousef was shackled again, this time his legs as well. He could only move forward a few inches at the time. Climbing the steep stairs was impossible, so he was carried up to the deck, where he was led to the bow between two sailors. The major personally saw to it that he was strapped tightly in a harness with a loop and hook above him.

"Read in the Quran, where Mohammed states that all of Abraham's children are chosen, Hebrews included, and you may want to come to our side to help produce peace for all Muslims and Jews." While shouting those words into his ears, she signaled the chopper to fly overhead and lower its line. She expertly caught the rope and attached the sling to the loop of Yousef's contraption, and within seconds, he was swung up and away, being hauled up into the disappearing helicopter.

Ten minutes later, at the Madeira airport, his legs were unshackled and he was guided to a waiting jetliner, a three-engine *FALCON*. The plane had no markings on it whatsoever, only some numbers on the tail and *Falcon* on its nose in small print. The inside was different from any airliner he had flown. It seemed more like a little apartment with a living room and kitchenette. At the far end was a door that probably led to a bedroom, he surmised.

Unceremoniously, he was placed in a club chair, and the sailors who brought him aboard were replaced by two civilians, husky men in tan slacks and short-sleeved white shirts.

Without a word, they buckled him in and the engines started to turn over, the top rear one first. While his guards seated and buckled themselves on either side of him, the plane started to roll. Minutes later, the hum of the engines became a roar and the jet gathered speed.

Shortly after it left the ground, the pilot rolled into a right bank and Yousef could see the prettiest island he had ever observed from the sky.

"Which island?" He asked the man to the left. He asked the question in English and to his surprise, the man answered in the same language, "Sunny Madeira."

He had assumed the two guys didn't speak French and he really hadn't expected an honest answer. Apparently, his location was no secret anymore, at least not to them. He wondered why he was being treated so civilly. Hezbollah wouldn't treat its captives this way. He shuddered at the thought of what might still be lying ahead and the reception he might get from his superiors in Beirut if he ever made it back there. Might they torture him for weeks, trying to make him spill any information that he might have coughed up for the Israelis? Might they suggest that he commit suicide in order to endear himself with Allah? Plant a bomb on himself and destroy a tank or a house?" The voice of Ankie's father Hendrik still rang in his ears, *"innocent women and children."* He shivered involuntarily.

"Try to sleep," one of the guards suggested. "It's at least a three-hour flight."

Yousef took his advice.

When the engine noise receded and the plane slowed for its landing approach, he awoke and started to study the scenery through the little windows on both sides. They were approaching a brown dusty landscape, and he immediately thought, "Lebanon" but realized that Israel probably was just as sandy and desert-like along its coast. In a wide sweeping turn he could see the built-up region along the entire waterfront and he knew that they had to be in the vicinity of Tel Aviv. He was right. After touchdown, they passed the passenger side of the field and taxied all the way to the military section, where slim fighter jets were lined up by the dozens. They resembled the American F-16's, but there were additional little wings ahead of the cockpit and the fuselage above the wings was more square than rounded, the way he visualized the Falcon Jets. "Additional fuel?" He guessed.

From the plane he was moved into an armored vehicle without air-conditioning. It became an hour-long drive through winding streets and into the foothills east of the city. He was sweating profusely, but so were his guards, so he didn't say a word.

In complete silence he was led from the car through an immense steel gate and into a big block building that might have been built by the Romans. It had one advantage: it was cool. After a long march through several corridors, a cell door was opened, his handcuffs unlocked, and he was gently shoved inside while the door shut with a loud clang.

Not a word had been spoken.

8

SECAUCUS, NEW JERSEY.
FBI HEADQUARTERS.

"Mr. Bongers, a Mister Dagan on the phone for you. He wouldn't give me any details, but insisted you knew him."

"I'll take it in my office." The bureau chief walked from the break room to his desk and picked up the receiver. "Hello, Meir? How are you? Have you finally decided to retire?"

"Are you kidding? Who can do my job here, and what do you want me to do? Go shopping with my wife all day or pull weeds in our garden? I'd rather be dead."

Bruce Bongers chuckled at that answer and asked, "Then what gives me the honor of your call?"

"This is confidential, Bruce. I cannot go through channels with this, because I don't know who I can trust. I'd like you to do some unofficial snooping for me for old time's sake."

"For old time's sake, like in Fort Bragg, when we . . .?"

"No, no, no! This is business. Somewhere in the system, in the U.S. or in Palestine is a broken connection that I need to find, and I need to know how I can fix it. Now, this is totally off the cuff. This is strictly between you and me, and I don't want you to stop any other important business for this, just nose around when you can."

"This sounds serious. We're on a secure line, right?"

"I am. Supposedly, so are you."

"Yes, I'm okay. Now tell me what you have in mind."

"Remember when I fed you guys information about terrorists moving into America with big plans, back in 2001? You were still in the Army then, weren't you?"

"Yes, how could I forget?"

"Well, with all the infighting and distrust between Homeland Security, the Naval and Army Intelligence, the FBI and the CIA, nothing was done, and the Twin Towers were destroyed on 9/11, right?"

"Right."

"Well, I don't wanna get caught in that web again. I know if I call your director, he'll have to delegate it to someone, or if I call Taylor at the CIA, he'll immediately put ten men on it and before long, we have no secret anymore, and leaks will be sprung everywhere and nothing will be accomplished."

"You certainly have my attention." Bruce wondered where all that was leading to.

"This conversation cannot be traced, I hope."

"Not from this end."

"Okay. Here's what I got. Have you heard about a Russian freighter being lost or captured by pirates?"

"Not officially. That's way off my beaten path, but I remember a newsflash about a lumber freighter that was missing in the Baltic. Russian, I believe."

"That's all you heard?" Meir Dagan was incredulous.

"Remember the FBI solves domestic problems and we have plenty of them."

"Oh, well . . ., We took the vessel . . ."

"YOU DID?" Bongers was flabbergasted. "If you needed lumber that badly, why didn't you buy some?"

"We didn't need the lumber. That's back en route. We took the missiles and guns that were hidden underneath the wood."

"Missiles and guns? From where?"

"From China and Russia, loaded in Saint Petersburg."

"Great Scott! Did the Russian authorities know?"

"Did they know? They made the deal."

"They couldn't! They wouldn't! The Russians wouldn't get involved in such a stupid international incident."

"But they did." Dagan remained as calm as could be while Bongers was getting more excited.

"Who paid for it and where was it headed?"

"That's where you come in. You won't believe this, but it was heading for the Gaza Strip, and it was paid for by American money."

"Oh no! Couldn't be. America might smuggle their own weapons in for a good price, but not foreign-made weaponry. No way!"

"Like I said, that's where you come in. How did money for housing in the Gaza get into the hands of Hezbollah, and how did they transfer it to Russia?"

"Oh, God. We have an international crisis on our hands!" Bongers stood up, phone in hand.

"Not yet, Bruce, not yet."

"How come?"

"You see, we have the weapons. Nobody knows that. The Palestinians will receive the lumber as scheduled, well, maybe a little delayed, and we'll unload the weapons in Israel, thank you very much."

The FBI man sat back down. "This is near fiction, so what can I do?"

"For the moment, put your ear to the ground. Pick up rumors. Show no particular interest. In another week, the armament will be in Tel Aviv, the lumber in Gaza, the money in Russia, and Hezbollah will be totally embarrassed. To the whole wide world, it may just have been a fizzle unless we, or the Palestinians, run our mouths, and we're planning on clamming up. The important thing is, Bruce, how does that money get funneled from the U.S. to Palestine and how did it get into the hands of the terrorists?"

"Like I said before, good God! Do you have any plants in the Hezbollah organization? Anyone at the upper level?"

"Not really, but we're working on it. We have a young twenty-two-year-old man in custody, who was to guide the shipment to the Gaza. He was on the ship when we snagged it. He was educated in Holland and in the U.S., Hoboken as a matter . . ."

"Hoboken? Right here?"

"He has a mixed Catholic, Muslim upbringing and speaks Arabic of course, plus fluent French and English. I'm hoping we can sway him to go back to Lebanon . . ."

"Is that where he is from?"

"Yeah, indeed. And I hope I can train him to become a double agent."

"Wow!"

"The thing that worries me; will they kill him for having failed his mission and how do I get him back in there without arousing suspicion. I can't let him escape. Nobody escapes from Israel."

"How about a prisoner exchange?"

"An exchange? On what pretense? Do you know how these things work? They release one Israeli soldier for three hundred of their terrorists, and they're always handled by our bureaucrats. A bunch of crybabies. I never have any say in it. Remember we released Mohammed Atta ten years ago under pressure from the American government? A year later he flew into the Twin Towers. I don't know, Bruce. How do I entice them to deal with us about this one young Lebanese?"

"Can you be patient and see if they'll approach you, Meir?"

"Slip a word into Beirut that we have him and that he may talk? It depends on how much he really knows, because that determines what he's worth."

"Worth a try. At this point I don't know if I should congratulate you on a successful mission or feel sorry for the pickle you're in. Any chance of you coming State side sometimes, so we can talk about our first parachute jump together?"

"Over a beer?"

"And a cognac."

"I'll look for an excuse. Shalom, brother."

"Shalom."

Bongers leaned back in his chair. "Those Israelis have more guts than anyone I know. Capture a ship on the high seas? Unbelievable." He was talking to himself as he pushed the intercom. "Bruno? In here a minute."

When his good-looking Latin assistant walked in, the Senior Agent pointed to the chair alongside his desk. "Sit. You wouldn't believe what I just learned, and I don't know how to proceed."

"Well, Boss, that's unusual for you. You normally always have the answers."

"Right now I don't know if I understand the answer. Who's our financial genius in D.C.? Isn't that Sol Adamson?"

"The one who valued the diamonds?"

"Yeah, that's the one. Let's think up a reason for him to come up here."

"Audit our books?"

"No, no. Don't we have a case that one of our agents is working on that involves some financial shenanigans?"

"I can find out."

"Let's work up an excuse for him to come here so he can baffle us with his expertise."

"What's this leading up to, Bruce?"

"We'll go to Angelo's for a beer, and I'll tell you about one-tenth of what I just learned on the phone under condition that you don't pressure me for all the gory details."

"Who's buying?"

9

TRIPOLI, LEBANON

Smoking hash was supposed to make Ahmed feel better, but not this morning. He threw down his pipe and started pacing the floor. "Where are those lazy bastards? They were supposed to be here an hour ago. How can a man run an efficient organization with lazy and incompetent people?" He was addressing the little Filipino servant, who added boiling water to his tea and stirred the mint leaves.

As a student he had been involved in the uprising against the Christians in Lebanon and he had put to use everything he had learned in Iran when the students captured the Americans and ousted the Shah. He became known as being ruthless, but intelligent, and had risen in the ranks of Hezbollah. Smuggling the weapons to the Gaza was one of his most brilliant moves, and the way they had manipulated the *"building"* money from Gaza to Saint Petersburg had been a stroke of genius.

Now, however, it seemed that his plan was about to falter. He sat down and lifted the hash pipe to his lips again. At that precise moment, two of his trusted teammates walked in, and he jumped up again. "Where the hell have you been? You're supposed to have been here an hour ago. What have you found out? What news do you have? I'm living in suspense, on the brink of hell and . . ."

"Do you mind if we sit down?" Hassan Nasrallah, the taller of the two motioned to a pillow next to his leader.

"Of course, of course. Allah il Allah. I forgot my manners, but I'm so deprived of information in this hole. No good television reception and my phone hasn't rung. Tell me, what have you learned?"

"Nothing much and nothing good."

The little oriental servant brought tea for the new arrivals. The speaker waited until he had left the room before he continued. "The ship *Vladivostok* was seized by an unmarked warship. The radioman got a brief message off to his home base, but was stopped. The boat was steered to Scotland, where the weapons were transferred to an Israeli freighter and the Russian ship was reloaded with the lumber and is sailing toward the Mediterranean . . ."

"May Allah strike them dead. What about the young boy and his girl?"

"The reports from Scotland to Russia to Arabia and then to us are very sketchy and they do not mention anything about the couple. They weren't noticed. They must have been transferred to the warship."

"Oh dear Allah. What if they talk?" Nasralah wanted to know.

"Talk, what could they add to the story? The Israelis must have known every detail of the operations, and the Russians may have sold us out. Why else would the captain steer due west toward Iceland instead of turning south to the channel? He must have known of a rendezvous before they left Riga. The Russians have their money, the lumber companies in Latvia have most of their money, the ship's captain saw to that, remember? So what could our young couple possibly tell them that they didn't know already?"

"Are you saying that Yousef and his girl did not betray us, but are victims of the same scam by the Russians?"

"Careful how you use the word 'Russians.' The Russian government may not be involved at all. It may be just a bunch of enterprising individuals."

"How can we find out?'

"Who made all the initial contacts, and who negotiated the whole deal, the weapons, the money transactions, the lumber cover up?

Who in Beirut had all that organized before they contacted us to execute their scheme? Who? And is there a leak in the organization, a traitor?"

"Allah forbid. What you're saying is that you don't think the young couple betrayed us?"

"That's right. How do we get them back?"

"Get them back? From the Mossad? Never happen. They will pump them for years about every little detail about our organization. No, don't count on that." Ahmed shook his head, as if to add conviction to his statement. "It'll never happen. They're too happy that they've caught one of ours red-handed."

"How about a prisoner exchange?" Nasrallah had been involved in this before.

"Exchange? Who do we have that they may want?"

"We have a wounded corporal, who we captured near the Golan Heights. They keep screaming for his return."

"Good thought. How do we propose it to headquarters in Beirut? They'll act like we screwed up the whole deal by putting it in the hands of some novices."

"No! We have to lay the blame on them from the beginning, and maybe we can flush out the traitor in their group."

"Let's go for it!"

TEL AVIV, MOSSAD HEADQUARTERS.

"Lev, you come with me. I want to talk to that Lebanese boy in person. Leva Weisman informed me that the young fellow may not be as fanatic as he pretends to be and that we may have a real chance of converting him to our cause."

"And forsake Allah?"

"Maybe not entirely, but at least get him to see the contradiction between what he now believes in and what the Quran really spells out. Let's find out. Let's take my car. You drive."

MEZIDDO MEMORIAL PRISON.

"Bring the man into the small interrogation room and have cameras rolling." Meir Dagan needed no introduction. As head of the Mossad, he virtually owned the building. It's "maximum security" designation clearly indicated that the most hardened criminals and terrorists were harbored within those sixteen-foot walls.

While waiting outside the mirrored wall, sipping coffee, the chief investigator in all of Israel, scanned through the secret file on *Josef Saban,* as his passport stated. "Must be real fluent in French," he said to himself. "Wonder how his English is? Would make it easier on me."

He looked up as the prisoner was brought in on the other side of the soundproof mirror.

Yousef was clean shaven, but his shirt obviously hadn't been washed or ironed in many days. He wore no tie, and his top three buttons were undone, exposing a fairly hairy chest.

"Nice looking kid," Dagan observed as he turned to his assistant Lev. "Doesn't show much Arab blood in him. Mostly French I guess. Let's see how he behaves."

Inside the little room without windows, Yousef looked around. Just steel walls with two metal doors, one on each side. Bright overhead lights made him blink a few times after the long walk through a dark corridor. He slowly examined his surroundings and compared the room with the one on board the Israeli frigate. "About the same," he figured, "except that huge mirror on my left." He stared at it for a minute and decided, "That's where the cameras are and they're probably sizing me up right now. Well, come on. I can take anything you dish out."

The door opened and a middle-aged man walked in. Slightly balding, but very erect and athletic looking.

"Meir Dagan," went through Yousef's mind. "They brought in the head honcho? Boy, I must be important to them. I wonder what's up?"

The intelligence chief seated himself across from the prisoner at the big wooden table.

"Good morning, sir!" He greeted him in English.

"Bonjour," was Yousef's reply.

"I know you've studied in Holland and the U.S, so it's probably easier if we conduct ourselves in English, agreed?"

"Pas pour moi. Français ou Arabique est plus facile pour moi."

"But not for me, buddy, so I'll continue in English. You've spoken English with Major Weisman aboard ship, so why don't you quit trying to fool me and cooperate. You know we have you here, and we can also keep you here. Maybe forever or at least till you're old and grey. That would be a terrible waste of a young life, wouldn't you agree? So let's start over. "Good morning."

Yousef couldn't help but smile under the circumstances. "Okay. Good morning." He stopped short of saying "Sir". He didn't want to show any respect.

"Josef, as you know, your whole mission fell apart and it may have international implications. When the Kremlin learns all the gory details about the underhanded weapons transactions, without their knowledge or approval, heads are going to roll in Russia, and when Hezbollah finds out who informed the Israelis, additional heads will be chopped off in Lebanon. If you were there now, your head might already be on the chopping block. Thank Allah that you're here . . ."

"But I had nothing to do with the betrayal and . . ."

"We know that, Josef, but some eager Hezbollah officials might lay the blame on you, just to keep the suspicion off themselves. You may not live very long in your home country."

"They wouldn't do that to me!" He rose from his chair.

"Yes, they would. You know they would. They will interpret the Quran in such a way that they'll feel totally justified in their decisions. Just like it doesn't say anywhere in Mohammed's words that you should KILL all infidels. That's just a way a fanatic Muslim can incite dumb youngsters into giving their lives for promises of paradise and many virgins. That's not at all what the Prophet said . . .,"

"Since when are you so learned about Islam and . . ."

"Since Abraham is the father of your race as well as mine and since we study our Bible right along with your Quran, we get a better understanding of what God really wants."

"You can't . . ." Yousef tried to get a word in edgewise.

"I'll tell you what I can. I'm going to upgrade your conditions. I'll schedule lessons for you, and an Imam will instruct you in the true meaning of Mohammed's writings. I'll also keep you posted on what's happening with the shipments and the heads that will be rolling in Beirut."

"Why would you do that?"

"You're exceptionally intelligent, and I hope you'll come over to our side . . .,"

"You're kidding? Never." He stood up and repeated; "Never!"

"Au revoir, mon fils." Dagan stood up.

"Don't call me your son, *mon fils*. I'd rather kill myself than becoming your son."

"You have your options. *Au revoir*." He walked out.

10

BETWEEN FOUR WALLS

As promised, Yousef was transported to a different cell. It had high windows on the south side, making it bright most of the day. The walls were at least three feet thick, built with giant blocks of limestone. Each one must have been a cubic yard. The walls were covered in graffiti, scratched in the soft stone over hundreds of years. The temperature was comfortable and the young Lebanese enjoyed himself for hours, deciphering many of the names and messages. That wasn't easy. At least a dozen different languages appeared on the walls and in more than five different scripts. Arabic, Hebrew and Gothic were some that he could work with, but even Chinese and Japanese prisoners must have been housed in the same room in the past, because there were hundreds of very complicated letters and symbols all over the room.

After hours of reading, he lay down and tried to sleep. There was nothing to read and not a sound penetrated the ancient walls. His mind was in turmoil. He hated the thought that the Israelis so easily intercepted and confiscated his ship. The Mossad had to have enormous resources at their fingertips in order to pull off a hijacking like that a thousand miles from their homeland. Compared to them, the whole Hezbollah was nothing but a bunch of amateurs.

The worst part was that he was so easily led by the nose by

that beautiful agent Lavana. He had really fallen for that girl. She seemed so genuine, so sincere, and all of that was just an act to entrap a young and upcoming terrorist. Her dedication to her home country must be so complete, so all encompassing that she would do anything, including laying her life on the line.

He himself totally believed in the Quran, but Lavana must also totally believe in her Bible in order to develop such dedication. "Unreal," he muttered to himself.

After six restless hours, the door opened and a guard removed his food tray and introduced a white-haired individual as, "Mullah Benjamin Samara." Without another word the jailer withdrew and left the two alone.

"Salam Aleichem, my son."

"Aleichem Salam." Yousef stood up.

"Sit, my boy, sit. After all, we're brothers. I'm named after the youngest son of our great father Jacob, and you're named after his second youngest one. The wise one. So let's be brothers and friends."

Yousef was not that easily sold. A Muslim Cleric in a Jewish prison didn't seem entirely Kosher. "Have you come to convert me to Judaism?"

"On the contrary, my son. On the contrary. I've come to make you a better Muslim, if at all possible. Why did you ask me that kind of question?"

"The Jews would like me to become an agent for them, and that would only be possible if I believed in their cause and their religion."

"Well . . ., I wouldn't put that past them, but that's out of my league. I'm strictly a cleric who interprets the writings of the Prophet, and that's what I came to see you about. I know virtually nothing about your background or your mission. Including your 'crime' as the Israelis call it and that is none of my business. My calling is to make you a true believer and follower of Mohammed."

"Then why do you work for the Jews?"

"I was born in this town, and I've lived in this town all my life. I've been an English citizen, a Palestinian, and now I'm an Israeli, simply because of where I live and work. I do get paid by the prison authorities to look after the religious welfare of the inmates, but let me assure you, they don't pay me enough to cover my rent or food bill, but every little bit helps." He had made himself comfortable next to Yousef on his bunk.

The old man continued. "I'll give you my interpretation of the Quran and what is wrong with the many ways it's being misunderstood."

"Misunderstood? It's plain enough, isn't it?"

"Is it? Then how come in this morning's papers it tells of a suicide attack in Bagdad, where seven people were killed, six of them women and children. They were Sunnis. The killers were Shiites, all Muslims, all brothers and sisters. Where in the Quran does that receive the Prophet's blessing? No, that is what causes most of the friction, most of the wars, the evil messages created by vicious, evil minds. That is what I'm against." Yousef started to say something, but the Mullah lifted his right hand. "Right here in Israel, we have no problems, Palestinians and Jews live and work together because we are all Israelis of different religions. In Jerusalem, there are also Protestants, Catholics and Orthodox Greeks. There's even an Armenian section. That's fine. We're all natives of this land and we can live together . . ."

"Then why are you fighting all the time?"

"Because some hotheads get hold of a missile, fire it across the Gaza border, kill one Jew and the Israeli jets are overhead in minutes to retaliate and clobber twenty houses, killing dozens. Does that make sense?" He shook his head. "This has been going on for sixty years already and nobody learns, especially the young fanatics, who are swept into a frenzy by some zealots."

He put his hand on Yousef's shoulder. "You are from the Lebanon, right? You ought to know. The Lebanese moved down into Northern Israel, and within days, the Israelis had beaten you guys back a hundred miles and still occupy a big portion of your country, including parts of the Golan Heights. Did all that make sense?" He shook his head again. "Who dreamed that up? Was it Hezbollah, or was it Hamas, or are they working together now instead of killing one another?"

Yousef had a dozen arguments ready, but was caught off guard. "I don't know that much about Hamas."

"They're supposed to be speaking for everyone, but it never comes across that way. I think they hate each other, and again, how do they justify that through the Holy words of the Prophet?"

The old cleric put his hand on Yousef's. "Young man, all I hope to accomplish with you, whether you're here for a year or fifty years, is that you learn to love and understand our religion and become a faithful believer."

"A year? Fifty years? What have they told you?"

"I know nothing about your case, and I don't care about your infraction. I only care about bringing the word of Allah to you, so you'll become a most devout and true believer."

"Can you give me any idea of what they have in mind for me?"

"Not a clue." He removed his hand. "All I heard rumored was that the Americans have an interest in you because moneys involved were allegedly American dollars, but that's a rumor, that's all."

"Great Allah. I hate Americans."

"Why?"

"Because they try to impose their will on the entire world and deny the existence of Allah and don't allow their citizens to worship . . ."

"Where do you get such nonsense?"

"I lived there for two years and . . ."

"And you didn't see their mosques?"

"Yes, but they have this superior attitude that the whole world should bow to them and they hate all Muslims . . ."

"How can you say that?" The Mullah interrupted. "When the Serbs and Yugoslavs went on a "cleansing" spree, killing all Muslims, some 1,400 of them, the Americans got involved in their so-called Kosovo war and brought all that back under control and our brethren now live in that region undisturbed, and we should be eternally grateful that they were willing to lay their lives on the line to help our faithful."

"Big deal!" Yousef wasn't that easily swayed. "They wanted to protect their oil interests in the Balkans, and some of the locals got in the way . . ."

"Do you really believe that crap? You don't think that they had real humanitarian interests? Well, I do, because those are the facts. So what did we do? We said, 'Thank you very much' and blew up their twin towers and killed nearly three thousand innocents. Is that something we're supposed to be proud of? Is that what the Prophet had in mind when he wrote the Holy pages of the Quran?" He put his hand back on the young man's shoulder. "No Yousef, this is not what our religion is about and I would like to start with the basic of our beliefs, from the beginning. That Allah is God, Almighty, all encompassing, and we have to worship and adore him. We have to spread his word through example and devotion, not by the sword. Let us start with . . .'

"I don't know that I'm interested in your help." Yousef moved away a few inches. " I think I'm man enough and know enough to take care of myself, and I don't need any help from you or anyone else. So . . ." He stood up. "Tell the Jews that I'm fine and that I want out of here." He walked to the door and continued, "I think you're a fine man, but you've been living with the Hebrew Devils too long to have an opinion of your own. You just repeat what they feed you. I don't need that. So…, thank you very much and tell Mr. Dagan that I want to talk with him." He knocked on the door, trying to get the attention of a jailor. "And please, Mullah Benjamin, my brother, do not call on me again. You're a prime example how the Israelis brainwash their victims." He knocked again. "Well, it won't happen to me. I will not betray my brothers in Beirut, and I will not rot in this hell hole either."

The old man remained seated. "I'm leaving my Quran. You're an intelligent man, you can read Arabic, so learn by yourself." With that, he took a cell phone out of his robe pocket, pushed a few buttons, and the door opened. "Peace be with you. Salam Aleichem." He strode out the door.

11

SECAUCUS, NJ, FBI HEADQUARTERS.

"Mr. Bongers, a Mr. Dagan on the secure line!"

The intercom interrupted a conversation with one of his chief advisors and he pushed a button. "I'll take it in my office." Turning to his agent, "Sorry, Sol. I'll be right back."

The 6'2" bureau chief hurried through the hall and engaged the blinking light on his phone before sitting down. "Bongers here."

"Bruce, good morning. Meir here. I'm not calling you for any earthshaking reasons, but I felt you needed to remain informed."

"Oh, sure."

"We had a surprise visit here in Tel Aviv at our main office, which is quite unusual."

"What made it so unusual?" Bongers was all ears.

"Well, normally, diplomats meet at embassies, not in intelligence dungeons. This time the Russian ambassador and his main spy, or should I say, 'chief intelligence officer' walked into my office?"

"Really? Must have been important."

"Important for two reasons and the second reason involves you. I'll tell you number one first. They came here to protest the capture of 'Russian hardware' and a demand for its return."

"The weapons on the ship?"

"Exactly. They were taken aback a bit when I explained we did not steal any of their war materials, that they belonged to Hezbollah and the Hamas Authorities in the Gaza. I said that we would never take anything that belonged to the Soviet Union as it was, or Russia, as it now functions. It's too important that we keep them on our side."

"Good thinking. How did they react?"

"Well, the ambassador stayed on the offensive until I said we would lodge an official complaint against his government through the U.N. about the fact that they knowingly participated in the sales of weapons that were destined to destroy Israeli lives."

"Hoorah for you!"

"That changed his tune somewhat, and he stated the real reason for their visit. He wanted to know if we had details of the financial transaction from the States to Gaza, to Hezbollah and then onto Saint Petersburg for the armament sale. Apparently, they want in on that kinda deal if they could, and until now, they have no clue. Well, I told them we don't either, but are willing to exchange information that could be of mutual benefit. So that left him none the wiser, but he had calmed down a lot."

"Did he demand the weapons back?"

"At first he did, but he left understanding that they were not his to demand, and then he switched to the second part, the part that may involve you or at least interest you."

"Me? Us? In what way?"

"He's trying to open a door between you, America that is, me, the Mossad, and their own Secret Service, the former KGB."

"That's nice. What's in it for him?"

"He's going to pump us for info in exchange for some input from their end. Like how do you get a hold of U.S. money, the way Hamas did? And he fed me a little tidbit for your end of the line, kinda to butter us up, I figure."

"What did he offer?"

"He claims that in Uzbekistan, on a foreign U.N. support base, they've captured some al-Qaida operatives, who were sent there to gather information and sabotage the place if possible."

"I'm not surprised, Meir."

"Not surprised? How?"

"As long as Osama bin Laden is still around, they'll try to infiltrate and murder any which way they can. No, I'm not surprised, but what's the connection with us over here?"

"Bruce, that's the whole point. One terrorist snapped. New wife and baby boy at home and he wants to get back. He's heard of Guantanamo, and he doesn't want to end up there. So he talked. According to the Russians, he claimed big plans are in the making in the U.S., bigger than 9/11. This time huge chemical explosions and..."

"Chemicals? Where?"

"He claims he doesn't know, or maybe the Russians don't want to feed us everything they found out. They may want to use their knowledge to milk information out of us."

"Sounds logical."

"Now excuse me, Bruce, but I don't have much faith in your CIA. They screw up too often, and they act like they're superior to all other intelligence agencies, so I want to feed you the information as I get it, and then you can slip it to the CIA, Homeland Security, Secret Service and the U.S. Marshalls. It'll force them to work together, rather than keeping all the glory for themselves as they've done in the past with disastrous results, as you well remember."

"Boy, oh boy!"

"What's the matter, Bruce?"

"What you're telling me is of the utmost importance, but what you're asking me is going against the grain of any ethics oath I have ever taken."

"Just remember two things, Bruce. What I've just told you is just a two-minute summary of what we hassled out in three hours, and number two-, what you pass along may save thousands of American lives, and that should be on your priority list. As a matter of fact, on everyone's priority list. I'm just approaching you because I feel you will do the most good when it comes to disseminating information to all the security forces where they'll prove to be most productive."

"Wow!"

"This was just a brief introduction, Bruce. I hope to fly into New York next month, and we'll arm-wrestle each other once more for a round of drinks. Just start thinking. Where is a chemical concentration that will do the most harm and kill the highest number of people? Where in the States? Start thinking, and I'll keep you posted on new developments. By the way, the Lebanese boy that we have in custody is being demanded by Hezbollah. Any ideas for a favorable exchange?"

"Exchange? Whom do they still have? Your corporal and a civilian woman?"

"That's about it. Can you find out what people the U.S. wants returned?" Dagan kept pushing.

"Americans held by al-Qaida? Taliban? Hezbollah and Hamas? Meir, that's way out of my league, but I'll put out some feelers. How urgent is this? When do you want me to get back to you?"

"A.S.A.P. or sooner."

"I'll see what I can do."

"Thanks, buddy. Shalom."

• • •

"Sorry, Sol. I used to think I had a simple job. Solve crimes, bring criminals to justice and go home and have dinner with the family. Not anymore. You won't believe what I get involved in. Before we go back to our subject, money transfers, let me ask you a question. Who is our national expert on chemicals and the largest concentration of chemical production?"

"I would say Doctor Jay Price in our Cleveland office."

"Never met him, but I'll give him a call. Thanks. Let's get back to our money flow."

• • •

"Bruno? Can you come in here a moment?"

Bongers' right hand- man, Bruno Garcia, walked in, tie undone and shirtsleeves rolled up.

"What's up, Boss?"

"Sit." He pointed to the chair next to his desk. "Sit!" He flipped through a yellow pad and stopped at a page full of scribbles. The room was very quiet, except for the distant hum of the traffic on the Jersey Turnpike. "Remember the other day when we talked about that Russian freighter that disappeared?"

"Sure do. What happened? What's the end of the story?"

"Oh, it hasn't ended yet, and it won't end for a while. One thing is for sure. The Israelis must have an intelligence network that's second to none in the world. How did they find out about the money for weapons transfer? How did they know the shipping date? How did they get the captain to sail a perfectly western course? How did they pinpoint that ship under a solid cloud deck? How did they pre-arrange the weapons transfer in Scotland under the noses of the British and American intelligence agencies?" He shook his head. "They're unbelievable. Anyway, here's where we come in. You may remember that they captured a young Lebanese who controlled the loading and the shipping?"

"Right. You mentioned that."

"Well, Hezbollah wants him back and are looking for a prisoner exchange."

"Okay!" Garcia nodded.

"I'd like to get in on that in such a way, that we get a hold of that boy, even if just for a while, by trading one of our captives."

"Whoa, Boss! Isn't that more up the CIA alley?"

Bongers nodded. "True, it's completely out of our league, but the boy was a student right here in Hoboken, so his English must be nearly flawless, and I'd like to borrow him for a while and see if we can't sway him to come to work for us."

"Jeez! Good luck. How are you gonna arrange that?" Bruno was leaning forward in his chair, his bronze face and flashing brown eyes reflecting his excitement. "How do we get him here?"

"That's where you come in. Unofficially, or should I say unobtrusively, find out which infamous Lebanese or Palestinian we have in captivity, that Hamas and Hezbollah want back in the worst way."

"How do I go about that?"

"You have friends in other agencies, like in Cuba, right?" He smiled broadly. "Well, buy them a beer."

12

MEZZADE PRISON, ISRAEL.

For ten days Yousef had not heard or seen anybody. A guard would slip a food tray through the slot in the door and retrieve it later, after it had been shoved back out. Not a word was exchanged. The young Lebanese was about to go stark raving mad. He'd called at the jailer on the other side of the door, but got no reaction out of him whatsoever. He was starting to suspect that there was a camera hidden in the ceiling and that his activities would be watched, day and night. Acting like he had a heart attack crossed his mind, but he wasn't sure how to fake it to make it look real. He could choke himself by tying his pants legs around his neck and making gasping noises, but on the other hand, he wanted to impress his captors that he was tough, so he slept or read the Quran.

Pencil and paper would have come in handy, because he wanted to record some of the events and his thoughts for future reference, but he didn't have anything to write on. The cleric had not reappeared, and Yousef felt he should have asked the old man for writing utensils and he might have gotten some.

After a while he wasn't sure whether he had been in that cell for ten days or eleven. A plastic fork wasn't a very good instrument for carving dates on the wall, so he gave that up too.

Suddenly, the door opened wide. Two guards walked in, summoned him to stand up and in no time, had his hands cuffed behind his back, and he found himself walking through the damp ancient halls of the old prison. In a small room with wooden benches along the wall, he was unceremoniously dumped on one of them, and then nothing happened. For an hour, or maybe an hour and a half. He could stand and stretch his legs, but his arms remained pinned behind his back, and his shoulders started to ache. He cursed the Israelis under his breath and his associates in Lebanon as well. He felt they could have forced his captors to release him by now, but he really didn't know how they would go about that. Just as he sat down again, the door opened, and Israel's intelligence chief walked in with two uniformed officers, both majors, Yousef assumed. A table and three folding chairs followed and the visitors made themselves comfortable.

"Monsieur Saban, or whatever your real name is, I hope you've been fed properly? Yes?" Dagan turned to one of the military men and said in Hebrew, "Take his cuffs off." Yousef didn't understand the order, but he certainly appreciated it. He rubbed his wrists and sat back down again.

"You've noticed that your diet was in strict observance of your Muslim laws, which are about the same as ours. We don't eat pork either." He dug a folder out of his briefcase and looked up at the young man. "I do hope you enjoyed our facilities so far. They may be the most humane ones you'll experience during your lifetime. Most of them are just dungeons, shared with rats and roaches. Ours is like the Revan Hotel in Riga in comparison."

Taking a sheet from his folder, he continued. "We have a message here from Ahmed Bin Behumed. I guess they're mad at you for having failed your mission . . ."

"I didn't fail anything! I was betrayed." Yousef stood up and shouted.

"Sit down and be quiet. Your former partners have . . ."

"Former? What . . ."

"Sit down and listen. If you get up once more, we'll chain you to the bench! Do you understand?" His voice had gotten louder, and his accent became more pronounced. The conversation had been in English to that point, and the intelligence man continued in the same tongue. "No more outbursts, please. The gist of the communiqué is that they don't want you back . . ."

"But . . . Sorry!" He shut up immediately.

"They want one of your top leaders, who's in American custody in Guantanamo, in exchange for some Israelis that they're holding. The Americans are not dumb. They want something in exchange as well, and you will become part of the transaction."

"I what?" Yousef had become very subdued and his question was barely audible.

"Don't flatter yourself. You're not important enough to be the sole bargaining chip. There'll be two more men in a Beirut prison that the Americans want released and then they'll consider returning Fanouf Bahouie. You're just part of the whole shuffle. They want to learn from you how the American money got transferred to Russia for weapons instead of rebuilding houses in the Gaza Strip."

"But I . . ."

"Don't interrupt. I understand Guantanamo is not such a bad place and you'll be surrounded by hundreds of your fanatic brothers from all over the Middle East."

"But I . . ."

"Go ahead. Spit it all out. I'm ready to listen."

"Well, Sir, " Yousef leaned forward. "I can't believe that my friends in Lebanon would simply toss me aside. I did everything that was asked from me, but someone in the upper echelon of Hezbollah must have screwed up and leaked the information to the Israelis and that's how we got caught and . . ."

"You hit the nail on the head, Yousef. Some higher-ups in your organization screwed up and you are made the fall guy. You're lucky that you're going to America, because if you went home, you sure as hell would be decapitated, so you could join the infamous seventy-two virgins. You would be punished as an example for the rest of the Hezbollah volunteers. Your life isn't worth two cents to them now."

"But Sir, Mr. Dagan, I should have a chance to plead my case and prove my . . ."

"Are you kidding? And make an ass of one or some of your leaders? Never happen. No, no, you're better off where you're going. I had hoped that you could be of help to us if you went back to your home country, but that is obviously not gonna happen. We will let you write a letter to your parents, and we'll see to it that it will get into their hands, without the knowledge of the authorities, so your folks will not be in danger of getting persecuted . . ."

"They wouldn't do that. They . . ."

"Oh no? They'd gladly torture your mother as a means of punishing you. You ought to know how ruthless they are. Have you ever wondered why your leaders live in luxury while sending everyone else to their death? They know it's much better to live on earth than to be dead and at Allah's mercy." He stood up. "You'll be given writing materials and some books to read while we work out the details for your transportation . . ."

"But sir, can't I get any other options?" He also got back on his feet while one of the soldiers snapped his cuffs back on.

"From here on in you'll have to negotiate with the Americans. You're lucky. They're a lot more lenient than we are and certainly more merciful than your own people. Good luck out there." He turned and walked out, while the officers restrained Yousef until the regular guards reappeared and guided him back to his cell, while his brain was boiling.

• • •

Tel Aviv, Mossad Headquarters.

"Get me Mr. Bruce Bongers in New Jersey on the secure line. Wait, wait." He raised his hand. "What's the time over there now?" He consulted the world map on his office wall. "Call his cell."

"Bruce? Meir here. Am I interrupting a soccer match?"

"No, we just finished dinner, and I was finally going to read this morning's paper."

"Okay, good timing. I have this boy Yousef from Lebanon all prepped to come your way. He thinks that he's going to Guantanamo in exchange for this character Bahouie, who was in on the 9/11 plot. He may be ready to be converted. He's certainly shook up that his own people have deserted him and are willing to sacrifice him. But first, you may need to get his parents out of the country for their own protection, because you know how those clowns are. They'll hold them as martyrs to keep their boy from working with you. I'll send you the details by fax, and you'll need the cooperation of the CIA, but I'm sure we can get them to Crete overnight, and then you folks take it from there. Okay?" He stopped a moment. "Am I rambling too much?"

"No, no. I was busy scribbling on the edge of the morning paper. Go ahead."

"You'll find it all on your desk in the morning. Any questions so far?"

"Not really, although I'm getting further and further involved in international affairs that are not really my department . . ."

"Just keep thinking about chemicals and all the lives you're gonna save."

"Sure! I'll keep that in the forefront of my mind. Shalom."

"Shalom, Bruce. Good night."

The tall FBI man stretched and yawned, thinking back about his days in U.S. Army intelligence when he and Meir Dagan had worked side by side in the Sinai Desert during one of the many Israeli wars. He had gotten to know him as a tough, straight-shooting individual and a hell of a courageous soldier. Those were memorable days, but he was glad that after twenty-six years, he had traded the Army for the FBI, and at least now, he was home fairly regularly and finally got to spend some quality time with his four sons.

His dad had joined the American Forces in the southern part of Holland at the end of '44 and had received a field commission as an Intelligence Officer because of his knowledge of Dutch, German,

French and English. For two years he was assigned to the Army detail that interrogated German SS officers and finally ended up in Northern New Jersey, where he became a U.S. Citizen and settled down with his sweetheart from Maastricht and raised five children, the oldest one being Bruce, who followed in his father's footsteps: Army Intelligence.

He sighed a contented sigh as he took his notes into his office. "It never stops being exciting."

13

SECAUCUS NJ, FBI HEADQUARTERS. 8:30 AM

"Mr. Bongers, I have a Doctor Price on the line for you. On line five."

"Thank you." Click. "Doctor Price. Thank you for calling back so promptly."

"My pleasure, Mr. Bongers..."

"Call me Bruce."

"If you call me Jay. How can I help?"

"I have the strangest situation on my hands. You are our key chemist, or should I say chemical expert, right?"

"Within the FBI? I guess so. Why did you ask?"

" Jay, at the moment, all I have is a vague rumor. So vague that I don't even want to inform the CIA or my own superiors."

"Why not?"

"If I do, they'll pressure me for my source, and I can't reveal that as yet. When I get some more concrete information I will pass it on, but like I said, all I have is a rumor."

"Where do I come in, Bruce?"

"Where within the U.S. is there a great accumulation of chemicals or a huge producer where a terrorist attack would cause the greatest loss of life?"

"Oh, my God!"

"You can say that again, Jay. Al-Qaeda is allegedly plotting another, but bigger 9/11, and this time it's supposed to involve a chemical explosion. Where would we be most vulnerable?"

"Oh boy! An attack that would kill thousands? In or near a chemical facility? Oh boy."

Bruce could hear a deep sigh on the other end of the line. "Bruce, I'll start scanning my computer right away and get back with you. I have your fax. I'll get back."

"Thanks. Thank you." But the line had gone dead. Bruce scratched his head and pushed back his chair. "I better talk to Lester." He dialed the direct line of the FBI Director in Washington.

"Lester, good morning. Do you have a minute?"

"A minute and a half."

"Okay. I have a tip of an impending terrorist attack on the U.S., but all I have is a tip. If I call the CIA, they'll want the name of my source, and I can not reveal that at this time. Personal, you know. What's your advice? Explore some more on my own? Get more facts?"

"Go slow. Tread easy. Contact me immediately when you have something more concrete, okay?"

"Okay. Have a good one."

Bruce leaned back and uttered to himself, "Good, that gives me a little leeway." He pushed the intercom. "Bruno, come in here, please."

When the good-looking Latin, Bruno Garcia, had settled in, Bongers started, "Buddy, we've tackled many problems before, but this new one is a doozy. We have no authority or authorization in what we're planning to do, and yet I'm scheming to go ahead and do it anyway."

"Sounds exciting already." The tan descendant of Dominican immigrants was always ready for action, regardless of the source or the danger involved.

"Do you have any personal acquaintances in Gitmo?"

"As guards or prisoners?"

"Guards, of course." The bureau chief laughed in spite of the serious matter. "How would you personally know any of the prisoners? Been in training camps with them? No, no. Any of the guards?"

"One of my Cuban school buddies is an interpreter at Gitmo, or at least he was. We were on the same high-school basketball team at Saint John's in Jersey City. I can find out where he is. What do you need to know?"

"I need to know more about the requirement for release of that facility. The Justice Department right now is so clammed up about those releases and transfers to U.S. prisons, that I can't get a whisper of information out of them. They're suspicious of everybody, and yet, out of every five that they return to the Middle East, two of them immediately go back to terrorism in Pakistan, Afghanistan or Yemen. I need to find one that we can cultivate into a double agent."

"Like the one that blew up seven CIA men?"

"Yeah! Wasn't that a bummer? No, that's the difficult part, who is really converted and dedicated to a peaceful life? How can you trust those clowns?" He shook his head. "As an interpreter, does your buddy speak Arabic as well as Spanish?"

"He's fluent in Arabic. He was a Marine guard in Saudi when he was in the service, and he made it a point to learn the language and some of the dialects. You should hear some of his stories. With his dark skin and big mustache, he could blend right in with the Arabs . . ."

"Okay, okay. Find him and put him in contact with me. On the Q.T. of course. Okay?"

"Sure thing." Garcia was gone.

"Meir?" Bongers had gotten through to the Mossad director on his cell. "What time is it out your way? Am I calling too late?"

"Well, no. It's 9:30 and the sun just went down over the Mediterranean. A beautiful sunset and I'm sipping a wonderful *Chateau Neuf Du Pape* on my terrace in the company of my daughter and grandson."

"Do you want me to call back later?"

"No, I'm walking into the yard as we speak. Go ahead. What's being stirred up in your mind now?"

"I keep saying to myself, 'Bruce, this is not your department,' but I can't help thinking about the fact that so many terrorists are still out there, trying to do us harm and specifically, the U.S."

"So?"

"This Lebanese boy in your custody, is he still being considered for an exchange?"

"Of course. Why?"

"Who's this man Bahouie that Hezbollah wants returned? What's so important about him? Was he one of their leaders, or do they wanna crucify him?"

"He was one of their top geniuses, but got caught by the Americans after the *'Cole'* incident in Yemen. What's your interest?"

"I'd like to have this young man Yousef planted in his cell in order to put a seed in his mind."

"Interesting. What kind of seed?"

"The thought that young Yousef will turn double agent and work with us in Jersey so that Hezbollah can feed him information that will mislead us, and in turn, info from here that they can use, directly from the FBI."

"Good God. How long would that take?"

"I realize we don't have much time, but I'd love to give it a shot. If I can have that boy for three days before he's shipped to Gitmo, I can get things started."

"How do you expect to get him in the same cell or even the same building? Do you have connections out there?"

"I'm working on it."

"I must say, you certainly have a fertile mind. How soon do you want that boy?"

"How soon can you fix a transfer?"

"Can you get the Air Force to stop over in Tel Aviv and pick him up?" Dagan chuckled as he watched a rising moon over the mountains.

"Wouldn't that be great? I'll work on it. I'll talk to you tomorrow."

"Shalom."

• • •

"Mr. Jarvis, please." Bruce dialed the FBI director's office. "Bongers here."

"Yes, Bruce. What's up?"

"How's your schedule for the next few hours?"

"I'm tied up till five, and I had planned on a lonely dinner after that, because my wife is at our daughter's, preparing for the next baby."

"Can we eat and talk at a secure place?"

"Do you know the Red Rooster on E street?"

"Sure do."

"Meet me there at six."

"We'll be there."

Lester Jarvis started to say, "We? Who else is coming?" but was already too late.

"Oh, well. Beats eating alone. Wonder what he's up to this time?"

• • •

"Bruno, we're taking my car. We're eating in D.C."

"I'm in favor of that. I hope you picked a good place. Any entertainment?"

"You and I will be the only entertainment. Let me call my wife and tell her I'll be home late. He picked up the phone, pressed # 6. "Susie, I'll be on my cell the rest of the day. Get my wife for me, please. Thanks."

14

WASHINGTON, D.C. RED ROOSTER RESTAURANT.

While waiting for their prime rib, Jersey Chief Bruce Bongers along with his assistant Bruno sipped their California Merlot as he spoke to his boss, FBI Director Lester Jarvis. "You can tell me that I'm way off base, but I'd like you to hear me out anyway. There is a plot in the works to send more terrorists to America . . ."

"That's not unusual." Jarvis, sixty-four years old and, balding and tan, looked more like a school principal than a G-man.

"But I may have a way of spoiling their game and . . . "

"Can't you just turn it over to the CIA?" Jarvis hated to cross the invisible line of responsibilities.

"I remember distinctly, when I was still with Army intelligence, that I informed them of the presence of Mohammed Atta in flight school in Florida and they did nothing with it. They just stood by and watched the Twin Towers burn to hell. I don't like a repeat of that. I think I have a plan that can cut them off at the pass, but I'll need your permission and a lot of help."

"Okay. I'm all ears."

"In Uzbekistan, the Russians have captured a group of Taliban fighters and one of them is singing . . ."

"What are the Russians doing in Uzbekistan?"

"Theoretically, they're working with local intelligence to protect the NATO forces that are flying out of there against Afghanistan, but realistically, the Russians operate all over the world to gather information and use it to their advantage. Our waiter may be working for the KGB for all we know." He smiled as he said that. "Anyway, the former Communists are having a favor called in by the Israelis, and I'm getting info that the CIA is not privy to."

"Ah! That's your source?"

"Can we keep that between us?" Bruce was afraid he had already said too much.

"Sure. Here comes our steak." The intelligence threesome, Jarvis, Bongers and Garcia stopped talking as the prime rib and salads were placed in front of them and after the waiter refilled their glasses and departed, Bruce took up the thread again.

"This is what I have in mind. The Israelis have a young Lebanese Hezbollah member in custody, who is not wanted by his leadership in Beirut, but may be a principal in a prisoner exchange scheme . . ."

"Come again . . . , slowly."

"Okay. Hezbollah wants Emir Bahouie returned from Gitmo. The Israelis want one of their soldiers and a civilian returned from Lebanon. America needs someone in return in this three-way swap. I want the Lebanese from Israel."

"Why? What good would he do for the U.S.?"

"This is my whole point. The young man graduated Stevens Institute . . ."

"Here? In Hoboken?"

"Correct. I want to make them believe that he can become a turncoat and work with us, while they'll exploit him as a double agent."

"Oh, man. This sounds like a spy novel."

"Well, it is. If we play it right, the young man will believe he's feeding info to Hezbollah, while we monitor his behavior and communications, and that way we know exactly what they're planning, which is a lot more than we know now. We're groping in the dark most of the time."

"Why couldn't the CIA or Homeland Security handle this?"

Jarvis was still cautious.

"Because I'm confident that I can do a better job than they can. All they believe in is handing out money, lots of money, and I don't think this young man can be bought. I bet you that money is not that important to him. Pride is. He has something to prove to his brethren in Beirut. He failed in his first mission, and they don't even want him back. That smarts."

"What do you want me to do?'

"Get with the various authorities and have this young man Yousef become a cellmate of Bahouie in Gitmo before he's returned to Lebanon."

"Bruce, do you know what you're asking?"

"A lot, but a lot of American lives will be saved if it works."

"Ayayay! The other agencies are gonna love me."

"Well, Lester. I will for sure." Bongers burst out laughing.

"Where do we start?"

"With your permission, we'll have young Yousef flown into McGuire Air Force Base, and I pick him up and nurture him for a few days before he goes off to Gitmo."

"Just like that? We get the Air Force to provide a taxi service and make a stopover in Tel Aviv on their way from Kuwait and pick up a prisoner to deliver to New Jersey?" Jarvis was astounded.

"Why not?" Bruce smiled broadly.

"Because it's going to be impossible to pull that off without Homeland and the CIA getting involved in the operation and asking a lot of questions."

"Would you let me worry about that? If you just pull the right strings to get Bahouie returned in a three-way exchange between Beirut, Tel Aviv and Gitmo. I'll take it from there."

"Oh boy. My steak got cold because I forgot to eat."

"Put some horseradish on it." Bruno suggested.

"Forget that." The director resumed eating. "What time frame are you talking about?"

"A week, ten days?"

"You're asking a lot."

"A lot depends on it, Lester."
"I know, I know."

• • •

Speeding north on the Jersey Turnpike, Bongers turned to his assistant Garcia, who was driving. "What's the time difference again between here and Israel? Eight hours? Ten? I always forget. If it's eight P.M. here, then it's four in the morning there, right? I better wait a bit before I call."

"You have the man's cell number, right?"

"Dagan's?"

"Yeah. He may get up at six his time. Call him from home. You'll be okay."

"Damn. I'm too anxious, but I might as well try to sleep."

"You'll wake up when I stop." Bruno rolled down his window and put the blinking red light on top of the car, so he could speed through the toll booths without stopping.

• • •

When Bongers had made himself comfortable in his home office with a Dewars on the rocks, he dialed Meir Dagan on his personal cell.

"Good morning, Meir."

"Shalom, brother. You're up early."

"Wrong, I haven't gone to bed yet. Listen. I have the unofficial okay from Lester although he doesn't like it. The friction between agencies is still very much in existence despite the threats from two different presidents. Do you have contacts in the U.S. Air Force so you can have a jet stop over and pick up Yousef?"

"I'm sure that our Air Chief, Hymie Aartman, has close contacts. When do you want him?"

"A.S.A.P. That way I can work on him for a few days. Then I'll ship him to Guantanamo and two weeks later we can have Bahouie flown to Beirut, as soon as you give us the word, that you have your men, or man and woman, as the case may be."

"Seems workable to me. I'll start on it the moment I get to my office, which will be an hour from now. When should I call you back?"

"Ten hours from now. I'll hit the sack in another thirty minutes."

"Will do. Shalom!"

Bongers strolled into the den and was just in time to say goodnight to his second son, who, at sixteen, was already two inches taller than dad.

His wife, Helen, still youthful and blond, waved him over to the couch. "Honey, do you want to watch the news or do you wanna sit and talk a little?" She knew that his brain was on another planet. "Lots on your mind?"

"Yes, but the good news is, I don't have to carry a gun or worry about actions against me or my men. It's all theoretical and paperwork. No bullets or missiles, so nothing for you to worry about."

"That's good. Yet I know you're worrying about something." She smiled and her face lit up when she did, while her eyes sparkled at the same time. She knew him well.

"It's just that if too many people get involved in this upcoming action, something is liable to get screwed up and leaks will start interfering with the overall effectiveness of the operation." His brow wrinkled as he spoke.

"Can't you do most of it by yourself?"

"That's the sad part. It'll take a lot of different people in various parts of the world to coordinate everything, and it may go smoothly until another agency gets wind of it and things go haywire."

"What is it all about, or can't you say?"

"Actually not, but in a broad sense, another 9/11 is in the making and . . ."

"God, no!"

"I'm afraid so. As long as these terrorists have endless supplies of money coming in, they can afford to plan anything they want anywhere in the world."

"Oh my! When will this ever end, Bruce?"

"When they run out of money. When we stop buying gas from them and that's a long way off. We're many years away from being self sufficient. Many years!"

"Goodness. Can I refresh your scotch?"

"Half of one."

15

BEIRUT, HEZBOLLAH HEADQUARTERS.

In the bath house of the Hazmieh Rotana Hotel, four bearded men were huddled together in the sauna-like setting with nothing but a bath towel to cover them, if they so desired.

"Before we go into our meeting upstairs, I want a vote from you. Do we allow Sheik Azballahad to attend the conference or do we dismiss him? Or discard him, maybe?"

"Ahmed, discard him? What has he done?" The gray-haired man with skinny legs addressed the bulky leader of the group.

"He has not shared his wealth or his power with us in six months, and we suspect him of screwing up the deal with the Russians." His eyes blazed and his voice became high pitched. "We still don't know how Yousef and the weapons were intercepted and by whom, but someone in our inner circle is a rat, and I have checked everyone and cannot find fault with any of them."

"That doesn't mean the Sheik is the culprit."

"But it doesn't prove that he isn't."

One of the other men spoke up. "Ahmed, it's up to you. If you don't trust him, get rid of him. What excuse are you going to use to dismiss him?"

"I've got it all arranged. Are we in agreement?" They all nodded.

"Okay, let's go."

As the six leaders of Hezbollah settled down in the comfortable cushions of the penthouse, Sheik Azballahad entered the lobby of the hotel and waved at his chauffeur to go ahead and park his Mercedes. He was dressed in the fashion of the old Bedouins, totally covered in a camelhair robe with a loose fitting hood. All seemed quiet. A bellhop in old-fashioned pantaloons and a red fez pointed him toward the last elevator in the row of three on the east side of the entrance. "To the penthouse, Sir."

Two workmen and a laundry cart shared the ornately decorated elevator and as the doors closed noiselessly, a thin piano wire was slipped over the head of the chubby Sheik and although he struggled with all his might, the noose tightened around his neck, and by the time the elevator reached the basement, he was dead. His lifeless body disappeared under the laundry and the cart was wheeled to a waiting SUV that pulled away as soon as it's backdoor was closed.

"We should have removed his ghutra. It took too long to choke him. Look at where he scratched my face." One of the "workmen" pointed at his left cheek.

"Blame it on your wife," the other chuckled. "Let's get to the meeting."

"What happened to your face? Did one of your wives get jealous?" Ahmed laughed at his own joke. "Well, everyone is here except the Sheik. So let's begin." After making sure that every man had his mint tea, he started the meeting.

"We have opened up negotiations with the Americans and Israelis. Emir Bahouie will be released in exchange for the Israeli woman and the corporal that we captured in the Golan. Then Yousef will replace our esteemed brother Emir Bahouie in Guantanamo."

"The Americans agreed to that?"

"They probably feel that they'll get more out of Yousef than they've gotten out of our Emir in three years. They have no idea as to how little the young man really knows. They will regret the exchange later, because they have no idea how much Bahouie has accomplished inside those walls on that Cuban island."

"Like what?"

"Through their exchanges of their Qurans, they have established a complete network of delegates from different nationalities. Some are already working in Yemen, training new volunteers for our Holy Jihad, and some have returned to Saudi, Iran and Iraq to establish pockets of resistance fighters. The movement in Iraq is going extremely well, and when- or if-, the Americans leave, they'll be ready to overthrow the existing traitors and install an all Shiite Government. Unfortunately, the Kurds don't trust our people as yet, but they will side with us when they see our successful overthrow of the present parliament."

"Why are they releasing the Emir now? Don't they have any idea of his value to our cause?" Burook, the thin old man, had his doubts.

"Why are the Americans releasing him? They made him swear on the Quran that he would not plot against the United States, once he's released . . ."

"He did?"

"Yes, but the stupid Americans didn't understand his Afghan dialect, so he actually swore that he WOULD take up the sword again against the infidels."

That brought a round of spontaneous laughter.

"Anyway, he should be with us again in a few weeks."

"Do we have any word on Yousef?"

"He's in an Israeli prison. Has been seen by our Mullah once, but the young man is difficult to deal with." No one questioned how Ahmed might have obtained that news. "Apparently, the Jews got nothing out of him, but then again, he didn't know much."

"How about his wife? His girlfriend?"

"She hasn't been heard from. Probably in jail." He sipped from his scalding tea. "But now onto the real call for this meeting." He gingerly put down his glass. "We are on schedule. On September 11, 2010, the United States will experience a greater calamity than the old Twin Towers operation. Several of our operatives are already in place, and all the plans are being finalized right now."

"Are we going to be privy to those plans?" The younger, black-bearded man seemed anxious to get involved.

"Yes, and because we don't want a repeat of the *Vladivostok* disaster, none of you will know the entire plan, just the details of your particular section." He looked around the room. "One of you is the direct contact with the Master, Osama bin Laden, and you know who you are. In your case, you'll be working with a devout Muslim on a supply boat in the Gulf of Mexico, based in New Orleans . . ."

"How will I know him?" A young man jumped up, giving away his identity.

"Patience, dumb brother, patience. Let me just say that he's a Filipino sailor, who fought valiantly with our group in the Philippines and now handles chemicals up and down the rivers in the southern United States. You may have to shave that beautiful black beard of yours and learn to smuggle hand-held rockets across the border from Mexico into Texas."

"My beard?" He literally jumped up and stroked his beautiful proof of manhood. "My beard? Must I do that?" The whole room burst out laughing.

"If Allah wills it so? Allah il Allah." He waved at the young man to resume his seat.

"Everyone here will have a definite assignment, and if we have another leak, like the Russian disaster, only a small part of our plan will fail, but the overall plan will succeed, and the whole world will realize that Islam is unstoppable. The whole world will kneel before Allah and our Prophet."

"Why are we picking that same date, 9/11?"

"Because on that date the Allies declared war on us, and this will prove to them that they are not winning this war. Not even close to winning the war." His dark eyes sparkled with fire. He lifted his glass again. "Death to the Infidels."

Everybody stood. "Death to the Infidels."

When order had resumed, the questions started up again. "Will we be able to get to their leaders?" One of the men asked.

"The Israeli President is scheduled to visit Washington, so that is very convenient. Many Senators and Congressmen may happen to be in the vicinity and enjoy a fast trip to hell with their Commander in Chief."

"How will you arrange for all of them to be near New Orleans?"

"Did I say that? Did I say that all of this would take place in New Orleans? Do you see what's happening here? You're already jumping to conclusions, and you're showing your impulsiveness. All I mentioned is that one of our devotees operates out of New Orleans. That's all I said. Don't misconstrue anything I say. Just do your job when you learn what it is and execute it to perfection. Just like Atta and the Twin Towers, he had it perfectly coordinated, and the only thing that went wrong was that some so-called heroes on one of the planes tried to overpower the pilots and it crashed in a field instead of on top of the Senate building in Washington. Other than that, it was perfect planning and perfect execution on our behalf. The prophet had been planning it for years, and the Americans and their foolish pride made it all possible because their Intelligence Agencies worked against one another instead of with each other. The same thing will happen this time." He got up, and his tone became more and more excited as he got into his speech.

"This time we'll feed the Infidels little bits of information, that will have them scrambling all over the country looking for false clues and then . . . 'BOOM!', right in their faces. It's going to be beautiful. Bin Laden may be here in person to brief everyone and . . ."

"How will he get here?"

"Hasn't he been hiding now for eight years while the Americans are offering twenty-five million dollars for his capture? He goes anywhere he wants. His health has been a problem for a few years, but the finest surgeons in the world have restored him to near perfection. He may be here and outline the details of our mission. Meanwhile, each of you will learn what your part of the plan is, and you'll select your associates carefully. Submit to me a list of your prospective operatives, and we'll start the screening and training process." He turned to the young man. "And do shave your beard. It'll grow back."

Other questions and remarks were floored, and twice more someone asked about the Sheik and his whereabouts, but no one seemed to have a satisfactory answer.

"Let's move to the terrace for a dinner of leg-of-lamb and couscous and enjoy the sunset that Allah presents to us each evening. The beautiful sunset over the Mediterranean will confirm that Mohammed and Allah are blessing our motives and our actions. Let's bow toward Mecca and express our thanks."

"Allah il Allah."

16

SECAUCUS, NJ. FBI HEADQUARTERS.

"Bruno! Quit what you're doing. We're going to McGuire." Bongers hung up the phone and grabbed his jacket. When Agent Garcia walked in, he said, "We'll have to check our guns at the gate, Bruno, but that's alright. The guy will probably be cuffed anyway. Were you in the midst of something important?"

"Just checking the files on this character Jason Julliard. A nut case if I ever heard one. I don't know yet how many aliases this guy has used in his life. Anyhow, Alice is continuing the rundown. What's up?"

"Our exchange prisoner is about to land, and we'll pick him up as soon as we can get there. The CIA will have his transfer papers ready, I hope. Let's take my car. You drive."

In spite of all their impressive IDs, the guards at the Air Force Base entrance made them turn in their weapons and wait for a military police escort before they were allowed to enter the gate.

The rest of the mission was easier. The civilian Homeland Security Officer who had accompanied Yousef all the way from Israel to the U.S. by means of Germany didn't even ask for the two FBI men to identify themselves. The fact that they were there to claim him seemed to be enough. Garcia took the handcuff off the young man's left hand and clamped it onto his own right wrist. Together they edged their way into the back seat of the military patrol car, and after Bongers settled into the passenger seat next to the driver, the vehicle eased its way to the gate.

The transfer of a shackled man into the back of a plain blue Buick aroused some curiosity in the parking lot, but that couldn't be helped. This time Yousef's left wrist was cuffed to the inside door handle of the back seat, and Bruce got in on the other side.

Until that time, not a word had been exchanged between the three men. When Bruno eased into traffic, Bongers spoke for the first time.

"I'm Bruce Bongers, Special Agent FBI from the New Jersey office. That is Bruno Garcia, my assistant." As he sat within inches from the young Lebanese, it struck him how much he looked like Bruno. Same tan complexion, same dark eyes and shiny black hair. The only difference was that the mid-eastern man's hair was not as wavy as Garcia's. They could pass for brothers or cousins with a ten-year age difference.

"You're going to be our guest for a few days or a long time, depending on a few factors." Yousef just looked at him with a wrinkled brow, but didn't say anything. "You're supposed to go to Guantanamo, as you probably well know, but I'm trying to delay that." Bongers continued.

"Why?"

"I want to learn more about you."

"Why?"

"Because ten years ago, I worked closely with a young Moroccan named Yousef, who could have been your twin brother, if you had been born earlier. I learned more from that young man about Islam, ethics, loyalty and devotion than I had ever learned from anybody, and I hope to continue my education with you."

"Where is that man now? That Yousef?"

"He's buried in a national cemetery in Bushnell, Florida, in the same grave with his adopted Peruvian brother."

The young Lebanese looked at Bongers, question marks all over his face. "Buried? In a national cemetery? Was he in the Moroccan Army?"

"No, he was in the U.S. Army. He died, trying to locate Osama bin Laden after the 9/11 attack on the twin towers. He died in Afghanistan."

Yousef still had a look on his face as if he had just heard a fairy tale. "He pursued bin Laden? Why?"

"Because his ancestor's beliefs couldn't condone the murder of innocent people for any reason. Political or religious."

The young man's voice reflected his antagonism. "What do you know of his ancestors and their beliefs and . . ."

"I visited his parents and grandfather in their home and . . ."

"Their home? Where's their home? In the States somewhere?"

"No, in Chefchouen, Morocco."

"Morocco? You've been to Chefchouen?" His tone of voice changed considerably.

"Yes, very devout, hardworking people. Weavers. They had . . ."

"Weavers? Like tapestry?"

"Yes. Why do you ask?" Now Bongers looked puzzled.

"My grandfather was a carpet weaver, and that's how my father learned his trade. But he prefers selling the stuff, rather than manufacturing it. He has a store in Tripoli."

"Tripoli? North Africa?"

"No, no. Tripoli, Lebanon."

"Well." For a moment neither spoke. It seemed that both of them wanted to absorb that new-found information.

Yousef was the first one to pick up the thread of the conversation again. "So how did your Moroccan Yousef get involved with the Army, and how did he get into Afghanistan in the first place?"

"Because of a childhood robbery accident, his leg bones were reset and restructured, so the Air Force turned him down for flight training, but the Army paid for his schooling at a civilian institute in return for a four-year enlistment agreement."

"A robbery accident? What's a robbery accident?"

"The teenagers that assaulted him threw him down the stone steps in the Kasbah of his hometown, crushing his pelvis and a bunch of his bones."

"Allah!" He seemed genuinely shocked. "And he learned to fly?"

"Yes, American doctors nearly perfected his body again, but it didn't meet Air Force qualifications."

"Allah il Allah! Where did his parents get the money? They were only weavers, right?"

"The Shriners paid for it."

Yousef looked Bongers in the eyes. "Shiners? What are Shiners?"

"Shriners, not Shiners. They're men who raise money to rehabilitate disabled children."

"Why?"

"Because they care."

"Because they care?" Yousef sat in the back seat, his eyes downcast and breathing deeply. Bongers didn't say a word. He hoped some of his message was getting through to the young extremist.

Bruno didn't use the flashing red light to speed through the toll gates, but instead moved through the *EASY-PASS* gates with the rest of the traffic. Finally, Yousef spoke up again. "Why am I not being shipped to Guantanamo in exchange for the Saudi?"

"You will be, but I'm trying to slow the process."

"Isn't this an exchange for some Israelis for the return of Bahouie and me being a pawn in the whole deal?"

"That's a pretty good summation. Who told you that?"

Yousef realized he said too much. He wasn't supposed to have known all that.

"Rumors . . . Just rumors. I wasn't told anything by the Mossad, but I heard whispers when we were taken from our cells."

"Hogwash. I don't believe a word of that. I'd rather believe that you were taken from your cell all by yourself and that you had no contact with any other prisoners. These Israelis are too smart to let you interact with other captives. Who told you about the exchange? The CIA agent on the plane?"

"No, no." The young man looked panicky. "Just rumors. That's all."

"Yousef, if we're to get along and you want favorable treatment by the United States, you have to start telling me the truth and in return I will be up front with you." He grabbed the young man's chin and put their noses close together. "Who told you that?"

The Lebanese shook his head loose from Bruce's grip and turned toward the door without saying a word. He looked at the door handle to which his cuff was fastened, and as if Bongers could read his mind, he said, "The door won't open from the inside, so forget about jumping out. Besides, your arm would be ripped off."

For ten minutes, no one said a word. The miles crunched away under the wheels, and finally Yousef spoke up again. "Where are we going?"

"To our office up the road."

"What will happen to me?"

"You'll be locked up with some real criminals, and they may enjoy the company of a good-looking young male. May be fun."

Fun was not what was reflected on Yousef's face. "Why don't I just go to Cuba?"

"And be trained to become a gutless suicide bomber who'll go into market places and kill women like your mother? Our A.C.L.U. will work to have all the terrorists turned loose again, so they can continue their so-called 'war' against civilization, be it Christians, Kurds or Shiites. No, if I had my druthers, I would gas the whole bunch and cremate them and use'em for fertilizer on the Cuban sugar plantations. No, if we send you there, you'll be out in ten years, so you can go back to the Golan Heights and lob grenades on the homes of hard-working villagers. I'd rather have you castrated and use you in an Arabian harem. That way you will suffer the degradation for the rest of your miserable life. The Saudis think you Lebanese are inferior people anyway, and they'd love to use you as a slave. Apparently this is the path you have chosen, and I'm glad to accommodate you."

"Why the sudden hatred? You seemed so nice a moment ago."

"I worked at the recovery of the victims of the Twin Towers, and I vividly remember digging out body parts of little children and pregnant mothers. I see in you the next killer, and I hope I will be able to prevent that. I'd rather shoot you myself, if I can convince myself I'd be saving American lives."

The car swung into the underground garage of the FBI building. "Bruno! Lock him up. I have some calls to make."

Bongers raced up to his office, dialed a number and told the voice on the other line, "Meir? You have a problem. You have a leak."

17

FBI, NEW JERSEY HEADQUARTERS

"Mr. Bongers, I have General Sullivan on the line for you on six."

"General, good morning. We had a hell of a time tracking you down. You're in the Pentagon now?"

"Again, Bruce, again."

"I hear you have your third star now, congr . . ."

"Hold that! I don't know yet if it's a blessing. It's good to be back in Georgetown in our condo, and my wife is in the middle of all her old-time friends again, but I'm going bananas with all the paperwork."

"Don't you have a huge team now that can handle all that for you?"

"No, Bruce, that's the problem. Thousands of pieces of information come in here and hundreds of people sort through them to see what is important enough to come to my desk and I may be missing out on some vital input . . ." He coughed and continued. "Like that suicide bomber on the Detroit flight? We had at least ten warning signals and they were never put together to become one aggressive piece that would trigger a warning shot. Very frustrating. Each one of the ten investigators didn't have enough evidence to warrant an alert. Very frustrating. Of course the press and the congress are all over us, and thank God, Homeland got most of the blame, but it was much simpler when I was at MacDill and just had to worry about Europe and the Middle East instead of the whole world." He coughed again. "Anyway, how are things by you? The missus and the kids okay?"

"They're fine and I really don't want to add to your problems, but do you also oversee Gitmo and the detainees?"

"All part of my deal. What are you up to?"

"Who's your man in charge, so I can deal directly with the head honcho?"

"Again. What are you up to?"

"I need to arrange for two men to share a cell, so I can receive and send out input about an upcoming terrorist threat."

"That's not your territory, Bruce, and you know it."

"That's true, but I have an inside source and information that a new 9/11 is in the works and my superior, Director Lester Jarvis, has given me some leeway . . ."

"Isn't it easier to give the info to the CIA and let them handle it?"

"Let them bungle it again? I still have vivid pictures in my mind of working in the ruins of the Twin Towers, because they ignored my warnings about Mohammed Atta and his flight-school cronies. No, I can't chance blowing my source until I have more facts and fewer rumors. When I add two and two together, you'll be the first one I'll call."

"Okay, Bruce. For old times sake. Call General Jake Watson, my old chopper pilot. I'll call him first and give you all the clearances you need. He's a good man. You two should work well together. Take this number down and wait an hour, to be sure I got to him first, okay?"

"Thank you and I will keep you posted."

"General Watson, this is Bruce Bongers, FBI, I . . ."

"I remember you, Colonel Bongers. At one point you were kinda my superior officer."

"I was? Kinda? When and where?"

"First in 'Nam, when my chopper detachment was assigned to

'Intelligence' and later when you headed up the group in Fort Bragg. We flew some of your assignments, but I don't think we ever met in person."

"So you stayed in and made general?"

"Well, you know how it is. Someone needs to do the dirty work. How 'bout you?"

"I got out after 9/11, and I get to spend more time with my boys."

"Good for you. What can we concoct together, the Army and FBI?"

"You have a man there by the name of Fanouf Bahouie, and he's about to be released to the Israelis."

"What about him?"

"He's one of the most intelligent, conniving terrorists that ever lived and Hezbollah wants him back for some of their exploits."

"And Israel is going along with that?"

"Reluctantly. I have a 22-year-old Lebanese here that I want to move in with Bahouie and get in his confidence. I need you to delay his departure as long as possible, and one of two things will happen. Either I get to convert our young man to our side, or he becomes the intimate confidant of that Saudi murderer, and one way or the other, I will get sensitive info from the kid or I feed them false information that will throw them off . . ."

"How do you expect to get an open line into my compound here?"

"There already is..."

"Oh, come on, Bongers. This is a secure facility, and nothing goes outta here that we . . ."

"You don't have control over the lawyers that the ACLU sends in there, plus all the other private lawyers that our do-gooders in government have walking in and out of your place to protect the rights of those killers . . ."

"How much do you know about that?"

"The media tells me that one out of every three that you release goes off to Yemen to receive further training from al-Qaeda. How do they know where to go? Who finances them? That's all arranged before they leave your camp, believe me."

"I could throw up, Bongers, but knowing your reputation and the high recommendation from General Sullivan, I'll work with you any way I can. Be specific." He sounded very annoyed.

"When that young Lebanese Yousef Sagan arrives, put him in the same cell under whatever pretense you can think of. Allow them a lot of time together. Bug their unit and have it translated and transcribed by someone you trust explicitly, and fax them to me as often as possible."

"What are you trying to accomplish, Colonel?" His tone was not friendly any more.

"I'm trying to avoid another 9/11, but one on a much larger scale."

"Holy Moses. When and where?"

"Same date, presumably, and in different locations in the U.S., killing as many people as they can."

"Good God. Not again."

"Again and again from the highest authority, Osama bin Laden."

"Bruce, sorry about my attitude there a minute ago. You can count on me 100%.

"Jake, that's what you were always known for. Look forward to working with you."

"Same here."

• • •

"Bruno, get me our prisoner. We're going for a ride."

This time, the seating arrangement was the same, but the destination was different. They headed for Hoboken. Instead of heading through the Lincoln Tunnel, they moved north along the Boulevard. The car cruised into Weehawken, where Bongers pointed out, "Here's where one of the best Americans, one of the best people in the world was shot. Right here along the river."

"I know. I lived here!" Yousef looked triumphant.

"You know? You lived here? When you went to school in Hoboken?" Bongers was genuinely surprised. "And you know about Burr and Hamilton?"

"Yeah. Some stupid feud and Hamilton lost."

"That's exactly the point I wanted to make. Two brilliant people, arguing over some silly point . . ."

"Not silly to them . . ."

"Good point. To the whole outside world it may have seemed silly, but to them it was important enough to demand a public duel and to kill one of them. Do you know that Hamilton is one of the few people, other than presidents, whose face appears on our money? He set up our entire federal taxation system that is still in use today . . ."

"And that most people hate . . ."

"And that has made this the most prosperous country in the entire world, and here is where he died." Bruce made a sweeping motion with his arm, as if the entire Hudson River had been involved. "Turn, Bruno. Hoboken."

While Agent Garcia circled the block, Bongers continued. "The message I was trying to get across is that all through the ages, people have killed others for no other reason than hatred and pride. So much suffering was brought onto the globe by that ego-maniac Hitler, who even after his death wanted people, women and children alike, to die, to die for nothing but his idiotic dogma. Millions and millions died. Many of them a horrible death. Why don't you take it upon yourself to help stop that."

"Me? By myself? What could I do?"

"You could, as your Quran prescribes, help stop the misinterpretations of the Prophet's message and help stop the killing of innocent people."

"But the Quran . . ."

"The Quran only talks in terms of bravery in battle, man to man. Not cowardly blowing up women and children. As a matter of fact, the Prophet Mohammed specifically instructs the men of Islam to be the protectors of women, not the slayers."

"What would you expect me to do? I will never give up Islam and I . . ."

"No, don't ever give that up, but join the thousands of Muslims who want to live in peace with one another for the benefit of all concerned."

"Why do you profess to have so much knowledge of the Quran and Islam?"

"I have worked with Muslims for more than twenty years. I truly believe that I know more about the Quran than the Bible I grew up with. That's why it's so frustrating to me to fight extremists because I know it's all so unnecessary. Just like the death of Alexander Hamilton."

Garcia had crossed the Lincoln Tunnel approach to the south, and Bongers pointed toward the waterfront and asked, "Does that bring back memories, good or bad?"

"Mostly good. Some bad."

"You're staying with us a few more days, and I hope you'll commit yourself to stay with us forever and work with us toward the same goal, peace for all mankind. Think about it. You could have a good future with us."

18

FBI HEADQUARTERS, NEW JERSEY

"Bruno, come in here a minute." The Special Agent in charge sifted through a pile of papers in a maroon folder. When his number-one assistant walked in, he pointed to the chair next to his desk. "Sit."

"What have you got?" Bruno Garcia could hardly wait to be clued in.

"For weeks we heard nothing, and all of a sudden we are inundated with info. I'll break it down as I sort these messages chronologically. Write down numbers and brief notes, so you can make head or tails of it.

First, report from Gitmo. It seems it took ten days before those two finally talked to one another."

"Which two? Yousef and Fatuoie?"

"Fanouf Bahouie."

"Isn't that what I said?"

"Right. It reads like . . . sounds like . . . Bahouie got a message from somewhere that the boy was alright. To sum it up, he wants the boy to turn double agent, confide in me, get out and work with us in the U.S., no particular place, just U.S., and feed secrets to al-Qaeda."

"Isn't that what you wanted in the first place?"

"Kinda, except I wanted him to spy for us, but we can wire him and track him, so that's good news. I'll let you read through all the transcripts and see if you pick up something else."

Bongers looked at his notes. "Second. Are you writing?"

"Just a sec. Okay... Second. Shoot."

"The chemicals we were looking for, the large accumulations? Guess what? They are huge tankers, thousands of gallons."

"What are they gonna do with those?"

"You blow those up with a hand-held missile, and you create an explosion like a nuclear bomb."

"Cristo Mio! How did you learn that?"

"Mossad has leaks inside Hezbollah and they . . ."

"Where are those tankers?" Garcia was still shaking his head.

"Moving up and down our rivers, to Houston, New Orleans, Lake Charles, the Sabine River, et cetera."

"God God! How do we cover all those areas?"

"One thing is for sure. It's gonna be a huge headache and according to the Russians . . ."

"The Russians? Where do they come in?"

"Oh, they're playing footsies with the Israelis in order to avoid an international incident about that missing freighter with all the weapons aboard, and they're holding six extremists in Uzbekistan, one of them is singing like a canary. Anyway, they provided a lead that we can work with. On those supply ships that sail back and forth between the drill platforms in the Gulf and the main land, there are hundreds of Vietnamese, Filipinos and other nationalities, and apparently one of the Filipinos is an escaped terrorist from prison in his home country, after that deal with the American family that they held for five months, remember?"

"Cristo Mio! Does this never end?"

"Well, all we know is that he's a devout Muslim, but now we can narrow it down with the Filipino authorities to 'escaped' extremists."

"Boss, it's time to spread the info. It's getting too big for this little office."

"True! True! But I wasn't finished yet. We're onto number three."

"Really? Number three? What else could you probably have up

your sleeve?"

Bongers laughed, "Sleeve? No, I have all this in front of me in a purple folder."

"Time to call the director. My head is spinning." He literally shook his head.

"I agree. We have to get together in a conference, just a small circle one, but you have not asked me about number three yet."

"Okay, I'm listening."

"Number three. All this disaster is to be choreographed to coincide with an attempt on the life of President Obama."

"You gotta be kidding me? Where is that supposed to happen?"

"Somewhere in our neck of the woods, probably New York City or D.C."

"How much time are you giving me to read all this and give you some sort of a summary?"

"Rush it. I'm calling Jarvis. We may chopper to D.C. or Langley, depending on what he suggests."

"Oh boy, give me the file. Can I read as you drive?"

Bongers didn't even hear him. He had picked up the phone.

"Lester, Bruce here. We need to meet quickly, with or without the involvement of the other agencies. We have an explosive problem on our hands. What do you suggest?"

"How explosive?"

"Three times 9/11."

"Jeez! Really?"

"Yep! Worse."

"Stay there. I'll call you right back."

"4:30 at Langley." The FBI chief called back within the hour.

"How many people present?"

"I don't know. Why?"

"Only the heads, please."

"Since when do you dictate procedures?" Mr. Jarvis was perplexed.

"Since I hold the strings and I know the results of too many players in the field. I buried people after . . ."

"I know, I know. 4:30 at the penthouse."

• • •

Langley Air Force Base, Virginia. CIA headquarters.

In the meeting room on the top floor, Bongers immediately objected to the setting. "This room is too big, too many recorders and too many people listening in. We need to move to secure and smaller quarters."

Jeb Taylor, the CIA chief, almost blew his cork. "Where do you come off dictating policy for this organization?"

"Mr. Taylor. The security of this country is more important than a simple company policy. We're going to talk about saving thousands . . . tens of thousands of American lives, including ours, so can we proceed?" Bruce remained stern.

"Alright! Johnson, prepare room 1102." Taylor spoke to one of his agents.

"No, no! Prepare nothing. No bugs. Just us, and pencil and paper." Bruce was out of his element, but he knew he was in control.

Reluctantly, eight people followed Mr. Taylor down a flight of stairs into room 1102, where Bongers dismissed three of them. "Not needed yet."

• • •

What Bruce had figured would be an hour-long briefing, turned into a three-hour session.

Many times they questioned the quality of his information, but in the end, Homeland Security, Army Intelligence, the CIA, and the FBI had divvied up their workload and assignments and agreed to involve the Secret Service as well.

Over dinner at the *Foxfire* restaurant, Bruce felt he had gotten to the softer side of the CIA Director and asked, "Jeb, obviously this whole thing is way out of my league and way over my head. Is there one person on your team, who you could appoint as the overall coordinator? Someone who has everyone's respect?"

"Anybody specific, Bruce?"

"I've worked well with several of your men and I'd feel better if I could continue with my everyday routine, while monitoring the info I get from or send out to my various contacts. Let's face it. There's no way that we could handle this whole operation from Jersey. The scope is simply too large. Does that sound reasonable?"

"Yes, you have a point. If each agency appoints one key man, then we'd have fewer chances of miscommunications or screw-ups. I'll make a decision in the morning and let you know."

"One small favor? When you have a team flying out west to check the tanker situation, can you fix me up with a ride? I'm not familiar with that part of the world, and I'd like to see first hand what the layout is and what we have to look out for."

"Sure, Bruce. Check with my main man . . ."

"Who?"

"The one I'll call you about in the A.M. By the way, how many pipelines do you have going? How many sources of secret information do you have?"

"Let's see. Russia, Uzbekistan, Gitmo, Tel Aviv. The Pentagon . . ."

"You've got more wires going than we do at Langley, and your territory supposedly only encompasses New Jersey. How do you manage that?"

Bongers nearly laughed out loud but caught himself. "I guess I've proven to be a good friend and a good listener to a lot of people."

"That's the secret? A good listener? Gotta remember that. Now I'd better head home. I had company tonight, but I think they drank my cognac all by themselves. Thanks, Bruce, even though you brought bad tidings. I'll talk to you in the morning."

"Good night, sir." To himself he mumbled, "I'd better find Bruno and my ride back to Secaucus."

The helicopter was still on standby and once he had found his assistant in the restaurant lounge, they caught a ride back to Langley for the flight home.

"Another long, long day, partner."

"You ain't just whistling Dixie, boss."

19

FBI, NEW JERSEY HEADQUARTERS

"A General Watson on line four."

"Thank you," Bruce stopped writing, picked up the phone and pushed the lighted button.

"Hello, Jake, Bongers here. How's it going?"

"Well, let me just say that the world is full of surprises. The order to close Gitmo was just countermanded, so I guess I'll retire here. That was surprise number one. Then I get an inmate who's returned to the FBI after just four weeks. Everyone else stays here for years. Then to top it off, the hardest criminal in the place is released back to his homeland."

"Bahouie? Directly to Saudi?" Bruce couldn't believe his ears.

"Oh, no! First to Israel, where they'll use him as a pawn to get some of their own out of Lebanese jails. Did you read all our transcripts?"

"Yes, I did."

"Isn't that funny how neither of them spoke for ten days or more. They must have been aware of bugs, or they thoroughly distrusted one another. Then all of a sudden the floodgates opened up." General Watson observed.

"Was Bahouie visited by a lawyer, just before they started talking?"

"Should be in the transcripts somewhere."

"It is, but I didn't get the whole gist of the conversation between the attorney and the Saudi." Bongers wondered if he'd missed something.

"Oh, that's by order of the government. The confidential conversations between lawyer and suspect are privileged and can't be recorded."

"Bingo!" Bruce shouted.

"Bingo? What do you mean?"

"That's your link. There has been a line of communication between Hezbollah, bin Laden and Gitmo for a long time, and now we know how. What's the name of the attorney?"

"Just a minute . . . Here it is. Amand Kalif from Chicago. I can't believe that. He's been cleared by the highest authorities. I'll hang that sonofabitch." His anger was obvious through the phone.

"No, no, Jake! Don't do anything. I'll get with General Sullivan and get an official okay to record all of Kaliff's conversations, and that way we get a direct line into the wolf's lair of Osama, Hamas and the Hezbollah. We've known that that line existed. We've known that the men who leave your camp have instructions where and when to report, mostly Yemen of late."

"Good God Almighty, and that has been going on right under my nose?"

"Don't blame yourself, Jake. Your hands were tied, but I'll get them undone. Just make sure that only your most trusted men are in on this. We don't want to lose a good thing, by blowing it, and we certainly don't want the media crying, *'Poor prisoners have their civil rights violated.'*"

"I'll get right on it. Great job. First major breakthrough in years." His smile became evident through the phone.

"What about my boy Yousef? What's his schedule?" Bongers wanted to know.

"It's your call."

"Okay. Hand him to the CIA. I'll take it fr,om there. Thanks Jake, you made my day. I'm calling Sullivan right now."

• • •

"After you track down General Sullivan at the Pentagon, find out where Mr. Jarvis is at this moment."

"Yes, sir."

Bongers stretched luxuriously. This was the best news he had in weeks. He leaned back and closed his eyes, organizing the whirlwind of thoughts that cascaded through his brains. Not for long.

"General Sullivan on six."

"Bruce, what's up?"

"What's up? Some of the best intelligence in years. Your man Jake Watson has been able to pinpoint the direct line between Gitmo and bin Laden."

"You're kidding! How?"

"The two, the Lebanese and old-time inmate Bahouie, didn't talk for ten days or more, not until Bahouie received word that Yousef was okay, and then the floodgates opened."

"The word from whom and by whom?"

"From whom? Hezbollah or Osama direct. By whom? This is top secret, okay?"

"Of course."

"Well, don't make any attempts to arrest the man and stop the communications flow. Let no one know who it is until we have all the wires and bugs in place. This is the source that we're gonna cherish."

"Are you trying to tell me how to do my job?" The general didn't sound pleased.

"No, sir, of course not, but this is the one source that may help prevent future 9/11's, and I'm sure you agree that's one incoming line that we can't blow, so I need to ask you one big favor. Can you please arrange to give General Watson authorization to bug all lawyer-client conversations in spite of the existing orders against that?"

"Man, Bruce. You manage to come up with the most unusual situations and requests."

"Well, look at it this way, Sir, you'll be the first to know what's happening in the sinister world of terrorism."

"That's a nice way of putting it. Do you know what hoops I'll have to jump through in order to work against directions from the Justice Department?"

"You can do it, Sir. If anyone can do it, it's you. Watson is awaiting your orders."

"Good God. I'm starting to dread your calls. I'll get back with you." Click.

"Mr. Jarvis is holding on three."

"Lester! We have a great breakthrough and an even greater problem."

"Give me the good news first."

"We figured out who our mole is in Gitmo."

"Really, who is it?"

"Sir, this is top secret, okay? Don't mention it to anyone, but your top officials and only to the top CIA, okay?"

"Are you trying to tell me how to run my job?"

"You're the second one to ask me that in the last three minutes."

"Who was the other one?"

"General Sullivan at the Pentagon."

Jarvis, the FBI director laughed uproariously. "Really? You're running the whole show now?"

"Not really, but I want to make sure that we don't blow this beautiful opportunity to get firsthand information from the horse's mouth."

"Okay, you got me. Clue me in." Jarvis kept smiling.

"A government-appointed lawyer from Chicago, visits the inmates in Gitmo and transmits the messages back and forth."

" Jeez! How come we never knew this before?"

"Lawyer-client privilege orders the system to shut off the bugs, and those conversations were never recorded." Bruce sounded sarcastic.

"Great Scott. Are we always behind the eight ball? Always a day late and a dollar short?"

"That's the price we pay for living in a free country."

"What's the man's name?" Jarvis was ready to take notes.

"He goes by Amand Kaliff. I'm sure the CIA can find out his real name or his full name and background, but again, he must have no notion that we are on to him. I can't urge that enough."

"You're on, Bruce, and I don't blame you for being overly cautious. Good work. I'll be back with you momentarily."

"Thanks," he muttered to a dead phone.

"The CIA on four, sir."

"Already?" Bongers thought the call was in answer to his conversations with the pentagon and the FBI director, but it wasn't.

"Mr. Bongers? We have a prisoner to deliver to you. Where should we bring him?"

"Where is he now?"

"We're about to take off from Gitmo. We should be over New York in three and a half hours."

"Can you drop him in Teterboro?"

"Sure. We'll call you when we're over Virginia."

"That would be great. We're standing by." Bongers pushed another button.

"Bruno, don't leave at five. I'll need you to pick up our young Lebanese."

"There goes my date! And man, is she a beauty."

"Call her and tell her you'll be a little late. Government business. It'll make you sound important and it'll make her more anxious."

"Since when are you an expert on women? Single women? You've been married so long that you don't remember how important a first date is."

"You're right. I'll call Helen and ask her to refresh my memory. I'll see you at about six-thirty."

"Oh, well."

20

TETERBORO AIRPORT, N.J.

"What are you gonna do with that boy?" Bruno was driving the short distance from Secaucus to Teterboro Airport.

"Funny that you should ask. I really don't know. We've never had a situation like this before. Here's a guy who is supposed to put on an act and try to convince us that he wants to work with us while behind the scenes he's supposed to spy on us and sell us out. How are we gonna handle that? How do we supposedly train him for our side, while we know he's a phony?" Involuntarily, Bruce scratched his scalp. "I have been given a lot of rope by Washington, but you know what that means, right? Lots of rope to hang myself. I don't know yet how we're gonna play it. Any ideas Bruno?"

"How about if we act very suspicious of him? Why the sudden turnaround? What convinced him to forsake his Islam cause and go to work for a bunch of Infidels? I'd say, let him convince us why we should accept him before we give him any freedom and offers of protection and money. I'd say let him prove himself while we act very suspicious."

"You may have a point there. Let's not be too anxious. Meanwhile, where do we put him, and what do we do with him twenty-four hours a day?"

"How did you talk yourself into this pickle, Boss?"

"My ego, I guess. I always feel like I can solve anything."

"Don't change, Boss. It works for you most of the time." Bruno hesitated. "This time?" He laughed as if he had just heard a funny joke.

"Maybe you should take him dancing? Introduce him to some of your swinging blondes. That might convert him immediately."

"Sure, I should sacrifice my night life for the sake of our country's security?"

"What a great cause, Bruno. You'd go down in history . . ."

"That's the problem. I may not go down as much. Hahahaha! Here's our turnoff. Which terminal?"

"Main one, I guess. It'll probably be an unmarked Gulfstream."

Bongers was right. Within ten minutes a sleek white passenger jet touched down smoothly and rolled to a stop in front of the modest little terminal.

"Bruno, roll the car right to the door." He didn't feel he wanted to walk through a public facility with a shackled man between them.

The New Jersey Bureau Chief walked across the tarmac toward the plane and waited for the engines to start unwinding and the door-stairs combination lowered from the side of the craft.

A man in a white guayabera shirt, that hid the pistol on his belt, stepped from the plane and approached Bruce, probably because Bongers was the only man around wearing a tie and a jacket. "Mr. Bongers?"

"That's me." Bruce extended his hand.

"Special Agent Karpo, I'm bringing you your long-awaited guest. Just a minute," He shook Bruce's hand and turned to re-enter the aircraft.

"No, no. Wait a minute. How's the prisoner, any problems?"

"No, we didn't talk much, but he's one of the most well-spoken inmates we've dealt with so far. Very polite. Why did you ask?"

"Just checking what his mood is like, whether nervous or calm, hostile or friendly?

"He's fine, like a traveler on a pleasure trip."

"Okay, bring him out. Here's our car." The blue Buick rolled up to the airplane door, and Garcia stepped out.

Karpo walked back up the steps and reappeared minutes later with Yousef between him and another agent in an identical outfit, black pants and a white guayabera shirt.

Bongers nearly gasped. The young Lebanese had a full black beard. "Well, whaddaya know? Are you the same Yousef?"

"Yes, sir!" His white teeth were accentuated by his dark beard and mustache.

"Well, come on! Agent Karpo, can you undo his leg bracelets? Thanks. Also, just the cuff on his right hand. Thanks. Do I need to sign something, some receipt?"

"Not that we know of. You're welcome to be our guest. We're heading back to Langley and a good night's sleep."

"Okay, thank you gents. Have a good flight."

The Buick rolled away from the plane and headed back to the FBI office.

"Did you eat or are you hungry?" Bongers asked after they had settled into the backseat. "We did have lunch aboard, but that was four hours ago."

"Bruno!" Bruce leaned forward. "Stop and pick up some pizza, okay?"

"Sure thing!"

Turning back to his prisoner, Bongers asked, "What's with the beard? Are you going to be a Mullah?"

Yousef grinned. "Not hardly! At first I had no way to shave, and then I didn't care anymore and let it grow. How do you like it?"

"I'm not sure, but I'm not sure about a lot of things. Like, why are you back here and what are we supposed to do with you?"

"Oh, I told them in Guantanamo that I didn't want to go back to Lebanon and that my life might be in danger anywhere in the Middle East, and they told me that I might be able to stay in the United States."

"Who are 'They'?"

"The Navy Psychologist that I worked with. A nice young man about my age."

"About your age?"

"Well, maybe 25, 26."

"Really? Navy? Are you sure he was not Army or civilian?"

"No, he was Navy, just out of school for one year."

"Well, that's nice. Maybe they felt you weren't a hardened extremist yet and that the Navy Psyche needed experience. Who knows? Maybe it's a good thing." Inwardly, Bongers was shaking his head. "How do they accomplish anything out there?" He muttered to himself.

Bruno pulled over and reappeared after a while with a couple of pizza boxes.

"Boy, that smells good. The food was not bad in Cuba, but the Americans tried very hard at feeding us mid-eastern dishes, but that was not too successful. Of course, we ate no pork, but very little lamb. Lots of chicken and some turkey, all in all, not bad. This smells better though."

"Five more minutes and we'll be eating. Stand by."

In the office break room, they enjoyed pizza and sodas after taking all the shackles off the prisoner. Bongers had walked to his office and came back after ten minutes. He sat down across from the bearded young man and said, "Couldn't reach anybody. I guess you're here for the night. What are we supposed to do with you?" He tried to look worried.

"Aren't you supposed to talk to me about staying in the States and working with you?"

"According to whom? The young Navy man?"

"No. An Army colonel listened to me for hours and said that my future back home was probably reduced to a suicide bomber if I wasn't shot before that. I tried to tell him that I wasn't at fault in the hijacking of the ship, but he showed me a dozen cases, where failure of an assignment immediately ended in torture or death. He scared the hell out of me."

"So they played you between a young psychologist and an old psychiatrist. Sounds like an old flim-flam game."

"Huh?"

"Then why did they send you here? The CIA trains converts, puts'em in protection plans, involves them in counter espionage and all that good stuff, but we are just a bunch of local problem solvers. We're not equipped for any of that. I don't even know where to put you tonight, but don't worry about that. Tomorrow we'll send you down to the CIA big shots, and they'll handle it from there."

"No, no! I want to stay with you!"

"With me? Do what and why?"

"You told me about the other Yousef, the young Moroccan man who's buried in Florida. I think you're an honest man, and you'll be honest with me and give me a chance at . . ."

"You told them that in Gitmo?"

"I told them that? Of course. I told them I wanted to stay in America, but I wanted to stay with you."

"Good God. After ten years, I've again become a baby-sitter?"

"Beg your pardon?"

"Forget it. Bruno, call North Bergen Police. Reserve a cell." Garcia got up and left the room.

"Yousef, I don't know what to say. A month ago, you were a hardened criminal, a devout Muslim and a hater of all infidels, and all of a sudden you're willing to work with us. Don't tell me you're also considering becoming a Christian."

His dark eyes flaring, Yousef stood up. "Never! I just have learned a lot about Islam, the Prophet and the Quran that I never knew before, and I'm anxious to make amends and work for peace for all people."

"All this in just one month? A complete turnaround? What prompted that?"

"Four weeks in Guantanamo. Four weeks between imbeciles who can't think for themselves. Imbeciles, who can be swept off their feet by fanatics with an impassioned speech and who can be influenced to kill their own mother and their own children. What a sick bunch of humans. I'll never become a part of that mentality."

After Bruno took Yousef to North Bergen, Bongers said to himself, "Very sincere? Or very rehearsed? We'll find out more tomorrow."

21

NORTH BERGEN POLICE HEADQUARTERS.

Bart Morgan, the North Bergen chief of police greeted Bruce Bongers with a warm handshake. "What gives us the pleasure of your presence here and the unusual visitor in our cells?"

"Where can we sit and talk a moment?"

"My office is secure. Follow me."

It was 9:30 in the morning and Bruce had finished a long conversation with his chief, Director Lester Jarvis in Washington. Neither one was sure of the best way to handle the situation, knowing that the Lebanese would act as a double agent and betray every secret action of the CIA and the FBI to his cronies in the Middle East. How to get information from him without arousing suspicion that they were on to him was one problem. How to have him around and keep him from finding out things that were considered top secret and FYEO, (For Your Eyes Only)? The result was, Bongers was to play it by ear.

Seated in the chief's office, overlooking the wetlands and the Meadowlands Stadium in the distance, Bruce started the conversation.

"Bart, I really painted myself into a corner this time. I suggested that we get a hold of this young terrorist and convert him into a double agent. That's not really my department in the first place and besides that, I really don't have time to play these games."

"Then why did you suggest it?"

"Huh . . ." He sighed. "Long story. I received some inside information about a potential 9/11 attack on the U.S, and . . ."

"Not again?"

"Yes, again. I can't really reveal my source or take a chance on blowing it forever, so I got stuck with the job."

"What can I do?"

"I want to rent part of your facility. Temporarily!" He added hastily.

"Like what?"

"Your old office building has this totally boxed-in burglar-barred cell-block, right?"

"Yes, it's been vacant for months. We . . ."

"Can part of that serve as some sort of an apartment, complete with phone, TV, computer line, et cetera?"

"It's already set up that way."

"Really, how come?"

"The mayor put his accounting office in there until the new City Hall was finished."

"I didn't know that. That's great. This is what I have in mind. We rent the place from you, install high-class listening devices and board our new canary in there. Do you have time to take a look at it in a little while?"

"Sure. What time?"

"A half hour?"

"Just a sec." He pushed the intercom. "Jane, what's on my schedule . . .? Oh, yeah. Thanks." Turning back to the FBI man he asked, "How about an hour?"

"Okay. One hour from now." He glanced at his watch. "Now I'd like to visit our newfound friend."

"Come on."

In the cell where Yousef had spent the night, Bongers sat down next to him on his bunk. Bruno made himself at home on the single plastic chair that he had carried in.

"Well, is this better than Gitmo or an Israeli jail, Yousef?"

"This is smaller than any of them, but the cot is better. I slept well. How long do I stay here?"

"I don't know." Bruce shook his head. " I don't really know how I'm gonna treat you. As an arch-terrorist, who's liable to blow himself up, killing everyone around him, or just a suspect for the moment, who needs to be interrogated day and night for details of some of the underhanded activities that Hezbollah is involved in? I don't know. How much information have you already given the Israelis, and how much was recorded in Gitmo? How much more do I need to know? How much more do I want to know?" He stopped talking and asked Garcia, "Have you had coffee yet? How'bout you?" He looked at the bearded young man.

"Can I have tea?"

"Bruno, get some coffee and tea. Maybe the guard can handle this for you. Check it out." Turning back to Yousef, "What did they promise you in Gitmo? Tell all you know, and we'll put you in a safe house and an income for life? What did they promise?"

Yousef looked baffled. "Promised? Nothing. I was new with Hezbollah and I don't know much."

"Then why did they send you to me?"

"I don't know. I told the young Navy doctor that I didn't want to go back to Lebanon because I fear for my life because I failed my mission."

"That's all?" Bongers had read all the transcripts and knew exactly what Yousef had told his investigators. "Why did they send you to me and not directly to the CIA, who are geared for this type of thing?"

"Oh, I did mention about the discussion we had about the other Yousef from Morocco, remember?" He looked Bongers in the eye, "And I felt I could trust you, that you don't hate me because I'm a Muslim and that I would have a fair chance at a better life outside of prison camps. Does that make sense?"

"And based on that they decided to send you here?" With a puzzled look on his face, he held the door for Bruno, who carried a tray with steaming mugs. "What did you learn from the other inmates in Guantanamo? Did you feel at home with them?"

"They were weird. Most of them are very uneducated. One of them, an Emir, wouldn't talk to me . . ."

"Why not?"

"He thought I was a spy."

"A spy? Inside the prison camp?"

"That's what he said when he finally talked after ten days or two weeks."

"How did you meet him? Was he in the same compound, or could you mingle with other . . .?"

"No, he was in the same cell and that is what made him so suspicious. He was moved from his other cell and put in with me. He thought that was a setup, so he said nothing. Then all of a sudden, he started to talk to me. He said he might be going home."

"Home? Where is his home?" Bongers was checking details in his mind, and so far, the man was telling the truth.

"He said he was from Saudi, and his dialect confirmed that, but he was going to Lebanon, he said."

"Did you tell him about your experience, and did you ask him to tell your leaders anything?"

"I told him everything except..."

"Except what?"

"The one thing I didn't tell you either. That the girl, Lavana, was an Israeli agent."

"Your girl friend?"

"Yes. She and I went together for seven months. I thought she was in love with me, and I liked her so much, I even considered marriage."

"So Hezbollah doesn't know about her real identity? She might slip back into their confidence . . ."

"They never trust women. The only reason why she was involved was because I needed to look like an established legitimate businessman with a wife. No, she better stay away from the Hezbollah."

"Where is she now?"

"In Israel, I think. I really have no idea."

Bongers sipped some of his coffee. "Back to my question. What are we supposed to do with you?"

"The Navy doctor said I could work with you without denouncing Islam."

"I'd like to meet that Navy man and find out by what authority he makes decisions like that. I have my hands full with enough internal crimes, that I don't want a baby-sitting job on my hand. I may ship you back or on to Washington."

Yousef jumped up. "No, no. I want to work with you here."

"With that beard? No way."

Bongers got up and walked out without another word.

"But, Sir!" Bruce could still hear him halfway down the hall.

In the car on the way to the old police station, Bruno asked, "Why that remark about the beard?"

"Because, if he has an ounce of sincerity in him, he'll shave it off before I see him again."

"You think so?"

"Wanna bet?"

"Nah . . ., You win too often."

Walking through the converted old police headquarters, Bongers noted, "This'll do fine. We'll get him cable TV and phone line. As an engineer, he'll figure out soon enough how to circumvent the system and get messages in and out. Bruno, get on the horn and get our workmen out. I want to close off the southern corner, giving him a bedroom, sitting room with a desk in the corner and a kitchen with a stove, breakfast table and microwave. Tell'em everything should look like it has been here for months. Nothing should look new, okay? Have our Washington boys install listening and recording devices. The equipment will fit perfectly behind the north wall in that closet space."

He turned on his heels. "You call while I drive back."

22

FBI H.Q. N.J.

Back at his desk, he found a message to call the CIA Director at Langley Air Force Base.

After a few minutes wait, he was connected with a Special Agent, Gerald Swartz.

"Bruce! Long time since we worked together."

"Haggled together," Bongers thought. Instead he said, "Always a pleasure, Jerry."

"Gerald!" He pronounced it a definite "GE-RALD". "Mr. Taylor asked me to call you direct and . . ."

"Glad to hear that. What are we working on?"

"He wants to personally thank you for that lawyer in Chicago, Amand Kaliff. We have him and his whole office under surveillance, and you hit a jack-pot. He was born in Detroit, pretty poor Pakistani family. Drove a cab while he worked his way through school. Became a Public Defender in Ward Four in Chicago and met with some of the lowest low lives that city has ever produced. His parents had never been very devout, but young Amand got involved with some of the former Black Panthers, who hired him on the side to represent a few of their brothers. He set up private practice in 1997 and has done fairly well, representing mostly Muslims and Blacks, as well as, of course, Black Muslims. Farrakhan had him appointed to Gitmo, where, at a substantial salary, he defends the rights of some of our terrorists. He has been responsible for the release of four inmates after they swore they would never again involve themselves in any anti-American activities. Two of them have been spotted in Yemen, training with al-Qaeda."

"Wow, you found out all that in just this week?"

"Just about, but this is what I called you about. You had asked Mr. Taylor if you could come with us to the Mid West and Texas to personally see their possible objectives."

"Yes, I'd like to get some feel for what we're up against, even though I won't be working that end of the case . . ."

"I understand, Bruce, and I'm scheduled to leave with a team of experts on Monday morning from Langley, and we'd like to have you along. Can you make that, or do you have a heavy schedule?"

"I'll make that. What are we talking about? A one-day, two-day trip?"

"One day. You might stay here overnight, 'cause we may be back late."

"Okay! Thanks for asking me. I'll see you Monday."

"Is Bruno back yet?" The intercom confirmed that he wasn't. "Get him on his cell."

While fingering through the transcripts from Guantanamo, his buzzer rang, "Garcia on five."

"Bruno, check with North Bergen police if they have better ankle bracelets than we have, the type that can't be cut, no matter what they do and with the high-tech GPS. If not, I'll have to get some from D.C. Let me know."

"Anything I need to tell our young man?"

"Yes, tell'im that Washington is willing to give him some freedom in a two-county area but only during daylight hours."

"With the bracelet?"

"Of course. We don't want him to start travelling."

Bruce took the transcripts home. Bruno had underlined all conversation that seemed pertinent and that saved a lot of time. With four yellow pads on the dining-room table, he broke down the individual conversations, trying to pinpoint how and where Yousef was supposed to communicate with the Middle East or the wayward lawyer in Chicago.

One big black hole seemed to appear as time went by. Not a word about a local contact.

Unless Yousef managed to get some sophisticated state-of- the-art electronic equipment, he had no way to get any messages out or any directions in. Bongers restacked the papers, chronologically and by individuals. Again, no clue. There had to be a contact person in the immediate New York/New Jersey area. He picked up the phone and called the New York City office of the FBI.

"Mr. Andrews, please." He was connected within seconds.

"Andy, Bruce . . . Fine . . . Just fine . . . thank you . . . Okay . . . not really . . . Let me ask you something?"

"Shoot."

"Remember when we nearly eliminated a terrorist group along the shore a year ago?'

"How could I forget? I nearly got killed."

"Hope you learned something that day. We nearly got all of them, but two guys from Newark were not there during the shoot-out and were signaled in Penn Station a day later. Do you still have a bead on them?"

"I'll have to check. Did we have anything on them, something concrete, so we could get a warrant for their arrest?"

"I think that was one of the problems. All we had were suspicions and hearsay. I'd like to find out where they are now and what they're doing. Any other potential terrorists that you're keeping an eye on?"

"What are you cooking up, Bruce?"

"Unofficially? Preventing another 9/11."

"Good God, no!"

"Just working on it. See what you can find. Do you have my cell number?"

"Yes, I'll jump right on it. It's my city, you know?"
"Thanks, pal."

Bruce left the papers on the table. His kids were at school and his wife was somewhere. Where? Garden Club? Women's luncheon? He didn't know and he didn't care.

He lay on the couch and tried to put himself in the mindset of the opposition.

What good was it to Hezbollah or al-Qaeda to have Yousef in the FBI organization, if they couldn't extract important data from him or feed him instructions? They had to be planning something in the New York Metropolitan area. But what? Another tower? That seemed unlikely. What would kill more people? Flood the subway? If they killed three thousand people in the Twin Towers, their goal had to be much higher this time. Bruce said to himself, "They don't have nuclear bombs, so . . .? This drives me nuts. What could possibly be their target? I hate to drink so early in the day, but maybe a scotch might make my brain work faster."

As he got up, his phone rang. "Bruce? Andy. We've had a house under surveillance in Canarsie. We first suspected drugs, but a stoolie couldn't buy a single gram of anything, so that's not it. We tapped into their phone line and have been intercepting e-mail traffic to London, Germany, and Lebanon. According to our interpreters they're not saying much of anything. Just family chatter."

"Do you have those transcribed, Andy?"

"Sure."

"Can you fax them to me and to the Cryptology department in D.C.? They may contain secret messages."

"Sure thing. Should we do anything else? Jump the joint?"

"No, no!" Bruce jumped up and nearly shouted. "No, no. Don't do anything yet. Lay low. Don't draw any suspicion. This may be exactly the lead I've been looking for. Thanks, Andy. Talk to you shortly."

Back at the table, but this time with a scotch on the rocks, even though it wasn't four o'clock yet. "Mr. Jarvis, please? Okay, I'll hold . . ." He took one sip and put the drink on the windowsill. "It's too early. What am I thinking?" Whatever he was thinking, it was interrupted by the voice of his boss. "Bruce? Lester. What's happening? I haven't talked with you since this morning."

"Lester. Andy is faxing e-mail transcripts to Crypto and that's the reason for my call. Have the faxes and the ensuing reports labeled 'TOP SECRET' and don't have them handled by the lowest ranking yoyo in the office. It has to remain at top level."

"Would you be kind enough to tell me the reason for this?"

"Yes, sir. This is the missing link, I think, between Gitmo, my boy Yousef, al-Qaeda. and Hezbollah. If I'm correct, my boy will start transmitting to them . . ."

"Them?"

"Yes, a safe house in Brooklyn and we'll have a direct line to their intentions."

"Good enough. I'll make the call. I hope you're right." Click.

Bruce looked at his cell phone and said, "I hope so too."

Carefully, he tore off a sheet from each yellow pad and stapled it to a pile of white 8 ½ by 11 sheets and sighed a satisfied sigh that seemed to come up all the way from his midriff.

He retrieved his glass from the window sill and stretched out on the couch. Just as he drifted off into a light slumber, his phone rang again.

"Bongers."

"Hi, boss, Bruno."

"Guess what?"

"What?"

"Our boy shaved off his beard."

"Well, whaddaya know?"

23

HAZMIEN ROTANA HOTEL. BEIRUT, LEBANON

The bath house was guarded and protected. Seven men sat in a small circle, enjoying the steam and the perspiration. With towels casually draped across their laps, they resembled a Roman Caucus from 2,000 years ago, had it not been for the long beards and the shoulder-length hair. The Romans must have been smarter. They were clean shaven and sported very short hairdos.

The moisture in their facial pride and joy became more uncomfortable by the minute, but no one complained.

Ahmed took the lead. Addressing Fanouf Bahouie with the rank to which he was entitled, "Emir, we hope that your first night back in freedom, was satisfactory, yes?"

The Emir nodded. Having been in bed with two buxom girls and a ten-year-old boy had been most gratifying. He smiled as he nodded. He could not wait for evening and do it all over again.

"Five years in an enemy camp must have been humiliating and frustrating."

Bahouie nodded again. He shuddered at the thought of having slept alone without a companion, male or female. That last boy was appealing, but he was definitely not interested. Besides that, he had wasted ten days by completely ignoring the boy. He sighed. If he could only do it all over again. He was a nice-looking young man.

"Well, welcome back. We apologize for not having been able to get you released sooner, but you understand . . ."

"I understand! By Allah, I understand!" He stood up, his skinny frame a small replica of his former being, was nearly infantile, had it not been for his hairy head. "I understand that you had many meetings in this luxurious setting, while we rotted away. I understand that you had comfortable nights with warm partners, while we could only play with ourselves. I understand that you ate well, and your bodies reflect that, while we had to eat food that Mohammed would not have fed to his swine, if he had any. I understand that you did very little, very very little to persuade the Americans to free us . . ."

"Emir, if I may. . ."

"No, you may not! I'm talking!" He started screaming, his demeanor changed. "I understand that you enjoyed the pleasure of your children, while we didn't even know if ours lived or died. I understand alright. But I want you to understand something!" He sat back down. "We are going to take revenge. I spoke with the Prophet, Osama, and we're taking revenge. We will kill one American for every day that one of our believers has spent in Guantanamo. Add it up. 1,500 days for me, the same for every other fighter for Allah who was there for the same length of time. 300 times 1,500 equals 450,000 devil worshippers. We're going to kill nearly one half-million Americans, and then they will surrender themselves to the fact that they're dealing with a real enemy, and they will leave Palestine, Iraq, Iran, Pakistan and Afghanistan alone, because the people of America won't let their murdering presidents continue their savage persecution of innocent Muslims." He sat down, exhausted.

For a minute, there was only silence.

"Emir!" Finally Ahmed stood up. "May Allah forgive us. Tell us what you want us to do." He bowed and sat back down.

"What we have to do is as follows: We have to recruit and train the most eligible, most fanatic freedom fighters and train them for our next mission. Young men, who are willing to die for Allah and who can converse in different languages. English preferred, but Spanish would be helpful. They must learn rocketry, gun handling, and man-to-man killing. We have three months to prepare."

"How many do we need, Emir?" One of the others asked.

"We recruit thirty. Train twenty-five, and select the top ten for our mission." Bahouie stood up again. "Can we now go upstairs and eat, drink and smoke something."

"Of course, of course." Everyone stood up and took to the showers.

Up in the penthouse, in some regal robes, the Emir looked a lot more Royal than he had in his naked butt in the steam room. He strolled around the room, pulling curtains, moving furniture and checking lamps and telephones.

"Are you sure this room is secure?" He asked Ahmed, who acted as the head of the Lebanon organization.

"You can count on it, sir."

"What's above this?" He pointed at the ceiling.

"The roof. We're on the top floor."

"Take me to the roof."

Ahmed had to call hotel security in order to get the access door unlocked at the end of the long hall. Twenty steps up the stairs were tiresome for both. For one, because he was too thin, the other because he was too fat. Once on top of the building, the brand-new free man walked from one end to the other, shaking antennas and satellite dishes, while asking a million questions, from both the uniformed security man and from the robed Ahmed.

Finally satisfied, the two conspirators retreated to the luxurious penthouse room and some delicious lamb and couscous.

When everyone was satisfied with food and hash, they gathered in a circle, comfortably lounged out on pillows and cushions. Emir Bahouie took the floor.

"There are no recording devices in this room. There are no notepads, no writing material.

Everything I tell you will have to be recorded in your brain. If you can't handle that, if you smoked too much hash, if you don't think you have the brain capacity to remember everything, just get up and excuse yourself. No repercussions." He looked around the room. "Anyone feel too tired? Impossible to keep up the pace?" Nobody moved.

"Okay. We are spearheading the greatest operation for Islam, since we rose up in revolt and freed Jerusalem form the infidels, the Crusaders. The plan has been worked out by our modern Prophet, Osama bin-Laden, himself. It will be executed with the same precision as the attacks on the Twin Towers in New York, where we kept the American Security Organizations completely in the dark. It will take the same precise planning, like the many years our heroes went though flight training in the U.S. in order to learn how to handle the sophisticated airline jets and guide them right onto their targets." He reached for his glass of mint tea and continued after a few sips. His voice became high pitched.

"It took four years of planning and preparation, and the Americans never had a clue. We don't have that luxury now. On the anniversary of 9-11-2001, we'll strike again, and we'll have to be ready. We won't have time to waste, no time to play, no time to fail! With Allah's help, we'll succeed!"

Everyone stood up and bowed. "Allah il Allah!"

"Pay attention. Remember everything I say. We will assassinate President Obama in New York. President Netanyahu will be there, and they'll be able to hold hands all the way into hell." Everyone applauded. Bahouie raised his hand.

"We have to train four different teams. One team, that has to blend in with the New York population without arousing suspicion; three other teams to come in through Mexico into Texas and Louisiana complete with handheld rockets, probably Stingers. They have to become experts at assembling and disassembling those weapons, and they have to smuggle them in without getting caught." He smiled. "Obviously."

A hand was raised in the circle. "What are our targets?"

"I appreciate your anxiety, but I would more appreciate your patience." The asker slumped in his pillow, soundly rebuffed.

"One by one, tell me what phase of the operation do you feel most proficient at?"

After an hour, Emir Bahouie seemed satisfied that everyone understood their assigned tasks and wrapped up the meeting with a prayer. All bowed down toward Mecca and praised Allah and his leadership on earth.

"Till tomorrow in Tripoli. Salam Aleichem."

"Aleichem Salam Emir."

When alone with the local leader, Ahmed, Bahouie asked, "I didn't see the Sheik. Is he well?"

"Unfortunately, he met his doom and is in the company of Satan."

"Oh? Serious offences?"

"The most serious, Emir. Trading secrets with the Israelis."

"Allah forbid. Did you have proof?"

"The fact that you're here is part of the proof. You were released as part of a trade that was intended to avoid embarrassment of the Russian government in the weapons deal that was meant for the Gaza Strip."

"Is that the one that the young Lebanese Yousef was involved in?"

"Indeed, Emir. Indeed."

"Too bad. A nice boy otherwise."

"The boy was not involved in the treason. He was an innocent victim."

"Allah works in wondrous ways. He now will bring us detailed information about our next New York operation. Allah be praised."

24

NORTH BERGEN, NJ. POLICE HEADQUARTERS

Bruno was having a hell of a time. Yousef refused to let them install an ID ankle bracelet on his right leg.

"No no! In other words, you people will always know where I am exactly, right?"

"That's the whole idea." Bruno stood in the cell, with the metal GPS in his hand.

"Sir? May I call you Bruno?"

"No! You call me Mister Garcia or Agent Garcia."

"Mr. Garcia, I thought I was going to work with you people, and this is not a good way to inspire confidence in a coworker."

"You're not a coworker yet, and we don't know if we can trust you at all. You'll have to prove yourself, buddy, and the best way to do that is; fully cooperate. This is step one. This bracelet is step number one. We want to know at all times where you are and what you're doing. It's made of the hardest metal known to man, so you can't cut or saw it, so don't think you could simply walk away from it. It won't work."

"But how will that build trust and confidence and . . ."

"Trust and confidence? Let me tell you something, buddy. I don't trust you any further than I can throw you. And about confidence? You'll have to prove that you're worth it. I'm not particularly thrilled with this assignment, being your baby sitter and nursemaid. So either you cooperate or I walk out of here and let you rot." Bruno's voice was getting more and more high pitched, showing his annoyance.

Yousef was not about to give in that easily. "Do you really distrust me that much?"

Garcia pointed the GPS bracelet at Yousef and between clenched teeth started spitting out words. "Distrust? Let me bring you up to date, In '68, Bobby Kennedy was shot by Sirhan Sirhan, a young Muslim . . ."

"But he was paid by the Americans . . ."

"Where'd you get that? Paid by Americans?"

"Everybody in the Middle East knows that story. I was not even born yet. The Sirhan family received lots of dollars from America, and that encouraged other young men to sacrifice their lives for their family."

"I never heard of such nonsense." Bruno was getting very agitated. "Who in America would want him dead?"

"You don't know? The Unions and the Mafia. The Mafia came up with all the money. They didn't want Mr. Bobby as the President. Bad for business."

"Well . . ., just the same, the killer was a young Muslim and then at the Munich Olympics, the most peaceful assembly of nations, young Muslims massacred young athletes . . ."

"Israeli athletes."

"There you go again. Justifying in your own mind that killing innocent people is okay if your Mullah says so. They were unarmed. They were sports enthusiasts. They didn't harm anybody." Garcia waved the bracelet in Yousef's face. "A few years later, young Muslims stormed the American Embassy in Tehran and held innocent people captive, and a few years after that, Americans were kidnapped in Lebanon, and later the U.S. Marine barracks were blown up in Beirut."

"Those were soldiers," Yousef interrupted.

"Yes, they were soldiers on a peace keeping mission, stopping the Israelis from advancing further into Lebanon. And when terrorists hijacked the cruise ship *Achille Laura,* they threw a 70-year-old man overboard in his wheelchair. What cowardly bastards! Young Muslims again, and when a TWA flight was captured in Athens, they killed a U.S. Navy diver who was trying to rescue the passengers. Should I go on? The list is miles long." He answered his own question by going on. "In '88, I believe, Pan Am flight 103 exploded over Scotland. No military whatsoever, all innocent people. Then in '93 the World Trade Center. In '98 U.S Embassies in Kenya and Tanzania were bombed. Later, a reporter, Daniel Pearl, was kidnapped and murdered and of course 9/11 and the Twin Towers, the crown jewel of extremists success. All these acts of terror by young Muslim terrorists! Would you like to know why I don't trust you either? Because you've been trained and brainwashed by the same regime and will probably try to kill a bunch of Americans, especially innocent women and children."

"No no!" Yousef stood up, but Bruno shouted in his face: "Sit! Do me a favor and hang yourself, so I won't have to deal with you anymore."

"But I have the best of intent . . ."

"Sure! I believed that too one day, and I have a scar on my hip from the bullet that was meant for my heart. Sure!" He turned around, opened the cell door and walked out. "Go to hell." He slammed the cell door and walked over to a stunned Police Sergeant, who had overheard the whole exchange. "When he allows you to put the bracelet on, call me." Garcia handed him the GPS and was gone.

Once away from the headquarters, he headed for the old police station, where workmen were diligently installing recording and listening devices. Bruno walked through the room inspecting some of the equipment, and asked the lead engineer. "Would he be able to use some of these outlets to get out long distant messages?"

"Long distance, like overseas?"

"Yes."

"I doubt it. Of course he can always ask for a long-distance operator. Do you want us to restrict that?"

"No, we would like to hear what he has to tell his cronies in the Middle East. I wondered if he could somehow bypass the normal lines and that way get messages out that we don't catch."

" Well, you'll always be able to hear what he says on this end."

"Can he use the TV cable to get word out?"

"I doubt it."

"Okay, this is what we'll do anyway. We'll get you in here on regular intervals and check to find out what he has tampered with. Make sense?"

"Best way to do it."

From his cell phone, he caught up with his boss. "Bruce, I gave the young friend a stern lecture when he refused to have the bracelet put on . . ."

"I heard. I heard. Chief Morgan gave me the rundown, and if the sergeant relayed your message correctly, the whole precinct will salute you when you walk back in there."

"Really? All I told him was why I don't trust those SOBs."

"Well, you must have been very persuasive, because he's now wearing the darn thing."

"Good for him." Bruno grinned to himself. "But boss, I went by the new establishment and I wonder how we by accident found that place for him, so he doesn't feel we wired it just recently?"

"Give it a few days. We'll wait till he gets real fed up about living in that cell and then, by coincidence, we'll learn about a vacancy coming up in the old police building. Give it a couple of days."

"What do we do with him in between time?" Bruno was not too anxious to get back in touch with the Lebanese. He had really gotten himself worked up.

"You take him with you on a few routine runs. Like bringing paperwork to the Sheriff's office, so they can serve the summonses to the suspects. But first, take him to Wal-Mart and get him some clothes. Tell him he must look somewhat professional. Not too gaudy. Use the house charge card. I'll okay the bills as they come in. When do you want to start up with him?"

"Not right now. How's tomorrow morning?"

"Okay, when you come back with new clothes, take all the old stuff away from him. We'll open up all the seams and have the lab analyze if there's anything hidden in his clothes, codes, numbers, anything. If he gives you a hard time about it, tell that you're just having them laundered and that he'll get them back in a few days. The more he resists, the more we know we're on the right track."

"Okay, I have a few things to follow up on, but I should be able to clear my calendar by tomorrow morning."

"Good show."

Bongers sat back and thought a while. "Gotta make this work." He dialed New York.

"Andy, anything from Canarsie?"

"We have the wiring intact, and we have some communication between Canarsie and Beirut. We have our linguistic expert working on it now, but the rough draft tells us about ships in the Texas Gulf, and the name *"Limo"* or *"Leemo"* keeps popping up and the analysts feel that it is a Filipino name. Is that helpful at all?"

"Andy, everything is helpful. Is there any way they may contact our boy Yousef in North Bergen?"

"So far, no indication, Bruce. When everything is translated, we'll send you copies."

"Don't wait till everything is done. Send me tidbits that feel important."

"Okay."

"Mr. Jarvis, please." Bruce waited patiently for the director to come on the line.

"Yes, Bruce."

"Question, do you or I pass on a little tidbit to the CIA?"

Jarvis chuckled. "You tell me and then YOU pass it on."

"Okay. Communications with Hezbollah again mention a Filipino name and the waters off the Texas coast."

"Interesting. When are you flying out there?"

"Monday."
"Keep me posted."

25

LANGLEY AIR FORCE BASE, VIRGINIA.
MONDAY 7:55AM

"Morning, Jay! You're coming with us?"

"I sure hope so, Bruce. You've aroused my curiosity. What do you know that I don't about chemicals and storage?"

"To tell you the truth, I don't have a clue. I'm on a learning expedition. All I have is very little information, a little more gossip and no facts. By the end of the day, I hope to have a clearer picture. Jay, have you come up with any more information on large accumulations of explosive chemicals in close proximity to large population areas?"

"I don't have the foggiest. The only large storage facilities we have are usually in fairly remote areas. You have me totally baffled. I'm looking for some of the same answers you are. Let's hope we get some. Here's our ride."

The two of them climbed into the back of a plain SUV and headed for the flight line. An unmarked Gulfstream was waiting for them, and they were introduced to the captain and copilot as well as two other agents, both CIA. Within minutes, another car pulled up, and three more men, dressed in business suits, joined the team aboard.

The elder of the team took the lead. "Gentlemen, I'm Gerald Swartz, and I'm going to play the Devil's Advocate today. I'm gonna question everything you're doing and everything you're saying, narrowing things down to some actual facts. We're heading for New Orleans first, so while we have breakfast and coffee, we'll just bounce a few questions around, okay?"

Nobody objected to coffee, so they spread around in a circle as best they could and started a dialog.

"Bruce, you initiated this whole thing. Why don't you start?"

"A nagging rumor, nothing but a recurring rumor, that on the anniversary of 9/11 a major attack will be perpetrated on the U.S. An explosion or explosions like an atom bomb. But since nobody has access to that size bomb, we have to look for other areas that can be compromised. Another rumor is connected with chemicals. I have asked our top scientist in that area, Jay Price. Go ahead Jay, take a bow. I've asked him to search for large storages or deposits that could mimic a nuclear blast, near or in a densely populated area. That's why we're on this trip, chasing rumors. Go ahead, Jay."

Before Jay could say a word, another agent cut in. "What do you have to substantiate those rumors?"

"If your superiors were not convinced of their validity, you and I would not be on this flight. Go ahead, Jay."

The agent who had spoken up retracted into his shell, like a puppy that had been reprimanded.

Jay spoke up. "I've been baffled by that question for weeks. Not that we don't have large deposits of flammable or explosive material, but not in areas that would kill thousands in one blast. I hope to learn something today." He turned to Bruce. "Didn't you also mention tankers, off-shore drilling and refineries?"

"The rumors seemed to concentrate around the Gulf Coast area. One other reason for that is, a name of a known Filipino terrorist popped up and the staff is sorting that out, because apparently he escaped from captivity in the Philippines after having been captured in that raid in which they'd freed dozens of Americans."

"What does that Filipino have to do with anything?' Swartz wanted to know.

"Oh, I'm sorry. I forgot to mention that. The Filipino works on a supply ship on the Gulf, motoring back and forth to the drill platforms and back to shore. Right now I couldn't tell you what the connection is, but I do know that he's in touch with Hezbollah in Beirut on a regular basis. Let's hope that today we'll understand a little more about that."

Swartz took the lead again, "We'll fly slow circles around those areas and take numerous photographs. We can print these out as we fly and study them. Bruce, do I understand that their intent is to kill as many people as possible or do lasting damage to our infrastructure?"

"Killing as many people as possible is their main goal." A groan went around the circle.

"And they plan this for 9-11-2010?"

"A sort of anniversary celebration. Gossip has it that Osama bin Laden is the architect of the project: an attack on our president and some major explosions."

"How do they expect to get the operatives into this country and execute such a series of strikes?" One of the CIA people wanted to know.

"Don't get me started on that. I informed the authorities of the presence of Atta Mohammed in a terrorist click in Daytona at Emory Riddle, and it was totally ignored."

"How did you know all that?" The same doubting Thomas again.

"Because I had an Army undercover man in the group."

"Wow!" "Jeez!" "Com'on!" "Holy Moses!", Were some of the outcries from the agents in the circle.

"Anyway, to answer your question properly, there are already two known communication centers established, one in Chicago and one in New York. They'll smuggle weapons and personnel in by ship or across the Mexican border, especially if their targets are Houston or New Orleans, both accessible by water."

"Again, wow! Bruce, do we really live in a cocoon in this country?"

"Seems like it sometimes."

"Anyway, we'll start circling New Orleans, go as far north as Lake Charles, then the Sabine river, Port Arthur and Houston. Take note of everything that catches your attention, and we'll fly over some drills when we head back. Check your coffee. We'll land for lunch at the Navy base, compare notes and plan our afternoon flight. Okay?"

The weather cooperated beautifully, most of the time. Some patchy clouds obscured the ground here and there, but not enough to obstruct the view of the massive Mississippi and its delta, and armed with maps, the various agents circled buildings, towns and refineries with different color markers. The plane continued on to Galveston along the coast and turned north over Houston and west toward Lake Charles, Louisiana.

By 11:20, the Gulfstream touched down at the Orleans Naval Air Station, and in a private room at the O'Club, the team was joined by the base commander Captain Goodson.

Agent Gerald Swartz briefed the captain on part of their mission, omitting details of a potential attack. There was plenty of time for that later, he felt. Obviously, when he asked the captain's opinion on storage of explosive chemicals, he raised his eyebrows a few times, but figured it was all a part of Homeland Security.

The lunch was typical "Navy chow", excellent, and afterward, they rounded up their pilots again for the over flight of the drills in the gulf.

That was a surprise to almost all of them. None of them had seen the enormous amount of platforms before.

"With a few hundred more of these, we won't need Arabian oil anymore, and bin Laden won't get his twelve million dollar monthly allowance anymore." Bruce commented.

"Yeah, he won't be able to finance these terrorists' operations anymore and we might start looking for peace in this world."

"From your mouth to God's ears." Another commented.

"Okay, let's sit around and hear what each one of you have noted for yourselves and add it all up. Bruce, when we're done, I hope we're at least one step closer to a solution."

"What did he just say? From your mouth to God's ears."

26

SECAUCUS, NJ, FBI HEADQUARTERS

As Bruce Bongers, the Agent in Charge, walked into his office at 7:55 AM, the buttons on his phone were already blinking. Pushing the intercom button first, he asked, "Susan, which do I pick up first?"

"I would take line five, Mr. Jarvis."

"Makes sense." Pushing "5", he said, "Morning Lester. Up early too?"

"Well, I got to bed on time. When did you get in?"

"I was home by eleven-thirty, not too bad."

"Reason why I called, I'm looking over the reports that are coming in from the CIA about your expedition yesterday. What's your take on it?"

"What I was afraid of is that we now have more questions than we have answers, but that's always the case when we're working in the dark. We have some good people working on it though and some answers will start coming in, I'm sure. I don't . . ."

"We already have one answer for you. Remember the Filipino terrorist, who allegedly was working on a supply boat?"

"Sure do."

"Well, we've identified him and we already have two agents on the way to join him . . ."

"Join him?"

"Yes, one is a Vietnamese veteran, who'll join the ship as a deckhand, and one Indonesian radio operator. They don't know of one another's existence, but they both know the mission, keeping an eye on 'Meelo Gonzalo,' the terrorist. They are to intercept all his transmissions and watch all his actions."

"Great! And I hope that anything that pertains to a New York attack will immediately be forwarded to me."

"Of course, of course. By the way, Bruce, how are you doing with your babysitting job? How's the Lebanese doing?"

"Hard to say. He claims he wants to work with us and shaved off his beard, but refused an ID bracelet. I haven't heard the latest yet, but we'll prime him. He'll be put in a position where he can make outgoing calls, and we'll see what he has to say."

"Good luck with that."

"Thanks."

"Is Bruno in the building?" Bruce was back on the intercom.

"He's in North Bergen."

"Okay. I'll join him in a bit. What are the other messages?"

"Mr. Dagan called twice yesterday from Tel Aviv."

"Alright, get him on the horn for me."

While fingering through the files on his desk, the phone buzzed again. "Mr. Dagan on three."

"Meir, good morn . . ., I mean good afternoon out your way. What have you got?"

"Bruce, I have a persistent rumor that an attack will be orchestrated on our president, Netanyahu, when he visits Barack Obama in the late summer. We have to plan as if we're sure that an assassination attempt will be made on both of them. Can you find out what their itinerary is going to be, and I mean the exact movements of the two together? Ours here is still too sketchy. I doubt that they would try to bomb the White House, when they're having dinner. Or when he's addressing the joint session of Congress. Too complicated. What else is on their schedule?"

"I'll find out and get back to you, and by the way, your hint about a Filipino extremist on our waters is proving correct. His name here is Meelo Gonzalo. I don't know what his real name is, but we have two shadows on him already."

"Good for you. How's my boy Yousef doing?"

"Funny you should ask. He's doing so-so. Shaved his beard, refuses ID bracelets."

"Seems like par for the course, could have predicted that. Have fun."

"Thanks."

An hour later at the old police station in North Bergen, Bongers toured the facility with Police Lieutenant Hatchadoorian and asked, "Lieutenant, can you have some empty boxes, half-empty garbage cans and papers strewn around the place? Make it look like the secretaries just moved out."

"You want it to look like they packed up yesterday?"

"Right."

"No problem."

"The entrance is locked from the outside, right? And are there any walls that someone could burst through from the inside?"

"They're all concrete. Just don't give him a jackhammer or a pickax."

"Do you have the keys? How many? Can I have one? Make some spares. I'll be back in a bit."

At police headquarters, he found Bruno and Yousef having coffee in the break room. The young Lebanese looked again like he did when they first picked him up at McGuire more than a month ago. Except, he was better dressed. His clean-shaven face did have a natural tan, so he didn't look like he was just let out of detention and his clothes were casual, but tasteful.

"Well, how are the Bobsy twins?" Bruce sounded jovial.

"We're fine." Bruno answered.

"Yes, sir, we're fine, but I'm glad you're here."

"I'm glad to hear that. Are you wearing your ID?"

Yousef raised his right leg, pulled down his sock and showed a shiny metal anklet.

"Now you see, sir, that I'm cooperating, so must I stay in this little rotten cell?"

"Well, what do you expect? A penthouse along the river, overlooking New York?"

"No, no. Nothing fancy. I have no money and I have to prove myself first. I understand that, but a little nicer place with a shower and a television, maybe a radio?"

Bruno sat down and poured himself some coffee. "Like I told you before, we're not set up like the CIA, where they have all sorts of transit facilities to house defectors and criminals. We normally have nothing to do with your kinda guys, but we'll make the most of it, if you keep working with us. Let me ask the chief."

He got up and reappeared within a minute with Chief Morgan. "Chief, our friendly guest from the Middle East feels that now that he is fully cooperating with us, he should be treated more like an agent instead of a detainee. In other words, he'd like his cell expanded, a shower installed and a giant TV screen."

"No, no!" Yousef jumped up. No, but could I have a little unit with a shower and a stove maybe. I like to do some of my own cooking, you understand . . .?"

"What's the matter? Can't get used to Burger King and Wendy's?" The Chief also had a sense of humor.

"I couldn't eat that every day, and I'm never sure if they didn't put pork in their hamburgers."

"Pork? You don't eat pork?" The chief was poking fun at him. "Boy, there's nothing better than some spare ribs and . . ."

"No, no pork. I like beef and lamb, but no pork. So sometime I'd like to cook something for myself."

"So next thing you'll want is a refrigerator and a microwave, right?"

"That oughta be good." Yousef was smiling broadly.

Bongers cut in. "He has not done a lick of work and he's already demanding benefits. The next thing he'll ask for is a raise."

The young man jumped on that. "That's true. I don't have a cent."

Bruno suggested, "We may be able to get your parents to wire you a few thousand from Lebanon."

Yousef took him seriously. "Could we?" Everyone laughed out loud, but Bongers said, "That's not a bad idea. We'll explore that later. Chief?" He turned to Bart Morgan. "We can't turn him loose in town, and maybe we shouldn't keep him in this little hole. What other choices do you have here? A family cell?"

"I may have something. Hold it a sec." He flipped open his cell phone and pushed a number. "Lieutenant? Have the girls moved out of the old building? The finance department?" He listened for a while. "Oh, good, I'll send them over." He flipped his cell shut. "The city administration had part of their accounting staff in our old precinct. Go see if any part of that is suitable. It may need some cleaning and dusting, but that should be minor. Do you know where it is?"

"Off Bergenline near 68th street?"

"That's the one. Check it out."

"Thanks, Chief." The trio walked out the door.

"Hey, this section over here has a bathroom with a shower and a little kitchenette. Are there more like that down here?" Yousef was getting excited. After months in detention, he felt a breath of freedom blowing his way.

"No, that's the only bathroom down here. The others are upstairs."

They were strolling through the basement of the former police station and things were going very much as planned. Yousef looked in the adjacent room. "There are phone jacks in the wall. Are they live?" He addressed Lt. Hatchadoorian who was acting as the tour guide.

"I don't know. Let me find a phone." He returned with a phone unit and a cord, plugged it in and had a dial tone. "This one works."

"Great!" Yousef reached for the phone and asked, "What's the number?"

"I have no idea."

"There's no number on this unit."

"Stand by." the lieutenant dialed a number and when it answered he asked, "Can you tell what number I'm calling from? . . . Just a minute . . . 662-1511. Thank you." He turned back to the young prisoner and said, "That was simple. My wife has caller ID."

Bongers added his five cents. "That was indeed simple. Are there TV's upstairs?"

"I doubt it, but we can get one easily enough from the school system." Hatchadoorian seemed to have all the answers. "And we should be able to scrounge up a cot and some furniture."

"Can we lock this place from the outside? I mean separate from the rest of the building?"

Bongers wanted to be sure his jailbird wouldn't fly away.

"Oh, yeah, no problem. We can have this place ready for human habitation by morning. Is that alright?"

"Sounds good to me. Bruno, did you copy that number in your cell?"

"Sure did."

"What's the area code here?" Yousef asked sheepishly.

"The area code? What do you need that for? Do you expect any calls from home?"

"These lines are all restricted." The lieutenant added. "Local calls only."

"Oh!"

27

FBI, NEW JERSEY OFFICE.

Bongers picked up the phone, "Yes Andy, What's happening in your jungle?"

"My jungle? You could say that again. Sometimes I think I deal with untamed animals."

"That bad? For example?"

"I just received two mad calls from the Airport Manager at JFK and the Port Authority."

"What are they so mad about?"

"They think that I . . ., the FBI, ordered armored tanks on their properties and they're screaming, 'What are we gonna do with tanks and . . ."

"Tanks at the airports?"

"Apparently, Homeland Security feels that they need protection in the upcoming crisis."

"Upcoming crisis? What are they talking about?"

"Apparently, our impending attacks here and in the west . . ."

"You mean our operation against al-Qaeda?"

"I guess that's what they're talkin' about, Bruce."

"Do you have that manager's number handy? . . . 555-5000, extension 414? Thanks, I'll call you right back."

"Mr. Thompson? Bruce Bongers, FBI, New Jersey. What is the

word on those tanks that . . ."

"Yeah, my assistant received a call from Washington this morning that because of a terrorist threat we are going to receive a tank or tanks for our protection . . ."

"Who in Washington ordered that?"

"Well, she thought it was the FBI, but Mr. Andrews assured me, it wasn't your office, so I don't know, but what the hell am I going to do with tanks on our airfield? Place them in the terminals and then what?"

"Mr. Thompson, as far as you're concerned there's no threat against your airport and you will not receive any tanks. I'll call you back in a bit, but forget the whole thing, as if it never happened. I'll talk to you shortly."

Bongers looked at the phone and said, "Damnit! That's what happens when too many people get involved. I wonder which ass started this mess." He dialed his director's private line. "Lester? Bruce. Who in the world would order tanks to be placed at every airport because of a terrorist threat?"

"Are you serious?"

"Yes, the New York City airports were informed that tanks would be placed on their fields..."

"To do what?"

"No idea! That was the question of one of the managers. What are we gonna do with them and where should we put them? In the passenger lounges?"

"I still can't believe that, but I'll find out fast."

"They're blowing the whistle on our whole operation and . . ."

"I realize that. I'll get right back to you." Jarvis was gone.

Bruce hung up the phone and went to refresh his coffee. He was so mad, that flames could have shot out of his ears if that were possible. He would like to blow his cork at someone, but no one in his office was guilty of that stupid move, so he kept his mouth shut for the moment.

Jarvis was back on the line in five minutes. "Bruce, I put a stop to all that nonsense, so you can tell your airport managers to forget this ever happened."

"Great! Now . . ."

"Just a sec." the director interrupted him. "Do you know what started this?"

"I sure would like to know."

"Well, when you went on that flight last week to view the scene in the west, you had a man from Homeland Security aboard and he reported his findings to his boss, Mrs. Napolitano."

"So?"

"The report told her that hand-held Stinger missiles were being smuggled into the country and that al-Qaeda intended to kill half a million Americans, so, she decided that the whole country was in danger and that she should do something about it, so she ordered that all airports should be defended by the Army."

"You gotta be kiddin'!"

"No I'm not. You see, protecting the homeland is their business and that's why we have an Army, right?"

"Oh, God, no!"

"Yep, that was her reasoning."

"Did anyone explain to her the importance of secrecy in order to help our mission to succeed?"

"I did just now, but the agent who filed his report hadn't gotten that message across, apparently."

"Lester, when are we as agencies ever going to able to work together like a synchronized watch?"

"We're working on it Bruce, but it's not easy."

"That's why I wanted as few ears and eyes involved as possible, so this wouldn't happen. Thanks, Lester and I'll call the airports and put their minds at ease."

"Good going, Bruce. Everything else in order?"

"I'm still no closer to the targets that they have in mind and the way they're planning to assassinate those presidents, but we're making progress."

"Great. Keep it moving. Have a good one."

Phone calls to airport managers and his counterpart in Manhattan made everyone breathe easier and the Jersey chief could go back to his regular duties.

He shook his head as he sat down behind his desk, "People? I'll never know what makes them tick. I should call Andy too. He'd be relieved."

28

FBI HEADQUARTERS, NEW JERSEY.

Bruce Bongers, Bruno Garcia, Yousef Saban, Jack Wieland, (anti-terrorist-specialist from D.C.), and Sheik Mashid al Momahammed from the mosque in Middletown were sitting around the conference table. Bruce did the introductions.

"The reason we're here is you, Yousef, because you may indeed be of great help to us.

The Sheik is an Imam, an instructor at a mosque, and agreed to help us again, as he has in the past." Bruce made a slight bow in the direction of the holy man.

"We had several situations where Muslim extremists set up recruiting facilities with the intent of hurting the U.S.A. We had a professor at the University of South Florida, we had Atta in Daytona before 9/11, we had another professor right here at Rutgers University, and there may be other such fanatics working anywhere in the United States. We'll ask you to attend religious classes in the various mosques and evaluate what the context is of their preaching. In the case of the Sheik, you'll be attending one of his workshops on Friday in Monmouth County. We know that he's on the side of the true interpretation of the Quran and that he abhors violence and the bad name it has produced for his believers. Most Americans are suspicious of Muslims, and that isn't right. He's a shining example of what a true believer should be."

He looked around the room and sipped some of his coffee. "Everyone okay with coffee and tea?" Each person nodded and he continued, looking at Yousef, "Dr. Wieland here is our expert, and the CIA borrowed him from our department after the fiasco at Fort Hood, because he had recommended that the Army major be removed from his duties, but he was ignored, and you know the rest of the story, thirteen dead. Dr. Wieland will evaluate you as well and make his recommendations: do we actively employ you or do we send you back to Gitmo? He'll look into your mind and your soul, and you better be honest with him. For the next few days, Sheik Mashid will take you to the mosque in Middletown and introduce you to the Clerics in Brooklyn. Meanwhile, you will still spend the evenings in your luxury dwelling in North Bergen, but you'll have a chance to shop for some of your favorite foods. Did you get a microwave or an . . ."

"Yes, a microwave. Very nice."

"Okay, any questions from anyone? You all have his itinerary for the week, right?"

All nodded. "Okay, thanks for helping again, Sheik."

"Bruce, I tell you time and time again, America is my country too." He bowed as he left the room, saying, "Salaam Aleichem." with Yousef on his heels.

Back in Bongers' office.

"Bruno, what have the tapes revealed so far?"

"He fiddled with one of the other phone outlets. It didn't interfere with his dial tone on his regular phone, so it must be another number. He asked for a local phone book, and he immediately learned the local area code, which is what we expected. He checked through the yellow pages, but I think he looked for mosques and couldn't find any. He has to establish contact with the team in Canarsie, but he hasn't figured out how yet." Bruno looked at his notes.

"He also played with the TV cable coming in. He's a bit handicapped, because he has no tools, just an ordinary table knife. I think he'll work on bypassing the regular phone lines and getting out nationally and internationally. Of course, we watch his progress on camera, and we check it out when he's out of the house. Seems we're on track."

"Thanks, Bruno! Dr. Wieland . . ."

"Call me Jack."

"Okay, Jack, we didn't have a chance to talk before, but thanks for coming. We are pretty much convinced that he's a plant and that he has no honest intentions toward us whatsoever, but that's good. That's just what we need him for."

"I don't understand." The dear doctor looked puzzled.

"Well, we need him to work against us and betray us." The doctor raised his eyebrows even further.

"We need to monitor him and all his communications, so we can find out what al-Qaeda is planning here in the U.S. and specifically, here in this area. We are already convinced that an attack will be made on the Israeli President and Obama, when Netanyahu visits here in the fall or late summer. Right now, we don't know any details, but we're tapping in on a line in Brooklyn and in Chicago, and when Yousef starts getting involved, we may pinpoint times and places. Our purpose, of course, is to prevent any murder attempts, but also to capture as many of the extremists as possible and that way put a considerable dent in their armor."

"Oh, boy. You have your hands full."

"Now, we expect that our young Lebanese will do his damndest to convince you that he's loyal to us and to get us to take off his ID bracelet, so he can move around undetected. So be prepared for a song and a dance, although I don't wanna tell you your business."

"How'd you get him here?" He put the emphasis on *you*.

"You wouldn't believe it if I told you. Call me just lucky." Bongers grinned from ear to ear.

"Do I detect a certain amount of sarcasm here?" The doctor smiled back.

"Right! In your business you should question everything."

"Unfortunately."

"Let's go find some lunch. You coming, Bruno?"
"No thanks, boss. Too much catching up to do."

Over lunch at Mama Mia's, Bruce clued in the doctor some more. "Jack, when you asked me how did I end up with this boy instead of the CIA and Home Security, I didn't answer you completely. You see, I served in Army Intelligence for twenty-six years, and I fought many battles in many different faraway countries and made friends with military men of all sorts and ranks. Many of them are good friends. They'll tell me things they wouldn't tell their wives or their superior officers, and those are sources I cannot reveal. To make it worse, I had direct information in 2001 that Atta Mohammed was training pilots and extremists in Daytona, Florida, and I passed it on. I had no authority to act on it myself as an Army lieutenant-colonel, so I had no choice. I didn't understand why the Israelis were forced by the U.S. to release that miserable S.O.B. . . . ."

"He was in Israeli captivity?" The doctor raised his eyebrows again.

"For eight years and the Clinton administration pressured Israel to release him."

"That's unbelievable."

"That's the truth, but anyway, what hurt me most is that my warnings to the Intelligence world were totally ignored, and you know the result. The Twin Towers and 3,000 lives. I get sick, just thinking about it. So now, I do things differently. If I give information to more than two people, I might as well put up a billboard and advertise it or announce on the evening news. Then the various agencies start competing for the potential glory of cracking the case and in the mean time, leaks start springing up all over the place and before long, the bad guys are as knowledgeable as all the top officials. Let's order. Do you know what you want, Doc?"

"It's Jack. Yes, I'll have the eggplant parmesan and a glass of Chianti. How about you, Bruce?"

"That sounds like a good choice, except, you have Heineken on draft, right? I'll have that." He nodded at the waitress. "Getting back to my story. I seem to get more direct pertinent information from sources than what the whole U.S. Intelligence family is privy to. So I dish it out more carefully. I tell nobody anything unless I first clear it with Lester Jarvis, and then we keep it in a small circle."

He savored his glass of beer and continued. "Take this case. If too many people get involved, too many people will talk to subordinates, wives, girlfriends, and before long, Good Morning America is sending reporters down our throats, because the public 'has a right to know' and the whole mission will be compromised. That's why I'm handling this boy personally, even though I really don't have the time to deal with him, but he'll lead us to the assassination location and other details, the hows, the whens, the wheres. All the details that we need to prevent it."

"Isn't that really the job of the Secret Service, Bruce?"

"That's one of the questions I wish you didn't ask, Jack. They'll cancel appearances, shoot a few people, and the main culprits will get away to do it all over again. No. We're gonna do it right and you're gonna help us do it. Here's your food. Eat while it's hot."

"Thanks."

After a leisurely lunch, Bruce suggested, "Are you in favor of returning to the office and study whatever papers we have on the case, or . . . Do you want to retreat to a hotel and do the reviewing there, or do you want to take advantage of my hospitality and spend the night at my home?"

"I'll be here for at least three days, right?"

"At least."

"Then this is what I'll do. I'll gather up all the pertinent paperwork from your office, check into my hotel, go to work and drive to your house for a family dinner. How's that sound?"

"You're on."

"I still don't understand how you got to know this boy in the first place and how . . . ."

"Those are some of the questions you're not supposed to ask."

29

FBI HEADQUARTERS, NEW JERSEY

"Bruce, this is Meir. I have some bad news and some bad news. Which do you wanna hear first?"

"Good God, can't you make up some good news, like, how's the weather in Tel Aviv?"

"Blue skies as always, but seriously, I lost my contact in Lebanon. Last I heard, he was going to a Hezbollah meeting and never reappeared. They probably got wise to him and knocked him off. That was my inside source. Irreplaceable! Takes years to cultivate a good contact."

"That's tough. No details?"

"Not a word. Disappeared from the face of the earth. Not even a funeral or a death notice in the papers, nothing. Sounds like your Jimmy Hoffa in the old days. The other bad news is, a crate with self-propelled, handheld Stinger missiles was just loaded for delivery into Port Arthur. Where is that?"

"Texas, right along the Louisiana border. Do you have the name of the ship?"

"A Dutch freighter, *Stad Deventer*. Do you want me to spell it for you?"

"No, I know how to spell that. That's actually good news, 'cause that narrows it down for us. Delivery date about ten days?"

"Twelve to fourteen. He's stopping in New Orleans and then on to Port Arthur."

"Thanks, Meir."

"How's our boy?"

"I think he's on track. We're counting on him to provide details of the attacks on the presidents. If September eleven is their target date, then we have time. Not too much, but we're comfortable."

"I'm coming with Netanyahu."

"Great. Plan to stay awhile when it's over."

"Yeah, I'd like to play on a green golf course for once. Shalom!"

"The director, please." Bongers made some hasty notes before Jarvis answered. "Yes, Bruce."

"Lester, pass this on to the elite group. A crate of Stinger missiles have been loaded in Beirut for Port Arthur on a Dutch freighter *Stad Deventer*. Let me spell that for you s-t-a-d, separate word, 'd-e-v-e-n-t-e-r'. Stopover in New Orleans, missiles dropped in Port Arthur. Would it be possible to get an expert aboard ship in New Orleans and de-fuse the rockets?"

"That's a great thought. I'll pass it on. Anything else?"

"Yeah, seems like Netanyahu is scheduled to be here for the anniversary of 9/11, and Dagan is coming with him personally."

"Wow, would be fun to see the old bugger again. How's the progress with the boy wonder from Lebanon?"

"Coming along nicely. I'm sure, he'll cut his ID bracelet before 9/11 and disappear, but that will be according to plan."

"Good going. Thanks."

Half an hour later the Director was on the phone again, "Bruce, you speak Dutch, don't you?"

"Well . . ., pretty well. A bit rusty, I guess."

"Could you talk to that captain aboard the freighter and get him to cooperate without arousing the suspicion of any Hezbollah agents that might be aboard?"

"I could try. Do you have a number yet?"

"I'll call you back."

Three hours later. "Lester, Bruce. I spoke with a delightful Dutch captain by the name of Leen van Nood, who was shocked to think that he had Hezbollah weapons on board and maybe even some extremists amongst his crew. Thank God, nobody was near the captain's quarters when we had our conversation, but very few of his crew speaks Dutch anyway. He has a few Germans, one Dutchman, his First Mate, and two Filipinos, that's it.

"Not a large crew."

"No, but that's all you need on a 265-foot ship nowadays. Anyway, he'll be glad to cooperate, but nothing can be done until they've unloaded in New Orleans, because the suspected crate is in the bottom of the hull."

"What's he carrying?"

"A lot of textiles, dates, olive oil, palm oil and an assortment of gems that he has in his vault. He thinks the missiles must be in the crates that are labeled 'Olive Oil'."

"That's ironic that he also has Filipinos aboard. Maybe part of that same terrorist group that has been fighting their government over there for years."

"Sounds like it."

"Do you think we can get him to take on another crewmember in New Orleans at our expense?"

"I'm sure he would. The Dutch are pretty anti-Moslem nowadays after the murder of a popular politician and an artist. I'm sure he's very much on our side."

"Great. I'll work on that. Thanks, Bruce. You have many facets to your talents."

"Thanks." He smiled broadly as he hung up the phone.

• • •

Tripoli, Lebanon
Hassan Nasrallah, Ahmed Bin Benhumed, Bahouie and three

others were celebrating with large helpings of succulent lamb and chilled grape juice. Apparently the meeting had gone well, and all the plans were coming together.

Bahouie spoke between bites. "We have not heard directly from my former roommate, Yousef, but it seems that everything is pretty much on schedule. That traitor, Sheik Mashid, has taken him under his wing in order to indoctrinate him in peaceful Islam. What a laugh. That Sheik works with the Americans all the time, but our boy is too ingrained with the true meaning of the Quran and our goal, *'death to the infidels'*, that the Sheik might as well be pissing in the wind. Our operatives in Brooklyn, Canarsie, will soon be making contact when the Sheik takes him to the mosque over there. Yousef already dropped a phone number in our Monmouth facility, so we'll soon know how to reach him."

"Won't the Americans tap his phone and listen in?" One of the Hezbollah members cut in.

"Not likely, because they think he's working for their cause."

"Are they that dumb? Has he already fooled them completely?"

"Oh, they may be cautious, but we will be more cautious. We'll send some unimportant messages and see if they react. If they do, then we know that we can't use that line of communication again. Kaliff in Chicago has been getting away with that for years. By the way, he's defending two more of our gallant fighters in Guantanamo, and it looks like they may be released back to their homeland."

"Who are they and where are they from?" Ahmed wanted to know.

"One is from Iraq, one of Saddam Hussein's trustees, and the other is from Jordan. Both should be flown to Egypt and then back to their homes, but they will be deferred to Yemen, to train with Bin Laden's instructors."

"Will they be involved in our September operation?"

"No. No time. Besides that, they are not needed. We have the teams pretty much in place already. The two Filipinos on the Dutch freighter will join Meelo, and two more of our operatives are in Venezuela, working their way toward and through Mexico."

"And the New York operation?" Hassan wanted to know.

Ahmed spoke up. "Hassan, it's too bad that you cherish your magnificent beard so much: otherwise, we might be able to shave it off and send you there in person." That created a chuckle all around the room. "If you appeared like that at JFK, you would immediately have a tail of five undercover agents following you, and you wouldn't even have any privacy in your bathroom." He grinned at his own joke. "So far it seems pretty sure, according to our Imam in Israel, that Netanyahu and Obama will be in New York together to commemorate our successful attack on their beautiful city. The exact itinerary is not known, but we suspect that they'll lay a wreath at the monument of the Twin Towers. and that's probably our best bet."

"The area will be crawling with security personnel . . ."

"True, they'll seal off every roof, every hotel, every apartment building in the area. They'll block every street, so a car- or truck-bomber won't be able to get near to them, so we have to think of something more clever."

"A paratrooper or a bomb?"

"Hassan, you may have a point there. We nearly pulled that off at Camp David, remember? It might work this time."

"Don't you think that they'll have fighters all over the sky, ready to intercept anything suspicious?"

"They passed a law after 2001 that authorizes American fighters to shoot down civilian airlines, when they behave suspiciously. So that might not be the right answer."

"We're making good progress, though. Where are the hash pipes? I feel like celebrating."

"Allahu Akbar, brother."

"Death to the Americans."

30

FBI OFFICES, NEW JERSEY.

Dr. Jack Wieland had many difficult cases in the past, but this boy Yousef was an unusually hard one. In Gitmo, most of the inmates were defiant, demanding immediate release, accusing the United States of violating their rights and comparing the Americans with filthy pigs. Some would simply clam up and respond to nothing at all, some would talk incessantly, and some would even threaten him right in their cells. Not but one percent would actually cooperate. This Lebanese man was different. *Too cooperative,* he wrote on his pad, *too anxious to please.*

Had the intelligence efficiency of the Israelis and the Americans impressed him? Had the time in the Israeli prison and Guantanamo made him see the light, that a lifetime in prison was not too darn desirable? Was the Sheik's interpretation of the Quran overcoming the hatred of the past? Or was it all a show for the benefit of fooling Bongers and his team and convince them to release him early from his ID bracelet? If he was indeed putting on an act to deceive the Americans, he was doing a good job of it.

The dear doctor could not make a definite analysis, and it bothered him. The Muslim man was definitely an intelligent, well-bred individual, and his knowledge of the English language was nearly phenomenal, considering that he had only studied in the U.S. for two years.

So, Dr. Wieland's report to Bongers was very brief:

Very clever individual. Potentially dangerous. Born charmer. Doubt that he has honorable intentions to our cause.

Jack Wieland, PhD.

When Bongers found Wieland's report on his desk in a sealed envelope, he grinned and said to Bruno, who was standing in front of his desk, "It took the brave doctor three days to come up with two lines?" He handed the note to Garcia. "At least we have him going in the right direction. What's the latest on the surveillance tapes?"

"He has the second phone jack rigged, so he can make outside calls, even out of the county. He has conferred with the guys in Canarsie four times, and they seem to have their timing in order. They are just about convinced that their D-Day is indeed 9/11, and they even discussed what the time-zone differences are between here and Houston. They don't have cell phone numbers yet out there in the west, but that may be because their operatives are not in place yet. Our friend is dying to get a cell phone, but they talked him out of it. Too difficult to hide, too difficult to apply for if you're not a registered telephone user and if you have no credit cards. Not to worry, though, they'll provide him one when the time comes, about two months hence."

"Any talk about what weapons they're gonna use? Rifles, bombs, rockets? What?"

"According to our translator, they're still very uncertain about that because Beirut is still uncertain." Bruno consulted his notes and shook his head.

"Damn. What do we prepare for if we don't know what and when they're gonna do it? We'll keep playing the game and we're still ahead of the game, but I hate to find out at the last minute that we didn't prepare properly and they pull it off."

"We have two months yet, Boss. We'll get them. We always do."

"Yeah, but the more unprepared we are, the more lives it may cost us and I mean, lives of our agents." He finally took off his jacket and sat down. "The more they lean toward 9/11, the more I feel that they'll plan something at the monument. Are any speeches scheduled for that day? Any ceremonies and by whom? Check with NYPD if they have plans or the Fire Department, honoring their fallen brothers. Find out if any permits have been requested and if the media is already getting set up for any events. I may just stroll out there and take a look for myself. See what the layout is nowadays after all the cleanup and rebuilding." A smile crossed his face. "Bruno, just a thought. If we're on the right track, then Yousef may ask you to go and visit the Twin Tower Monument, and when he does, you call and clear it with me and take him."

"Really?"

"Sure. The more anxious he is to view the scene, the more certain we can be that we're on the right track."

Bruno smiled also, "You may have something there, Boss. You may have something there."

"Has our boy given you a hard time yet, Bruno?"

"No, the biggest problem is his shopping habits. He tries to convince me every day that he needs to go to Wal-Mart for milk, bread or something, and then he shows up with pliers, screwdrivers and mini-wrenches. I charge it promptly and keep the receipts, but he's obviously working on a way to unlock his cell door from the inside and eventually cut off his bracelet."

"What is that thing actually made of?" Bruce had never figured that out.

"Titanium, I think, with a core of Teflon."

"I'll have to dissect one of them in my garage."

"Good luck. Let me know how it works, just in case I ever get locked up."

"Bruce, This is Jeb Taylor."

"Oh, hello, Sir. What a pleasure."

"You can say that for real?"

" It's always a pleasure dealing with you. How's your progress on the conspiracy? We seem to be on track, all indications pointing toward September and the visit of the Israeli president. What do you have to add?"

"Well, we ran into a slight snag. The agent aboard the freighter *Stad Deventer* couldn't get into the crate with the rockets while they were still stashed in the hull under tons of olive and palm oil, but he's going to be there at the unloading at Port Arthur. We have agents on the docks, and they'll follow them anywhere they'll be delivered. We are still guessing at what they could possibly be after anywhere in that area, but the distribution of the rockets will tell us a lot more about the potential targets. Has your Lebanese added anything additional?"

"No, mainly that they're targeting something or somebody on 9/11, but we're still guessing at where and how. Do you have a fix yet on who will man and fire the rockets and where the large population congregations are near a chemical storage?"

"No, we're still puzzling over that one. All chemical compounds and refineries are away from any urban areas. If they hope to kill thousands, then we have to consider a different target. Yet the hand-held rockets on the freighter tell us they're aiming to shoot up something that will really rock, not just a storage tank or a tank park. Anyway, I was hoping your protégée would have given you some clue by now."

"I'll call you immediately when I get something."

"Thanks, Bruce." He hung up before Bongers could say, "You're welcome."

Without putting down the horn, he dialed the Hoover Building in D.C. and asked, "Mr. Jarvis, please."

"Lester?" He chuckled. "I just had a direct call from Jeb Taylor. To what do I owe such honor? Are they getting desperate?"

"I guess so. They're just as frustrated as we are, and they really have put a lot of people on it, which is exactly what you didn't want."

"True, the more people are in on it, the better the chance of a leak and alerting the enemy that we're on to them. We need to catch these clowns in the act, or otherwise we'll never get convictions in this liberal system. Have you or your team anything new to report?"

"No, I guess you receive the same input from the CIA about the lawyer Kaliff in Chicago and the team in Brooklyn."

"Yes, and it's helpful. We'll narrow it down over here. We'll catch'em. We're on track. It's just as frustrating as all the other cases, but that's par for the course. We'll get'em, Lester. We always do, right?"

"I have every confidence in you Bruce, just don't call in any F-15's without clearing it with me."

"Let's just hope there'll be time when the time comes."

"Make the time. Get ahead of'em."

Bruce laughed, "Yes, Boss."

He reached his right-hand man Bruno on his cell. "Bruno, what are you doing at the moment?"

"I'm explaining our training manual to Yousef here. He's very studious, although I think he'll attempt to rewrite it."

"Sounds familiar. He can study on his own, can't he?"

"Sure, what's up?"

"Can you meet me at the McDonalds on Bergenline in Union City in about twenty minutes?"

"Sure can."

"Okay."

Sitting in Garcia's car, heading for the Lincoln Tunnel, he sighed and said, "Bruno, I'm getting more and more antsy about that 9/11 memorial and I really want to look around the place and get a feeling for the layout. Park somewhere close and let's walk around and grab lunch. I have this unconfirmed nagging hunch that this is what they'll be aiming for. Can you picture bin Laden's statement, ' While the infidels celebrated the impact of 9/11, we celebrated by assassinating both enemy presidents right on the spot of our victory in '01?' I bet you he already has an elaborate statement printed up, ready for recording."

"Boss, I hope you're wrong, but the frightening thing is, you're right most of the time."

"Let's keep it that way. I hope you're hungry."

31

MANHATTAN

On his cell phone, Bruce reached the main office of the FBI in the Big Apple. "Mr. Andrews, please."

"Andy? Bruce. We're heading for the World Trade Center. Wanna join us for lunch?"

"Sure. Where?"

"You name the place. It's your city." Bongers grinned while he was talking.

"How about at McGregory's Irish pub on Vesey Street? They have great sandwiches."

"Sounds good. It'll take us about fifteen minutes, I guess."

"See you there. I'll grab a cab." Andrews hung up.

Over Irish stew and a Guinness draft, Bongers explained his reasoning. "As I see it, or should I say, as I smell it, if these two presidents are going to be in Manhattan on 9/11 of this year, they're going to be right here, laying a wreath and making a speech. If that is the case, then this is where the attack will take place. Do you know if wreaths are laid at the *Sphere* or at any other spot around here?"

"I'll check that out. For such events, they usually put up bleachers and a speaker's platform. The city fathers should have permit requests on their desks by now, because they'll need a lot of planning. Roads need to be blocked off, traffic diverted, facilities for Security Forces, you won't believe the amount of hoopla involved."

"Would a foreign-security detail like the Mossad need special permits to operate here in protection of their leader? Do they need special clearances to climb on a roof, like right here where we're sitting?"

"Probably. They are used to dealing with local police departments, wouldn't you think?"

"I'll check with Dagan." Bruce munched some more of his stew. "The Secret Service will man all the roofs and all the hotel rooms facing the monument, wouldn't they?"

"That would be a monumental task- forgive the pun. Can you imagine how many apartments and offices face this square? Then again; all the hotel rooms. I wonder how many of my men will be drafted for security purposes? So far I haven't heard a whisper about it, but I'm sure they're finalizing their itineraries as we speak." Andrews shook his head. "All that hullabaloo and all that expense. For what? To stroke the egos of some high-ranking yoyos? It's hard to believe, but what can we do? Play along, I guess."

"Dear Andy, the price of freedom and democracy. It doesn't come cheap. What I wanna do is, walk around the whole square, study the layout of all the buildings and access roads. I still wonder what they could possibly have in mind. A helicopter or small plane, loaded with explosives, diving down on the entourage? Not easy. Could be shot down before they ever get close. A truck bomb, car bomb? There's no way they could get in here, right?" He finished his beer.

"No, they'll have concrete barriers all over the place." Andrews shook his head in emphasis.

"How about a motorcycle or a walking person, strapped with plastic explosives?"

"Could be, but probably could not come close to the celebrities."

"Okay, let's take care of the check and start our excursion."

They circled the layout twice, studying all the building around the area that once housed the twin towers. "Weren't they supposed to have a huge building up by now, Andy?"

"You read the papers, you see the news. You've seen what a bunch of jackasses are fighting over designs, structures and permits? I believe they are on the fourth architect and now the Port Authority, that owns this property, is nixing everything that was agreed on earlier. In just nine years, they've managed to fall nine years behind schedule."

"So the only real monument around here is that *Sphere*, where we saw the flowers and the group of pilgrims?"

"Pilgrims?" Andrews stopped and looked puzzled.

"At least they were holding hands and praying."

"That seems the most logical place for a ceremony."

"Let's look at the buildings around there again, especially the roofs."

Bruno took pictures of everything in sight. At the *Sphere* the second time around, Andrews said, "You've heard the latest theories, haven't you?"

"Like what?"

"Because burning jet fuel could never melt steel, it doesn't get hot enough, there had to be other explosive material stashed inside the towers, to make the steel crumble and…"

"You gotta be kidding."

"Look at the films. You see the buildings explode, not just burning down, floor by floor.

Engineers have figured out that there were other elements involved. Jet fuel alone couldn't have done it. If jet fuel could burn hot enough to melt the steel structure you're looking at right now, we'd have another great invention on our hands. Look at it!" He pointed at the ball of twisted steel and copper that had become a lasting tribute to all of those who died in the inferno. "No way can you cut that or melt it unless you'd have an acetylene torch of at least 3,000 degrees. Kerosene doesn't burn that hot."

"In other words, what you're saying is that the Taliban or al-Qaeda had materials stashed in here long before the actual hits on 9/11?"

"Sure looks like it." Andrews looked very somber as he shook his head.

"Man, oh man, we're dealing with a very smart opponent!"

"We better never forget that."

"Amen, brother. Amen."

Back in the New Jersey office, they looked at all the shots Bruno had taken and made notes as they talked.

"You see that big building, facing south on Vesey Street? It has two levels. A roof garden on the twelfth surrounds nearly the whole upper structure, and then there is another flat roof on top of the building. If you had a sniper rifle, where would you be able to get off the best shot?" Bongers had his little red laser pointer dancing all over the screen.

"Forget the roof garden. That's gonna be crawling with onlookers, and I'm sure the Secret Service will be out there in force." One of the agents remarked.

"So the roof? Can someone google that area and print out a blowup of that building? Thanks. We'll have to ask the Manhattan office to check all those other buildings as well. Most of them have permanent solid hurricane-proof glass, right? Are there any windows that can open, facing the square? Any place a sniper can have a clear shot? Just remember Lee Harvey Oswald. You don't need a very big opening to stick a rifle through. Justin," he addressed one of the agents, "coordinate all those details with the New York office, will you? Let's hope we can narrow it down considerably."

Before leaving for the day, Bongers got through to his right-hand man on his cell. "Bruno, how's our boy doing?"

"He was annoyed that we left him in his cubbyhole all day. He wants to get out more. He has plenty of reading material, though, and he loves American television, especially celebrity programs and dancing. He asked me some more questions about his body-monitor and I explained that somewhere on a screen, every body movement is watched, and if he ran off, he would be located within minutes and caught within seconds."

"So he's thinking of going exploring?"

"Yeah, he also complained of the lack of money. I asked what he needed it for. I said, 'You have everything you want and when you really need something, I buy it for you, right'?"

"What did he say to that?"

"He said, "you make me feel like a prisoner'. And I said. 'You are. You haven't convinced us yet that you're really gonna work with us' . . .' And then he said, 'work as what?' . . . and I said, 'As an informer'. And he said, 'That's what you really want me for? To spy on my people'? . . . And I said, 'Only the bad elements, the murderers, the extremists, not the hardworking upstanding members of society'."

"What was his reaction?"

"He mumbled something about 'unfair', but I left at that point. But let me ask you something, Boss. That bracelet? Is it true, that it can't be cut? That it's too hard?"

"No. I'm sure a hacksaw or a torch can cut through it . . ."

"So what keeps him from splitting one day?"

"Oh, we expect him to do that, and we hope that he'll go straight to the point of the assassination or to Canarsie, to his extremist cronies. The moment he cuts it, the GPS will show where he is at that time, and we take over from there. We'll shadow him wherever he goes. We better be prepared for that event. I plan to be. We need him to pull that stunt no later than September one, so we have a few days lead time."

"Maybe I should give him some money next time and let him shop by himself in Wal-Mart and see if he buys a saw blade."

"That would be the smart thing for him to do. Buy a package of good hard steel saw blades and hide them in his socks. Then after you and he are on the road, I can search the apartment and see what he's come up with. Has he asked about calling home to Lebanon or outside the local calling area?"

"No, but he took the existing phone apart and found he couldn't do anything with it. He tried to call an operator, but that didn't work from that phone. Strictly local calls."

"Good going. I'm heading out soon. Two of my boys are playing on the Varsity Soccer team. Hope to catch a match for once."

"Too many long days, Boss?"

"I'm not sure they mentioned that when they interviewed me for this job."

"Funny, they mentioned all the benefits and all the reasons why I should join the FBI, but long hours didn't come up at all."

"Just wait till you retire, Bruno."

"Another twenty-five years?"

"Something like that."

32

CALDWELL H.S. STADIUM

The match had been exciting, so far. It was half time and the score was Caldwell 2, Essex High 0. One of the goals had been scored by Gene Bongers, the Senior. The other son, Elliott, a Sophomore, played defender, so he didn't get as many chances to score. Just penalty kicks, which was his forté. Bruce was at the vendor's window, when his phone rang.

"Just a moment, just a moment. Let me get to a quieter spot." He moved away from the crowd toward the parking lot. "Hello, hello? Who is this? Van Nood? Leen? The captain? Right? Oh, I'm glad I gave you my cell number. What's happening?"

"You've got to help me. I've cooperated with you folks all along. I took this extra man aboard in New Orleans and uh . . ."

"What happened? What's the matter, Mr. van Nood?"

"I just pulled into Port Arthur, and I need to unload tomorrow morning and head toward Galveston and . . ."

"And what?"

"They won't let me unload."

"Who won't let you unload?"

"You people."

"We people? Who's we people? What are you talking about?"

"Two men in suits and ties came aboard and handed me this paper saying that I have a *'hold on the cargo.'*"

"A hold on the cargo? By whom, what's the title of the agency on top of the order?"

"It says, Central Intelligence Agency."

"The CIA? Well, I'll be damned."

"Yes, but what you don't understand, if I can't unload, the delays will cost me $3,000 or more each day, and it'll put me into bankruptcy in a hurry."

"Mr. van Nood. Stay close to this phone. I'll call you back."

"$3,000 a day. Do you understand? That's a lot of money for a small operator like myself."

"I understand. I understand. I'm right on it."

"Please, this is a terrible . . ."

"I know, I know. Stay by the phone." Bruce ran back to his seat at the bleachers. "Helen. I'm taking the wagon home. Catch a ride with the boys, okay?"

"Okay. Drive carefully." She knew her husband when he was under pressure.

He needed to have access to a whole bunch of phone numbers that were not in his cell, but were on the rolodex in his home office. While driving, he punched Jarvis' number, but got a recorder. "Bruce here, 8:35. Call me back. Urgent, very urgent." Before he reached his driveway, he got a hold of the FBI headquarters in D.C. and left orders to track down the director, no matter where he might be. "National Security," he emphasized.

Inside his desk, he found the CIA Directory, and he called Gerald Swartz on his home phone. "Mr. Swartz? Bongers FBI. Would you kindly rescind the order to put 'hold on the cargo' of the freighter *Stad Deventer* and do it immediately?"

"Since when do you give orders to the CIA?"

"Since the CIA is violating inter-departmental trust between the FBI and the CIA. Get on it immediately, while I call Taylor." He slammed the phone down. To himself he said, "Those stupid bastards."

Next he called Jeb Taylor's direct line, but was told that the director had gone for the day, so he called his cell. Another recorder. "Mr. Taylor, have your agency rescind the hold on the cargo order of the *Stad Deventer* immediately. I'm now trying the White House." He kept muttering to himself. "These gentlemen don't like to be disturbed in their spare time, apparently."

He was about to call Homeland Security, when his cell phone rang. "Bruce, Lester here, what's the excitement?"

"As usual, the CIA screwed up. They delivered a 'hold on the cargo' notice to the freighter with the missiles, and that's gonna scare the terrorists away, who'll be there for the pick-up!" He was nearly shouting.

"Who ordered that?"

"I don't know and I don't care. That order has to be rescinded immediately, so the skipper can start unloading in the morning, and our agents can start following the rockets to their final destination or holding point, whichever comes first."

"Have you talked to Taylor?"

"Left a message. You've got to stop that order immediately, Lester. The whole plan will fall apart if you don't."

"I'll get on it."

Bruce walked to the kitchen to fix a drink when his cell phone rang. "Bongers, this is Mr. Taylor, and you are walking on hot coals when you're threatening and ordering my agents around. You may have your head in a noose this time."

"Sorry, Sir. It's your neck, and the president himself may apply the noose."

"The president? Where does he come in?"

"He'll be the next person I call if you do not cancel that asinine order in Port Arthur, to put a hold on the cargo."

"I ordered that injunction and it stands."

"I'm calling the White House." Bruce hung up. He continued to the kitchen, but this time he walked to the bar and pulled out a bottle of Dewars. Before he could even get to the ice cubes, his cell rang again. "Bongers, don't you ever hang up on me again!"

"Sorry, Sir, stand by. I'm on hold for the president." He laid his cell phone on the counter and finally got to open the freezer for some ice cubes. He could hear Taylor screaming while the phone kept making undecipherable noises. He finally picked it up. "Sorry, Sir, the president is at a dinner function. It'll be another few minutes, but I told them it's a national security problem, so he'll be . . ."

"Bruce, listen!" The CIA director was actually screaming. "Listen. Our operative could not defuse the missiles while on board, so we're simply gonna confiscate them . . ."

"And blow the whole operation?" Now Bruce was yelling into the phone. "Upstage everything we planned? Just a moment . . ." He put the phone down again and poured some scotch on the waiting cubes. He took a sip and picked up the instrument again. "Sorry Sir, it'll be another ten minutes. At what number can I call you back?"

"No wait, Bruce, wait! By grabbing the missiles, we disarm the whole plot and the threat is over..."

"Over for now!" Bongers was still hollering. "Just long enough for them to get some more rockets and pull it off after all. Are you people dense or something? We need these rockets picked up by the extremists, followed to their destination, so we know what they're after, catch them red handed and bring them to justice or kill the bastards. I prefer the latter."

"Yes, but . . ."

"And that's what we, Swartz, you, Lester and I agreed on and now you went directly against our mutual agreement and against all common sense . . . Just a moment . . . The White House again . . . Must be an important dinner affair if national security is put on the back burner . . ." The cell phone kept making noises, but Bruce leisurely took a swallow of that great scotch tradition called Dewars. Finally, he picked it up again. "Hate to make you wait. What number can I call you back at? Homeland Security will rescind your order, so you can go to sleep. It's all under control."

"Bruce, wait. Let's be sensible about this. What was the plan that you had in mind?"

"That WE had in mind? We'll trace the rockets to their destination, where they'll be stored. We keep an eye on them. More than likely, on September eleven or before, they'll be split between different operatives, two or three, I guess, and we follow them to their final destination. When they're ready to fire their missiles at their . . . , still unknown to us . . . , targets, we knock them off or arrest them with hard evidence that will stand up in court, so they won't go back to Yemen, like so many others. That's how we're gonna work it, with or without the CIA."

"Now hold it, Bruce. We can still play it that way. No harm has been done, just some miscommunication on behalf of my staff and . . ."

"Just a moment, the White House again." Bruce took another sip. "They'll call me back. What were you saying, Mr. Taylor?"

"Tell the White House, we've got it under control. I'll cancel that order, and my people will be watching the unloading and shipping, and we'll keep you and Lester posted about the destination. Just tell them, it's all under control."

"I'll tell'em." He clicked his phone shut, took a sip, walked to his office and called the skipper, Leen Van Nood. "Leen?" (he pronounced it 'Lane'.) This is Bruce. Unload on schedule in the morning.

"Really?"

"Yes. Act like nothing happened."

"But what about those guys . . ."

"Just a little misunderstanding, something about olive oil."

When his wife and sons walked in, Helen asked, "Trouble, honey?"

"Just a little snag. What can I fix you and what was the final score, boys?"

"Four to one, Dad. How about you?"

"About the same."

33

FBI, NEW JERSEY. 8 AM

"Mr. Bongers, there's a call from the White House on seven."

Those were the words that greeted the Senior Agent as he walked in the front door of his office building.

"Who is it?'

"The secretary of the Chief of Staff."

"Oh, what's his name again?"

"George Kopolosi."

"Thanks, I'll pick it up in my office." The 6'2" curly blond office manager smiled as he took off his jacket. "Wondering what they're up to?" He picked up the horn. "Bongers here."

"Just a moment, Sir. Hold for Mr. Kopolosi." Bruce loosened his tie and undid his top shirt button.

"Mr. Bongers? Kopolosi here. We want to know what the fracas is in Port Arthur, Texas."

"Texas? Sir, I'm in charge of New Jersey. Let me look up the name of the Special Agent in Charge of that area. Just a moment, while . . ."

"No, no. We understand that you interfered with security operations . . ."

"Interfered? I work for the FBI. I assist in security matters. Is that what you meant to say?"

"No, that's not what I wanted . . ."

"Then can you be more specific?"

"Apparently, there's been a security breech and . . ."

"Sir, this is not a secure line, and I suggest that you connect me with the president directly, after I get clearance to discuss this matter from Mr. Jarvis at Headquarters, because I cannot and I will not reveal anything without permission, you understand that? So give me your number and I'll call you . . ."

"Mr. Bongers, you are most insolent . . ."

"You mean efficient, don't you? I'm breaking the connection now and I'll call the White House on a secure line, once I have the proper clearance." He hung up.

"Those damn clowns," he said to no one in particular, because there was nobody else in the room. He pushed the intercom button. "Julie, get me Mr. Jarvis, please."

He got up to walk to the break room to fix himself a cup of coffee, but the intercom buzzed before he got to the door. "Mr. Kopolosi again."

"Tell him I'm on the phone with the Hoover Building and ask for his number." He continued out the door.

Before he had a chance to stir the fresh brew, the intercom speaker sounded again. "Mr. Bongers, Mr. Jarvis on one." With a sigh, he added some sugar and returned to his desk.

"Good morning, Lester."

"Just a moment, here comes Mr. Jarvis." A female voice responded instead.

"Good morning, Lester. Did you have a good night?"

"I had a good night, but you must have gone overboard again . . . "

"Me? What did I do?"

"You called the White House without any prior authorization . . ."

"Me? When?"

"Didn't you call the White House last night?"

"I wouldn't call them without clearance from you, and I told that clown Kopolosi the same thing this morning. I wouldn't give them the time of day unless you approved."

"You didn't call the White House?"

"Not since last year."

"Great Scott. What is all that hoopla . . ."

"While we're at it, Lester, I don't want to talk to anybody in the White House concerning our present mission, because they'll leak it to the press and gum up the works. Nobody but a very small circle should be involved, and that's what we agreed on. You, I, Taylor and the rest of the agents involved. So, if I have your permission, I'll get word to Koloposi, or whatever his name is, that I cannot talk with him. Orders from Headquarters."

"Good God, the problems you get me involved in . . ."

"Sir, we're talking about the life of the president and thousands of innocent Americans. We have to protect them at all cost."

A deep sigh came across the phone line. "You're right, you're right. Go ahead. Talk to nobody. My orders. I'll call you back."

"This emphasizes again why I hate to work with the CIA, because they always want to do things their way, stupid or not, without consulting their partners."

"Bruce, one of these days I'm gonna retire from this pressure cooker."

"When you do, we'll play some golf."

"Sure."

Bongers finally got to drink his coffee.

Leaning back, he dug out his cell phone and called the freighter captain. "Leen, Bruce Bongers here. Are you prepared to unload?"

"It's only just past seven here, but the cranes and the dockworkers are already lining up to start the process."

"Any problems?"

"Problems? No, except two of my crewmembers didn't return from shore leave last night, and I need them here, but I'll roll up my sleeves and pitch in. In this business, the captain does whatever is needed. One day, I'm an electrician, the next day I'm a welder and . . ."

"The sailors who didn't return, were they Filipinos?"

"How'd you know?"

"Lucky guess! Anything unusual on the shore? Any unusual activity? Men in suits and ties?"

"No, except my stevedore is just walking up the gangplank, and I need to order supplies . . ."

"Call me immediately if something unusual happens, okay?"

"Okay and . . ." Bongers had already hung up.

"Get me Mr. Jarvis again, please." He picked up his mail and started browsing through it. Nothing that needed his immediate attention. He sighed and considered calling Bruno in to share last night's experience with him, but the intercom interrupted him again. "Mr. Jarvis on three."

"Lester, who do we have on the docks in Port Arthur? Are they our agents or are they CIA."

"Both."

"Do you mind if I talk to whoever is in charge down there?"

"I guess not. I'll call you back."

For fifteen minutes, Bruce walked back and forth between the break room, the reception area, the other cubbyholes and his office and back again. He smiled, joked and seemed relaxed, but his staff knew what was brewing. Bruce Bongers couldn't stand NOT being in control. Many of his staff wondered if the White House call had gotten him up tight, but nobody brought it up.

A second cup of coffee and a Dunkin Donut landed on his desk, just as the phone rang.

"Mr. Jarvis on two."

"Yes, Lester. The man in charge of our team is Foster Raims, 'r-a-i-m-s'. Here's his number. He's on site."

"Thanks. I owe you."

"You better believe it."

"Foster? Bruce Bongers here. Have we ever met or worked together?"

"No, but your reputation is such that I would look forward to it."

"Oh, that's nice. Where are you at the moment?"

"I'm in overalls in a garbage truck."

Bruce chuckled, "Making a buck on the side?"

The Texas agent laughed as well. "With two kids in college, I could sure use it."

"Where's the truck you're in."

"Parked across from the docks in front of a diner. My partner is getting breakfast."

"Great. Any of your people on the docks?"

"Yes, two. Working as longshoremen."

"Good. Do you know what we're looking for?"

"I've been briefed."

"They'll be unloading crates of olive oil, I believe in cans. Five gallons maybe, but I don't know that. Two of them will be extra heavy, because they contain rockets."

"Huh?"

"I thought you'd been briefed. Anyway, they'll be picked up by a different truck than all the other crates. The two with the missiles are what we're interested in. Follow them, wherever they go, probably a warehouse, but we don't know where. Maybe in Port Arthur, maybe Houston, maybe Timbuktu, we don't know. The point is: we have to know where they're going, and then they have to be watched, probably for two weeks. Maybe part of that load will go to a different point. Whatever, we have to have around the clock surveillance on those weapons. We have to catch them red-handed when they prepare to use them."

"Why don't we just grab them now and . . ."

"That's dumb CIA policy . . . Forget that. We have to find out what their targets are and we have to catch the bastards in the act. Foster . . . Listen . . . We are talking about hundreds of thousands of American lives . . ."

"With handheld rockets?"

"By the explosions caused by those rockets. Al-Qaeda is expecting to kill half a million people on September eleven, and you and your team can help prevent it."

"Good God. Are you serious?"

"Osama bin Laden is serious. Dead serious!"

"Ooy! "

"Foster, go aboard as if you're a longshoreman, see Captain van Nood, like 'von note,' and get the papers of two Filipinos that went AWOL last night and find them. Don't arrest them, just trail them. They're al-Qaeda terrorists. Ask the captain to give you some signal when the extra heavy crates come ashore. And call me regularly, okay? Keep me updated every step of the way, will you?"

"Sure will."

34

FBI OFFICE, NEW JERSEY.

"Bruno, how's our boy?"

"I'm in his place now. He's discovered how to play Free Cell and spends hours doing it."

"He's got a computer?"

"Yes, there were still several old PCs in the building, and we gave him one. He also tried to cut off his bracelet the other night, but the hacksaw blades barely scratched the surface, so he'll have to try something else."

"Where's he now?"

"The Sheik brought him back from a trip to Brooklyn's mosque and he's out now with a Sheriff's Deputy, learning how to serve summonses and warrants."

"Does he have a key to let himself in?"

"No, the local policeman locks him in and lets him out, when I call him. By the way, I gave him $50, like you told me."

"It'll be interesting to see what he buys with it. Okay, thanks Bruno."

"Our boy", Yousef was in a hardware store at that very moment, while the Deputy was on a coffee break.

A short, but attractive, young lady was waiting on him. She had a very round face with blue smiling eyes. Her hair was reddish blond, and he wondered if she were a blond who had died it red or the other way around. She was at least a foot shorter than he was, but well rounded. Not really chubby, but round in the right places. Her smile was infectious.

"What can I help you with, Sir?"

"Call me Joe. I lost a key to a padlock, and I tried to cut it with a hacksaw, but it's too tough. How can I cut the darn thing?"

"Come back here." She strode ahead of him to Isle 21 and pointed to a large chain cutter.

"This will cut just about anything."

"How much?" He twisted the price tag and fondled the cutter. "Aye! $34.95? I don't have that kinda money on me." The truth was, he couldn't possibly walk out with that thing and have the Deputy deliver it to his cell.

"Do you have a credit card?" She smiled from ear to ear.

"No, I'm a student here and . . . uh, at Stevens in Hoboken, and I get money at the end of the month."

"Where are you from?" They were still standing between Isle 21 and 22.

"I'm from Lebanon . . ."

"I wondered why you had such a suntanned face."

"I'm suntanned all over, and you?"

She blushed. "I'm starch white all over. As a matter of fact, with my complexion I burn in five minutes when I'm out in the sun."

"All over? Where are you from?"

"I'm from Wisconsin, but my parents retired down here, and I stay with them."

"Ah? You live with your parents. That's nice." He thought, "That's too bad." But he said instead, "When I get some money, I'll take you out to dinner sometimes. Would your parents object?"

"Oh, my parents are up in Wisconsin now. We have a little 40-acre farm, that they lease out, but the tenant walked off without notice, and now they're up there straightening things out, so they can lease it again. Pain in the butt."

Yousef's ears perked up. "So you now live by yourself. Near here?"

"A few blocks north in Fairview. I'm just in Bergen County."

"I'm working with a Deputy right now, so I have to go, but I'd like to take you to lunch sometime."

"Or I can cook lunch sometime. What are you doing with a deputy?"

"Oh, it's just a part-time job, delivering court summonses."

"Wait. Let me write that down. I live at 434 Fairview Court, Apartment 212. My number is 626-2023. Call me before you come. I work from three to ten, so at noon, I'm always home."

"Thanks, I will, I will. Thanks. Two days from now? And I'll come back for that cutter."

"Oh, I'll take it home and then you can pay me back later."

"Oh, great. What's your name?"

"Inge, I'm Swedish!"

"Beautiful. Inge! White all over?" His mind was spinning. "Two days." He spontaneously hugged her between the isles. Her arms tightened around him and held promise. He nearly floated out of the store.

Back at the office.

"Sir, a 'Foster' called while you were out. He said simply, everything's okay."

"That's good news. Thanks."

"And Mr. Taylor wants you to call back."

"God no! Did he leave a message?"

"No, just to call back."

"Damn, don't they ever give up.? Get him on the line for me, okay? I'll take it in my office."

By the time he walked in with a cup of coffee in his hand, the buzzer sounded. "Mr. Taylor on seven."

"Good afternoon, Sir."

"Bongers, the White House is on my tail again . . ."

"Sir, Mr. Jarvis forbade me to talk to anybody without his permission. Have you cleared it with him?"

"Don't give me that crap. I can talk to anybody in the world if I want to."

"But I can't. Call Jarvis." He hung up.

It didn't take ten minutes before the intercom sounded again. "Mr. Jarvis on five."

"Yes, Lester. What's up?"

"Please talk to Jeb."

"Is that an order?"

"Yes."

"Then I'll talk to him. Meanwhile, the two Filipinos that were crewmembers on the ship, all the way from Lebanon to Port Arthur, went AWOL, but Foster should be on their trail, and the rockets should be shadowed to their storage location as we speak."

"Great. Good work. Do talk with Jeb. After all, we have to work together."

"That's my whole argument. He doesn't realize that."

"Realize what?"

"That we're supposed to work together, not against one another."

"Bruce. Talk to him. We may all sleep better."

"Mr. Taylor, Special Agent Bongers."

"Bruce, don't hang up."

"No, I have permission to listen to you."

"How do we get the White House off our tail?"

"Tell'em, it's top secret and that Homeland Security has put a clamp on all communication, so we won't see a desperation outcry on CNN about national emergencies, that will alert our enemies."

"You don't have much faith in our top executives, do you?"

"Should I? All they do is stupid things. My parents live in The Villages in Florida. Are you familiar with them?"

"What about them?"

"They're in their eighties, and they received $250 stimulus money a few months ago."

"What about that?"

"My folks and thousands of others, maybe millions, have no idea whether their checking account has $4,000 or $4,250 in it. They didn't need that money. My father gave it to my boys and told them, 'Multiply this into $10,000 over the next ten years, 'cause you'll have to pay it back and it'll cost you ten grand by then,' and my mother spent it on Australian wine. Now does that make sense? Wouldn't it have been better if they had used two-hundred-and-fifty million dollars to help young people, who were losing their homes through foreclosure? Don't they have any common sense? All they . . ."

"Bruce, I can't help that . . ."

"But I don't have to listen to their stupid opinions and extravaganzas, like when they spent millions of our dollars to fly to Copenhagen, staying in expensive hotels and eating like kings off taxpayers' money, just to tempt Mother Nature to turn her thermometer down. Well, they could have saved our dough. We had the worst winter worldwide in ages. They . . ."

"Bruce, Bruce . . ."

"I wasn't finished . . ."

"You have permission to listen . . ."

"Okay, okay! I'll listen."

"I want you to get back together with Swartz and coordinate our activities. I'll pacify the White House."

"Does Lester know this?"

"Yes, I just spoke to him."

"Okay."

"Is everything under control in Port Arthur?"

"A-OK. I'll call Swartz."

"Good."

35

THE HAZMIEN ROTANA HOTEL, BEIRUT

Ahmed bin Behumed rose from his cushion in the Penthouse, and so did the rest of his entourage. "Gentlemen, a distinguished visitor from Afghanistan. His Highness, Mullah Sheik Ali Kamastan. The direct representative of our Prophet Osama bin Laden."

Polite applause and many bows greeted the honorable guest.

"Salaam Aleichem! Salaam!"

"The esteemed Mullah has brought some very good news . . ." Ahmed continued.

"First, I'd like to hear the latest news."

"Of course, of course. Please get some hot tea for the Sheik." One of the Hezbollah agents left the room in a hurry.

"What is that you would like to hear first, Your Highness?"

"Have the rockets arrived safely?"

"They have and are being stored for a few weeks until we need them." Ahmed showed his large teeth in a triumphant grin.

"Where are our Filipino operatives? Are they safe?"

"According to Chicago, they're on their way to Lake Charles, where they'll be equipped with cell phones." The Lebanese leader was well informed, obviously.

"How about Leemo on the supply boat? Thank you." The clergyman accepted a steaming glass of mint tea.

"He's at sea, due in Galveston in three days."

"How about the young man, Yousef?"

Bahouie answered, "He's working for the FBI in New Jersey. He's been in touch with our contacts in Middleton and Canarsie, but he does not yet have a means of outgoing communication."

"What's the opinion of the American intelligence? Are they indicating any suspicion?"

"So far, they still keep Yousef locked up at night and have a GPS device on his leg, so they still don't quite believe he's sincere." Fanouf Bahouie grinned as he spoke, especially when he said "sincere".

"That's about what you suspected, right?"

"Yes, Your Highness. We're right on track."

"How about our boys in Venezuela?"

"They're in Mexico. And now comes the hard part, getting into the States. They're dark skinned like Mexicans, but their Spanish is more of a Moroccan dialect than Mexican, so obviously, they have to be careful." Ahmed answered with a bow.

"How are they getting in?"

"On a fishing boat from Belize to Corpus Christi. They'll seem like poor fishermen from Guatemala."

"How will they get their money?"

"It's already in Corpus and our contact there is waiting for them."

"Is the Israeli president still scheduled for September eleven in Washington and New York?"

"As far as we know, it's still on for that date."

"Good." He sipped some tea. "Great. Allah is with us in our fight." The Sheik reached for his beautifully decorated leather bag.

"With compliments from our great leader, bin Laden, each of these pouches contains one- hundred thousand Euros." He grinned. "Funny how we don't deal in dollars any more. Take one each. These are yours and of course it will pay for some of the expenses you incur while working for Islam. Allah be with you."

"Allahu Akbar."

"Let's eat."

• • •

Mossad Headquarters, Tel Aviv.

"Lev? Come in here a minute." Dagan beeped his assistant.

"Yes, Meir?" The tall, skinny intelligence man was getting balder every year.

"Any news from Beirut?"

"Our new man is copying and translating tapes right now from a Hezbollah meeting. Lots of questions, but most importantly, Sheik Kamastan brought in a million Euros from bin Laden."

"Damn! Their money supply knows no end. How can we stop the world from driving their gas guzzlers?" He shook his head and tapped his pen on his desk. "Euros no less? Inform Switzerland and see if they can track where that came from. I'd like to divert some of that into our coffers."

"Yeah!"

• • •

FBI, New Jersey.

"Have Mr. Bongers call Dagan. I'll try his cell." The night watchman made a note.

"Bruce? Good evening. Are you in bed yet?"

"Nearly. It's eleven thirty out here. I'm catching the late news. What's happening?"

"Two extremists will come into Corpus Christi on a fishing boat from Belize. They're picking up money somewhere in Corpus and then on to their targets. I guess these are the rocket experts."

"Good God. Thank you very much . . ."

"Don't call me God. He may strike me dead."

"Thank you, Meir, and thank you God for blessing him."

"Shalom!"

Bruce turned to his wife, "Helen, do you know if Corpus Christi is on Central or Mountain Time?"

"Aye, without consulting a map, I would say Mountain Time. Doesn't the line cross the U.S. just west of San Antonio?"

"Well, let's suppose they're still awake. I better find my directory." He got up from the couch and retrieved his FBI listings from his desk drawer. Back in his seat, he lowered the volume on the TV and punched in a number.

"John Ballew? This is Bruce Bongers, Special Agent from . . ."

"I know who you are. Your reputation preceded you. What are you up to at this hour?"

"You may have heard rumors about an impending attack on the U.S.?"

"No, I haven't."

"Wow! Then our system is not leaking as bad as I thought. That's great. Let's keep it that way. Keep this Top Secret, and swear your agents to secrecy as well, because that's the only way we will grab all those bastards and prevent a tragedy. Do you have a pen handy?"

"Just a moment. I was watching the news." After a few seconds he came back on. "Shoot."

"Two Moroccan al-Qaeda terrorists will be landing in Corpus on a small fishing boat from Belize. They'll receive money and cell phones from one of their operatives in the city. I don't know who and don't know where. You got to figure that out. Do not attempt to arrest or arouse these men until September eleven or when given orders. Shadow the two, wherever they go. Their goal is to reach a location where handheld Stinger missiles will be waiting for them in order to blow up something that will cost thousands of American lives, like the Twin Towers."

"Holy Moses, you're kidding."

"Sorry, but I'm dead serious. Your job is of the utmost importance. If they get alerted in any way, they may chicken out and come back to do it some other time. This time, it won't be a repeat of

9/11 '01. This time we're gonna capture or kill the bastards before they can pull it off. So you see, you're going to be an important cog in this massive operation. Note down my cell number. Call me at any time something comes up, okay?"

"This is all cleared through D.C., right?"

"I'm under direct orders from Jarvis, and I report directly to him."

"Okay, Bruce. It's gonna be exciting."

"That's what I'm afraid of. Good night and good hunting."

"Good night, Bruce. I'm looking forward to working with you."

"Thanks."

"Helen, now I'm so wound up, I'm gonna have one more scotch. Are the boys still out?"

"It's not twelve yet. They'll be here twenty seconds ahead of schedule."

"I wonder where they got that punctuality trade from?"

"I guess from their grandfather."

"Paternal?"

"You better believe it."

36

NORTH BERGEN FORMER POLICE STATION.

Yousef was going crazy, trying to figure out how he would be able to get away the following day. The thought of a perfectly white, naked body had him walking the floor. He hadn't been with a woman for more than seven months, maybe more. The image of Lavana was still very vividly etched in his memory, and he was anxious to replace that with a picture of a zaftig Swedish redhead in the raw.

He had no idea what he could tell Bruno in order to let him get away for a few hours. He was not scheduled with the deputy again, and he had no way of contacting the Sheik, because his phone was restricted. His best bet was to ask his guardian, Agent Garcia, if he could visit his old school in Hoboken and maybe catch up with some of his former professors. That had possibilities. If Garcia said he was too busy, Yousef might volunteer to take a bus and return by bus. That might work. The public transportation in the area was excellent, he remembered, because he used it to go back and forth to his classes.

He couldn't wait for Bruno to arrive. The computer and Free Cell diverted his attention somewhat until his keeper showed up at 8:30.

"Ready to go?" Bruno spoke up as he unlocked the door.

"Where are we off to?" He had considered practicing his Spanish on Garcia, but he felt, it was better if Bruno didn't know he had some command of it. Could come in handy sometime.

"We're going to court."

"What did I do?" He nearly panicked.

"Not you. We're going to watch a jury selection and then maybe a trial, to give you some indication of the American Justice System and how it works."

"Oh!" The sigh came all the way from his midriff. "Who's on trial?"

"A bad dude who tortured his girlfriend, then shot two cops who came to arrest him. I finally got him in his spine during a stand-off. He's in a wheelchair and I have to testify."

"That might be neat. I'm ready."

The courtroom was a novel experience for Yousef. The magnificent dark paneling, the curved wainscots, the Judge's bench, high and elegant, and the massive wooden fan blades milling around noiselessly.

What he didn't understand was the noise of the people. While the judge was listening to a lawyer in front of him, another dozen lawyers were scattered around the room, talking to their clients, huddled in the church-like benches. Nobody seemed to care and nobody seemed bothered by it, including the presiding judge.

"What a madhouse," he whispered to Bruno. Garcia only nodded and said softly, "My case is on the docket in a half hour, and most of these people will be gone by then."

"The judge can hear all these cases in a half hour?"

"Most of them will ask for a continuance, and the rest will be scheduled for trial or dismissed."

Yousef shook his head and started studying the people. The only ones that wore a tie were the attorneys apparently. The rest were in blue jeans and T-shirts, it seemed.

"Don't these people have any respect for the court?" He wondered. Also, about all the people in the room, except the lawyers, were either black or Hispanic. "Don't white people commit any crimes, or don't they get arrested when they do?" He asked himself.

Bruno proved to be right. Some people would get up, the lawyer representing them would talk to the judge, then they would leave the chamber. By 9:30 the jury box filled up with potential jurors, and Bruno and Yousef moved to the front row. Now he could hear the proceedings. First one lawyer, then another, would ask a jury member some questions and they would either accept or reject them. He found that very interesting. Finally seven men and five women were seated, and it seemed surprising that ten out of twelve were white and two were Hispanic. No blacks. He decided to ask Bruno later if that was typical.

The trial was nearly an open-and-shut case. The witnesses testified that they had seen the shooting when the defendant resisted arrest. None of the witnesses had seen the torture of the girlfriend, so she was the only one who testified on that account. According to Yousef, she convinced the jury. She came across as a real victim. The others, including Bruno, testified to the actual shoot-out and how the FBI had been called into the stand-off. Garcia showed how he shot the man by returning his fire from an open window, and his demonstration was very effective, although he had turned in his gun upon entering the courthouse.

They didn't have to wait for the verdict, so they went for lunch.

"Do you have to go back again?" Yousef wanted to know.

"Only if they get a hung jury or they call us back in additional cross examination."

"So what are we gonna do?"

"We'll hang around."

"Can you bring me back to my apartment? I have figured out the computer. I can write something or play a game. I don't wanna sit in that courtroom anymore."

Bruno nodded. "Sounds okay to me. Let's finish eating and I'll call Mr. Bongers to ask if he has something else up his sleeve."

On the way back, Yousef saw his chance. "Do you have to stand by again tomorrow?"

"Possibly?"

"Could I go visit Stevens Institute and see some of my old professors? They may still be there. I doubt if any of my classmates are still around, unless they're going for advanced degrees. I can get there by bus. I did that for two years."

"I'll call Mr. Bongers and see. He may have plans for you that I don't know about."

"Okay."

When they got to the apartment, the "suite" as Bruno called it, Bongers wasn't in and Garcia left it with, "I'll get with him later. Write a love story about the FBI." He locked him in.

"Bruce? He's ready to break! He asked permission to go to his old Alma Mater because I may be tied up in court again, and that would be his chance to escape."

"Okay. How would he get his brace off and where would he go? Go ahead and schedule a shadow on him. He might ride busses, subways. He may go the Twin Tower site. He may go directly to his cohorts in Canarsie, we don't know. Make sure that you have a variety of people on his trail, so he won't get suspicious. I'm calling Andrews in New York and have his people to stand by if needed. We can't afford to lose him. It's a few days earlier than I expected, but that's alright. So, in the morning, before you go to court, tell him to call you on your cell when he needs to get back in."

"What if he says, 'they're not allowed in court'? He's sharp, you know?"

"Tell'im you'll have it on vibrate. He'll fall for it. How's the case going?"

"He'll get life for attempted murder of a LEO." (Law Enforcement Officer)

"Good show. Stay in touch."

"Andy? Bruce. Tomorrow, our boy is going to spring the trap. The Lebanese may take the bus to Penn station, he may transfer in Jersey City to the tube, he may go visit the 9/11 monument to familiarize himself, and he may end up in Canarsie. I'm betting on the latter, because he'll realize that we'll have an APB out for him, and he may want to get undercover somewhat. I wonder if he's gonna grow a beard again. Let me send you both pictures. With and without a beard. Remember, we still don't have a clue as to what they've got planned, so strict surveillance is of the utmost importance."

"How come the excitement always lands in my backyard, Bruce?"

"You're just lucky, Andy. Consider yourself one of the chosen few."

"Sure."

"Julie, get all available agents in the meeting room."

When twelve people were assembled, Bongers, his shirtsleeves rolled up, addressed the group. "Those who are working on cases that can't wait, you're excused." Two agents left.

"We're only going to interrupt your work briefly. How many of you have seen our Lebanese friend Yousef in here and feel that he could he recognize you?"

Three hands went up. "You're excused." They left.

"The rest of you, tomorrow, be prepared to run out of here on short notice. Yousef is going to escape." He hesitated. "We assume. At least he'll be given that chance."

"I thought he was going to work with us." A lady agent raised her hand.

"As a matter of fact, he is. By betraying us. Like Judas, he's gonna lead us to our goal, an assassination attempt." An audible gasp went around the room. "This is top secret. You do not speak about it to your wife, your fellow agents, your husbands or girlfriends, nobody." He raised his voice. "Do you understand? Nobody. The smallest leak may lead to a national catastrophe, costing thousands of American lives. Another 9/11 is being planned for 9-11, 2010.

We're going to prevent that, you and I and dozens of other agents around the country. So let's draw up a potential scenario. He may get on a bus in the morning, still hooked to a GPS. We'll be monitoring that closely. The moment he cuts it, we'll know, and we'll know his position. The hunt, or should I say, the tail, starts right thereafter. That's where you come in. There may be dozens of ways he may travel, but we think that his final destination is Canarsie in Brooklyn. New York agents will be standing by to continue the tail in the City, and we'll be excused the moment they pick it up. So there's no way we can predict anything. Just come in dressed as a tourist, a farmer, an office worker, anyway other than an obvious FBI agent. Any questions?"

"How about as a stripper?"

"You're on, George. You're on."

37

NORTH BERGEN, FORMER POLICE STATION

Yousef wasn't even dressed when Bruno showed up.

"Oh, I thought you'd be anxious to get out of here!" His voice reflected his surprise.

"No, I figured I'd find most of the staff in the cafeteria at lunch time, although some of them eat in their little cubbyholes. I'll find out what their class schedule is when I get to the Admin building."

"Oh well, I guess that would work."

"What time do you want me back?"

"Let's say, four? Four-thirty?"

"Okay. Are you going back to that court?"

"Yeah, I'm afraid so. See you later." Garcia was gone.

From his car, Bruno called Bongers. "He doesn't seem all that eager to get out. He wasn't even dressed, and he asked me when I would expect him back, can you believe that?"

Bruce chuckled, "I told you he is sharp. Anyway, we're ready for him. Our agents are in place. I'll be in the meeting room with an area map, so we can pinpoint his position at all times. You better come in here and stay out of his sight."

"Okay."

Yousef was in no hurry. Inge had said something about twelve, noon. "Call first." She said. He was talking to himself as he shaved and showered. He wished he'd bought some nice-smelling aftershave or something. Well, that couldn't be helped. He checked his pockets and counted the remainder of his money. He still had more than forty dollars. That should do well for the day.

A little after nine, he shut down the computer and the TV, looked around the room if there was anything he would miss over the next few days and decided against it. Carrying a bundle of his new clothes would make him look suspicious, so he took nothing at all. Once outside, he strolled to the nearest bus stop and waited for the next southbound local.

He had no watch, but he estimated that it took ten minutes for the #44 to arrive, and he bought a one-way ticket. In the middle of Union City, he got off, bought a newspaper and walked into Wendy's. A good breakfast for less than $5 was just what he needed and could afford. The menu was in Spanish and English. That surprised him. "No wonder they never get to know the language. Well, that's their problem." He had gotten into the habit of talking to himself, because most of the time he was the only one around.

When the restaurant clock told him it was ten o'clock, he wrapped up his paper and started looking for a phone booth. Wendy's didn't have one, but after two blocks he found what he was looking for, and he dialed Inge's number. She must've been sitting next to it, because she answered on the first ring. "Hello?'

"Joe here."

"Where are you?"

"On Bergenline in Union City. Should I come up or wait till twelve?"

"Come now. Take the number 44 and get off as soon as you're in Fairview. Walk toward the river, just two blocks, and you'll see Fairview Terrace on your left. Go to 434 and just buzz 212 and I'll open up."

"Alright. I'll be there in about half an hour."

"Okay." She hung up the phone. "Okay! Okay!" She danced around the room.

When her door opened, she looked so radiant, that he regretted not having bought flowers. That would have been the right thing to do, but it didn't matter. The moment he stepped in, she grabbed him in a bear hug, while kicking the door closed with her heel.

Yousef was ready. His mouth found hers, and for a few minutes, they just kissed and hugged. His hand moved under her blouse, and to his surprise, she wore no bra. His hand moved to her front and cupped the softest boob he'd ever felt. Their breathing became more rapid and her tongue explored the back of his mouth. When she grabbed his crotch, his manhood was already as hard as a rock, and she groaned with satisfaction.

Still embraced in a passionate kiss, she moved him slowly to the bedroom, sidestepping inches at a time. Standing in front of the bed, they tore at each other's clothes, falling across the bed, naked. Except for his socks. She was indeed as white as a sheet, while he was as tan as an Apache. His middle finger found her womanhood, and he inserted as deep as he could while her hand firmly held on to his erection.

"Put it in, put it in!" She shouted hoarsely, and he did.

He rolled on top of her body and penetrated her with a cry, "Ohohoho!" changing to "Ahahaha" as he ejaculated on his second stroke while arching his body like a bow.

Inge screamed as well, but in frustration, because he came much too fast, long before she was ready for an orgasm. She kept kissing him feverishly while he rolled off but still inside her.

They lay still for a moment, and then she rolled him on his back without disturbing the penetration. She sat atop of Yousef, his tool still hard, and started bouncing up and down, first slowly, while he twirled her beautiful pink nipples. Inge bounced faster and faster until she resembled a bucking Bronco and with a yell, climaxed, while Yousef came for a second time.

Locked together, they dozed off.

After twenty minutes or so, Inge stirred. Yousef had slipped out of her and snored softly, lying on his side. She made for the bathroom and retrieved two cans of BUD from the refrigerator, downing half of one in one long swallow.

She stood at the foot of the bed, staring at that beautiful muscular body. "What a man!" she thought. "I better fix some lunch, like I promised." She didn't bother to put any clothes on, and naked as a Jaybird, she gathered up ham and cheese, mustard and tomatoes, preparing an appetizing sandwich. Next came the coffee pot, and as she poured water in the contraption, he snuck up behind her and cupped her luscious breasts. Inge gasped and spilled the water. "You startled me." She whispered as she turned inside his embrace. "I brought you a beer . . .," but his lips interfered with her words."

"I don't drink." He pulled her into him as hard as he could, and she could feel his manhood rising again.

"I fixed you a sandwich," Inge murmured between kisses while Yousef edged her back in the direction of the bed.

"I'm not hungry."

This time, he laid her gently on top of the blankets and settled in next to her, all the time kissing and probing, probing and kissing. He seemed fascinated by her breasts. She was intrigued by his penis until they made love again, this time, gently, very gently until passion converted them to stallions in the wild.

They woke up at one o'clock.

"Are you hungry now? I fixed some food." She got up and returned with a plate and an attractive sandwich.

"What's on it?" Yousef wanted to know.

"Ham and cheese and . . ."

"I can't eat ham?"

"Why not? Are you Jewish?"

He laughed. "On the contrary, I'm a Muslim."

"A Muslim? I never met a Muslim before. So what can I fix you?"

"Cheese and tomato would be fine."

"And you don't want beer?"

"No. Same reason. Excuse me, is the bathroom that way?"
"First door in the hall."

For the next hour they discussed the pros and cons of going to work at three, because she wanted to spend the entire day with her newfound love.

Yousef needed her out of the house, because she had brought home a huge chain cutter, at least three feet long. He still hadn't taken off his socks and had slipped back into his slacks, so she wouldn't start questioning him. It was easy to see that there was something around his ankle if you looked closely, but Inge hadn't looked at that part of his anatomy at all.

Over food and orange juice, they worked out an arrangement. Inge would go to work and claim that she wasn't feeling well and would return as early as possible. Probably between seven and eight. Business was usually dead by then, and she was confident she'd get out early. A glance in the mirror confirmed that she didn't look all that well, bags under eyes and a general look as if she'd been in bed with a wild man for hours, which was true.

Inge was barely out the door, when Yousef dropped his pants and took off his sock. The cutting blades of the tool were about three inches long and an inch wide. He couldn't get the blade to slide between his bone and the bracelet. It would slip under it sideways, but it wouldn't cut that way. In desperation, he went through drawers and closets until he found two hammers and by using one as anvil, he laid his ankle on top of it and with the other hammer, banged the contraption into somewhat of an oval. It hurt like hell, it cut into his shin, but he now could get the blade under it. Not as far as he would like, but with the three-foot handles, he had a lot of leverage and in ten minutes, long painful minutes, he cut through it, and it came off, not easily, not without ripping his skin, but he got it off. A washcloth, wrapped around his ankle, stopped the bleeding, and tucked within his sock, nobody would notice. He pocketed another washcloth as a spare and was ready to go. Dressed, bracelet in his hand, newspaper under his arm, he turned the doorknob and peeked into the hall. Nothing.

"Good!" He smiled at himself and walked toward the stairs. Instead of leaving by the front door of the building, he turned toward the back, where the smaller door bore a warning, "Emergency exit only. Alarm will sound."

Yousef hesitated. "They're bluffing." He decided and turned the knob. Nothing sounded and he rushed into the alley behind the building, heading west toward the Hudson. At the street crossing, he didn't see a soul, and he disappeared into the alley across the street. Hurrying between the apartment buildings, he soon arrived at the Boulevard and found a bus stop, where he read the newspaper until the bus showed up. He had dropped the bracelet in a garbage can in the alley.

38

FBI HEADQUARTERS, SECAUCUS, NJ

On the map, Bongers put a green pin in the location of Yousef's dwelling. A red pin stayed in the middle of Union City for a long time, nearly an hour.

As the bus chucked its way up Bergenline Avenue, the red pin moved up with it. The stop in Fairview had not been anticipated, nor Yousef's trip back to the north. There was no agent present when the young Lebanese exited and started walking west. Everyone had concentrated on him going to New York, and agents were all over the place, ready to follow him.

No big problem, though. The GPS computer followed him every step of the way, and by the time Yousef and Inge went at it for the second time, the red pin was at exactly 434 Fairview Court.

"What in the hell is he doing there? Have there been any reports of unusual activity out there? Any Islam connections?" Bongers was flabbergasted. It was no real problem yet. Two plain cars were posted in view of the entrance, and now the waiting game was on. The man hadn't done anything illegal yet, except that he was obviously not visiting professors. Or was he? Not knowing, not having any intelligence about that location could drive Bruce up the wall.

"Bruno, while you were traveling around with him, did he mention that location at all or a name of a person living there?"

"No clue. We never even went above the county line."

"Alright, let's wait. We're still hoping for him to lead us to Manhattan and Brooklyn. Let's do something constructive while we're waiting."

Turning to one of his agents, "Brad, find out who lives in that apartment and get a plug on the phone line if you can."

"Okay. I'm on it."

"Bruno, you told him to be back at four, four-thirty, right?"

"Yes, Boss."

"Well maybe he'll stay there till four and take the bus back. Do you suppose he may have a girlfriend there dating back to his college days here?"

"Could be, but he never mentioned it." Bruno was searching his memory for any helpful hint he could think of, but he found no answers.

"Well, call off all the agents in Manhattan and at the bus depot. It looks like we went on a wild-goose chase."

Everyone relaxed or went back to their respective desks to catch up on paperwork, until . . .

Until . . . 3:16 . . . "GPS called. He cut the bracelet!"

"Holy hell! Who's at the site? Randolph? Get him. Who else? Bruno, get out there.

Have them get hold of the superintendent get into the apartment. Seal off the area. Find out who lives there." He was in his element, shouting orders, getting control of the activities.

"Randolph, you're at the front door? Call your partner, send him around back. What are you saying? The super does not answer? Ring every bell till somebody buzzes you in. Head for the floors on the south-west side. GPS couldn't tell what floor he's on, only what part of the building."

"Call the agents that we've just called off and watch the bus terminal in Union City and Jersey City. He may be heading for New York, after all." His assistants rushed out of the meeting room.

Bruno had his red flashing light on top of his car and his siren blaring. From Secaucus to North Bergen was just a short distance, but traffic and street crossings were aggravating the dickens out of the Latin agent. He made it to the front door and pulled behind the other plain sedan, light blinking. The front door was locked again. "Damn, I don't have Randolph's number." He pushed every button and the door buzzed open. He ran up the stairs, not knowing which one of the six floors was his target, but he lucked out. On the second floor, the door to 212 was wide open, and several people were inside, talking at the same time.

He rushed in. "Randolph, what's the situation?"

"This is Mr. Rodriquez. He's the super, but he doesn't speak much English."

"No problem. ¿Senor Rodriguez, Quien viven aqui?" (Who lives here?)

" Un hombre y su esposa y una muchacha, su ija, yo credo." (A husband and wife and his daughter, I think.)

Bruno continued in Spanish, "Where are they now?"

"They're in Wisconsin and the daughter is at work."

"Where does she work?"

"I don't know. In a restaurant, I theenk. She works the late shift. She leaves at three and comes back after ten."

"Is that her?" Bruno pointed at a picture on the dresser.

"That's her!"

"A redhead, eh?"

"Yes. Why are there two hammers on the floor and is that your tool?" He pointed at the chain cutter that was still on the living-room rug.

"No, I never saw that before."

Bruno turned around to Randolph and the other agent, who had also come up. "Call the office. Have the white coats come in. Don't touch anything. The cutter says, 'ACE'. Senor, is there an Ace hardware store in the area?"

"On Bergenline, just south of the county line."

"Kurt, go shopping there. Don't say anything. Check if there's a good looking redhead working there, and call me if there is."

"Right on." The agent left.

"See that spot. That may be his blood. He must have used both these hammers and the cutter to get it off. Madre Mia, can you believe that he nearly snowed us? He seemed so sincere. That shows, you can never trust those bastards. Have we searched the building? Might he be on the roof?"

"No." The super understood that much. "It's locked."

"Let's check it anyway. Mr. Rodriguez, could he hide out in someone else's apartment or in the basement?"

"I don't theenk so."

"Let's find out. Don't touch anything in here, including the bed. They must have had a good romp. I wonder how he knew her?" He walked out the door, following the super.

His phone rang. "Bruno, Kurt. She's here. She works here."

"Stay out of sight. We'll be there shortly." He pushed a code on his phone.

"Bruce, we found the girl he stayed with. She supplied the cutters, and do you want to come out here personally?"

"You bet your sweet bippy. Where is she?"

"Ace Hardware on Bergenline, just south of Fairview. Wait for me there. I'm walking out as we speak. Any sign of our boy?"

"Not a trace."

"Damn."

When Bruce came close to his destination, he turned off his overhead light and his siren. Bruno's car was half a block away. Kurt was behind him.

When he caught up with them, he spoke to Kurt. "Go around back in the alley. Don't let anyone escape. We'll walk in the front door in five minutes."

While they waited, Bruno brought Bongers up to date on the events at Fairview Court.

"Any ideas how he got to know this girl?"

"No clue. We never came close to this place." He pointed at the store.

"What a puzzle. I'll talk to the owner or the manager. You get hold of the girl."

"Cuff her?"

"Only when necessary. Let's go."

It wasn't very often that two men in jackets and ties walked into a hardware store. Most customers wore blue jeans, so the manager showed surprise as Bruce walked up to him.

"Sir, I'm Special Agent Bongers, FBI. Are you the owner?"

"No, the owner isn't here. I'm the manager. How can I help."

"We're taking your lady employee with us for questioning. Nothing serious. She may be back in a little while."

"What did she do?" He looked stage-struck.

"No, she didn't do anything. She may have witnessed something. She'll come peacefully, I'm sure."

"Anything I can do?"

"No thanks, sorry for the inconvenience."

"Glad to help."

Bruno came forward from the far end of the store, holding the arm of the young good-looking redhead. "She's cooperating, Mr. Bongers. Come."

Inge looked panic stricken. "Sir, what's wrong?"

"We just need to ask you some questions. You'll be okay. You're not under arrest."

Following Bruno and the girl out the door, he called Kurt. "Kurt, we have her out front. Come here and ride with Bruno and the girl to the North Bergen police station. We'll come back for your car later."

"Bruno, Kurt will ride with you. Follow me to the police station. I'll get things set up."

"In Bruno's car, Inge asked, "But, Sir, what did I do? Where are you taking me?"

"Well, for one thing, you stole a chain cutter, right?"

"No, I bought it. I paid for it. Honest!" She started crying. "Joe

said he needed one and would pay me back."
"He did? Good luck."

39

NORTH BERGEN POLICE STATION.

"Chief, I'd like to borrow your meeting room a minute." Bruce seemed breathless, but it was the frustration that was starting to show. He had seldom lost a suspect before, but today, it was happening.

"You want the interrogation room? Recorders and such?"
"Yeah, that might be better."
The chief was curious. "What's happening?"
"We lost our young protégé and I . . ."
"The one you were keeping in the old building?"
"Yep, that's the one and we're questioning an accomplice. Here they come."
"How'd that happen?"
"Look in and find out." Turning to Bruno and Inge, "Follow me."

Seated across from the scared young woman, Bongers touched her hand and said, "Relax. You're not under arrest. We just have to find out what happened to Yousef . . ."
"Joe?"
"Yes, Joe. When did you see him last?"
"About a quarter to three when I left for work."
"At your apartment?"

"Yes, he was going to stay there till I got back from work."

"How long did you know him?"

"Just two days, when he walked in the store."

Bruno, watching through the one-way mirror, made a note. "That was the day he was working with the Deputy."

Bongers continued, "You'd never seen him before?"

"No!" She actually blushed. "He came in to buy some cutters. What's the matter with him? He seemed so nice."

"He's nice, alright. He's also sharp."

"But what did he do?" She seemed on the verge of tears.

"He's a suspect, that's all. Did you sell him the tool?"

"No, he didn't have enough money with him. He's a student and doesn't get money till the end of the month, so I bought it for him and . . ."

"You bought it? Did he take it with him?"

"No. He would pick it up two days later at my apartment."

"You gave him your address, right there and then?" She actually turned red. She didn't just blush, she turned red, and Bruce was afraid she'd have a heart attack.

"He seemed so nice, and I wanted to get to know him better, so I told him I'd have it when he came. He said he had to cut a lock to which he had lost . . ."

"A lock? Did he show you the bracelet around his ankles?"

"No, he kept his socks on at all times." She turned crimson again.

"He didn't use the cutters while you were there?"

"No, his lock was in his apartment, I thought. He said he was a student at Stevens in Hoboken, and I guessed he lived there too."

Bongers got up and went to the door. "Bruno, get all the details from her. Social, et cetera, and take her home when the spooks are done with it." He kept on walking, but Bart, the chief, caught up to him. "That's weird."

"You're not kidding. The whole FBI force was out-snookered by a young terrorist. I'm never gonna be able to live that down." The chief had never seen Bruce so dejected.

"Coffee?"

"I feel like a beer."

"Don't tell anyone, but come into my office. All I have is Corona."

"That'll do." As they closed the door and the police chief reached into his little refrigerator, Bongers' phone rang. "Sir, we got him."

"You what?"

"We got him in sight."

"Where and who are you?"

"I'm Shirley Adams from the New York office, and he just got off a Jersey bus and is going down to the subway station."

"Wow! Can you stay with him?"

"Sure, and Agent Brown is behind me, dressed as a workman." She sounded triumphant.

"Great. Keep me posted. He may head down town to the Twin Tower site or to Canarsie."

"We're on it, Sir."

"Bart, you wouldn't believe this, but that Corona is gonna taste better than any beer I've had in my life."

"How so?" He handed Bruce a cold bottle.

"Because it'll wash the egg off my face."

"Huh?"

• • •

When Yousef entered the bus, he asked, "Are you going to Manhattan?"

"No, but I can give you a transfer. Just get off in Union City and catch the O-4. That'll get you to Penn Station."

"Great." He waited for his change and sat down in the back of the bus, hiding behind the paper as best as possible. Nobody paid attention to him, and he avoided looking at anybody.

At the transfer, everything went so smoothly, that he got suspicious. "Would the FBI really be so stupid as to let him go?" He didn't know if the GPS kept recording his location to be in a garbage can in Fairview or if it automatically stopped the moment he cut it. He never asked how it worked exactly, and nobody bothered to tell him.

"Well," he murmured to himself again, "so far, so good. I'm going to take a look at our greatest victory, the Twin Towers that were." He actually grinned. "Wait till I inform Hezbollah of my escape. That'll surprise them, won't it?" He sighed as he settled in the backseat.

At Penn Station, he looked at that confusing subway map that had puzzled him before in his student days and still baffled him today. The red lines, crisscrossing with green and yellow lines, might be simple for New Yorkers, but for Yousef it was like a jigsaw puzzle. He finally figured it out and bought some tokens. Once on the train, he studied every stop till he finally got off at Washington Square. He had memorized, as best as he could, in which direction he should be walking, and thank God, the sun was still out to tell him where southwest was, and so he walked toward the sun. The sun, directed by Allah, was as reliable as ever, and before long, he circled the area of the devastation. At the *Sphere*, he bought a Kosher hotdog with onions and stood there, nibbling at his leisure. He figured that the Jews shunned pork the way the Muslims did, so that was a safe choice. Several wreaths were laid at the foot of the monument and little groups were standing around, holding hands and praying, it seemed like. He couldn't hear what they were saying, but the meaning was obvious.

"Good, the more they grieve, the more we proved our point. We were victorious with the help of Allah Almighty." He involuntarily bowed to the east, forgetting that Mecca was actually to the west from that point.

Satisfied with his visit, he walked back to the subway station and, looking at the map again, decided that the easiest way to travel was to head back up to 42nd Street and change lines to Brooklyn. "Stupid system." he hissed as he shoved another token in the slot.

His directions weren't very exact, and he didn't know the phone number of the other operatives by heart, so he strolled for several blocks before he got his orientation and finally headed down the street which would become his final destination for the following weeks.

He had expected a great welcome, but instead, he was met with suspicion and worry.

"How did you get away? Don't you have an ankle bracelet? (They didn't know the Arabic word for GPS.) Have you been followed? We gotta get you outta here!" He couldn't get a word in edgewise, until he lifted his leg, lowered his sock, unwound the washcloth and showed them his bloody shin.

"Where were you when you cut it off? What did you do with it? You don't have it on you, do you?" They were worried silly.

"No, the remnants are in Fairview, New Jersey, in a garbage can, and I wish you would show me some respect for what I have accomplished."

"Like what?"

"I've escaped from the mightiest security force in the world. How many can claim that? Allahu Akbar."

"Allah il Allah. Welcome, brother. Salaam."

• • •

"Mr. Bongers, I believe he's at his final destination."

"Is this Miss Adams?"

"No, this is Eleanor Mendelsohn. I live on the next block, so I'm a fixture around here."

"Great. Are you part of the team that's had this house under surveillance for some time?"

"Yes, Sir, and I record all their outgoing and incoming calls."

"Beautiful. Do you speak Arabic?"

"Yes, my mother was born in a Jewish Ghetto in Jordan and I can understand most of their dialects."

"Like I said, that's beautiful. Eleanor, apparently you have my direct line, right?"

"Yes, Sir."

"Take my cell-phone number too. Call me immediately when

something breaks, okay?"

"That's what Mr. Andrews said. 'Call Bongers directly.'"

"He did? That's a good man. Shalom!"

40

FBI OFFICES, SECAUCUS

"Now comes the worst part, the waiting. Not knowing what comes next." Bongers was sitting in the briefing room with a few of his select agents, including Bruno Garcia.

"Let's write down what we know and what we suspect. I'll write the 'known' stuff in green, the unknown in pink and the suspected in black, okay?" He didn't expect any answers or comments and he didn't get any. "Okay, here we go." He stepped up to the big white board.

"In green . . . Yousef . . . Canarsie

Canarsie . . . Four extremists, planning an attack

In pink . . . Attack, where ???? When??? September 11, in green . . . what time . . . in pink.

In green . . . Kaliff in Chicago . . . Master planner, we think . . . Lake Forest . . . "

"What's in Lake Forest?" One of the agents wanted to know.

"That's his home, north of Chicago. He does a lot of communicating from there."

"In green . . . Port Arthur . . . Warehouse with missiles. Two operatives, one Arab, one Filipino.

In pink ... How many rockets? We assume at least a half dozen.
In pink ... Targets ... ???
In green ... Corpus Christi, Carpet merchant, money manager ... and ... cell phones.
In pink ... Two Moroccans ... Armed, with money and phones ... lost near Galveston."

"What do mean, 'lost'?"

"They disappeared in thin air. The Houston office is going crazy. I know the feeling." He continued.

"In green ... Two Filipinos in a casino in Lake Charles, Louisiana."

He looked around the room, "What else?"

"If we grab the rockets and arrest the known culprits, won't we defuse the whole thing?" A lady wanted to know.

"Jan, what could we hold them on or convict them of? They'd be out in a month, ready to plan all over again. We have to catch the bastards red handed or kill'em. The latter is cheaper. Saves court costs."

"Sometimes Mr. Bongers, you sound so brutal, so unlike you." Another lady agent spoke up.

"Wait till you dig through rubble, digging up pieces of women and children. You'll learn to sing a different tune." She hung her head and murmured softly, "Sorry, Sir."

"Okay, let's start with our own area here. New York and Yousef." What are they going to bomb with? Simply shooting with telescopic rifles seems inefficient, and they'll never come close enough. Any thoughts? I know this is frustrating."

• • •

Beirut, Hazmien Rotana Penthouse. Hezbollah meeting.

"This is most frustrating, the waiting. Let's go over what we know for sure, what's in place and what we must work on right now." He looked at his devout audience, confirmed extremists. "Mashan, are the explosives in place, or are they still en route?"

"No, brother, they're there. Safely in the trunk of a Cadillac in Queens, New York."

"Good, who will push the button, and who will call the others out west?"

"Well, we thought it best that one man calls on his cell, pushes the button, makes call number two immediately, so all the explosions should be simultaneous, just about."

"Who'll be doing that?"

"Well, Yousef is an engineer and he does not have a beard, so he doesn't look suspicious in a crowd like we would." That brought laughter to the whole room. "As a matter of fact, he grew a mustache like Clark Gable, not a proud one like yours, but a very thin line. He thinks he looks Italian." More laughter rocked the room.

"Oh, well. Has he studied the bomb? Does he understand the workings?"

"He's one of the brightest ones there."

"Allah be with him. Now we continue the waiting. Very frustrating. Hand me my pipe."

• • •

CIA headquarters, Langley A.F.B., Langley, Virginia.

"This is the most frustrating part. Doing nothing. Waiting. Damn. Is everything under control? Are all the agents in place?" Director Jeb Taylor was pacing back and forth, stopping on occasion to address an individual in his small group. Six of his top executives were gathered, pen and paper at ready.

"Wouldn't it be easier if we round up the whole pack right now and prevent possible . . ?"

"Don't start that again. " He snapped. "Any more details about Netanyahu's itinerary?"

"He'll fly in on September six. Will meet with movie producers in Hollywood, raising funds, I suppose, and move to Washington on the eighth, conference and dinner with Obama on the ninth, and a helicopter hop to Manhattan on the eleventh. They won't reveal as yet, where he's supposed to land."

"And then a speech at the monument?"

"That's the idea."

"Damn! Frustrating! Sitting on our hands! How many agents do we have out there now? A thousand?"

"Something like that, Sir."

"Very frustrating. Is there anything we're overlooking?"

He sat down. "I can't stand it. Very frustrating."

• • •

The Herbert Hoover Building, Washington, D.C.

Usually, FBI Director Lester Jarvis wore his jacket at all times and never unbuttoned his shirt. That was usually. On that particular September afternoon, he seemed stressed out, sleeves rolled up and tie undone. "This is so frustrating! Reminds me of my days as a field agent. Sitting in a car, drinking gallons of coffee and not knowing if your suspect will ever come out or make a move. Then another agent relieves you, and sixteen hours later you start it all over again. What a lousy way to make a living." He got up again, but looked at the phone that wouldn't ring.

"What have we heard from Bongers lately?"

"He's doing the same as you're doing, Lester, pacing the floor in frustration."

In spite of it all, Jarvis chuckled. "You're probably right. Let's look at that aerial shot again." The screen lit up with a close-up of downtown Manhattan. "If all of the streets are blocked with concrete barriers, no truck or car can get close enough to become a threat. Yet in Bagdad they managed to drive into that hotel, remember? How'd they do that? Find some details. If all the roofs are patrolled by security people, a sniper would never get a shot off, right? How about all the buildings that face the square? Are they secure?"

"Sir, NYPD and Andrew's office have scanned every floor, every office, every apartment that has a view of the monument. Everyone!"

"Remember how they once tried to crash into Camp David? Is that a possibility here? Could a chopper or small airplane be able to get in that airspace and dive down?"

"We're having all flight plans monitored for that day, but the problem is, they can file an hour ahead of time, or they can file no flight plan at all and just take off."

"Have we checked with every base operator at every little airport in the vicinity? Long Island, New Jersey, Westchester, upstate New York? Let's get word out to all airport mangers to report any suspicious activities, any airplane rentals for short periods of time. Homeland Security is scheduled to have fighters in the sky, right?"

"All the way from the White House to the monument. The presidential helicopter may well land in the middle of the square."

"Any attack helicopters around?"

"Sir, a whole squadron of Cobras is coming in from Camp LeJeune in North Carolina. They'll be stationed at the old Floyd Bennett Field in Brooklyn, seven minutes from Manhattan, loaded with Hellfire, heat-seeking missiles."

"Good God. Great! I mean!" He shook his head. "How many millions of dollars are we spending on this fracas?" Jarvis again shook his white-rimmed head.

"We're not supposed to think in those terms, just in total lives saved." One assistant remarked.

"Sure! Very frustrating, though."

Tel Aviv, Mossad Headquarters.

"This is it. I'm through twiddling my thumbs. I don't care what our Knesset says. I'm taking an additional twenty men with me, and we're leaving now. Get us the proper visas, the right U.S. IDs and accommodations in lower Manhattan and Hollywood. We're flying ahead on a military craft. We'll be in place when the president and his security team get there. I'm tired of waiting. Too damn frustrating. Let's roll."

41

FBI HEADQUARTERS, SECAUCUS, N.J.

"Dr. Price? Bruce Bongers here. We have narrowed down something, except I don't know what."

"That sounds intriguing already. What have you found?"

"There are between six and twelve Stingers, hand-held missiles in storage in Port Arthur, Texas."

"Chinese make?"

"We assume so. If we assume right, they can take down an airplane at a thousand feet."

"Goodness! Are you saying aircraft may be the target?"

"No, I'm just telling you how powerful these rockets are. Now here's the puzzle for you. These missiles have been in the same location for more than two weeks. In other words, we may disregard targets way up north or in the west, because they would have brought them in position up there, near their potential goals. Two known terrorists are in Lake Charles, Louisiana, and two more have been followed to and lost in Galveston. We are starting to deduct that the targets would be near those cities, so that they can load the missiles in the morning and have them on location early in the afternoon, to coincide with an explosion in Manhattan."

"It's still guess work, isn't it Bruce?"

"You're right, 60% of my work is guesswork, 30 % is my nose, intuition, and 10% is fact. I just listed the facts. Now can you tell me what chemical plants or storage facilities are in those areas, so we can narrow it down some more?"

"I'll get right on it and call you back."

"Mister Bongers, Mister Bongers, an urgent call on three." His secretary came rushing in, because Bruce had ignored the constant buzzing of the intercom. He pushed the button.

"Bongers!"

"Sir, we lost him!"

"You lost whom and who is this?"

"This is Agent Browning in Canarsie. A black SUV drove up, Yousef jumped in, and before we could get a car started or turned around, they were gone."

"Did you get a tag number or other description?"

"A black SUV, fairly new. Chevy or GMC, I think. Dark windows."

"Oh, boy."

"You see, Sir, no one in that household has a car, so they always walk to the subway or go to the store on a bike, so we were . . ."

Bongers hung up. "Damn."

"Bruno, get an APB out for a black SUV leaving Brooklyn. Do not, I repeat . . . do NOT stop the vehicle. Just shadow it and report its location. Get NYPD in on the chase as well."

• • •

Yousef had raced from the front door to the passenger-side door of the black Chevrolet Tahoe that moved before he even had the door closed. Without exceeding the speed limits by more than eight miles an hour, the vehicle moved about five blocks and turned into a garage that advertised, "FIRESTONE TIRES", and the overhead door closed behind it. Two men and the young Lebanese climbed out and walked to the next bay, where they climbed into an old Lincoln, vintage '94. The red vehicle backed onto the street and eased its way to the Belt Parkway. Yousef shook hands with the two gentlemen and at their suggestion, leaned back and relaxed.

"I'm Omar Alfantash, from Lebanon like you, and it's my job to train you. Listen as we drive. When we're at our destination, we will show you how to detonate the bomb when the time is right. You'll be carrying a remote control that has a safety cap, so you cannot set it off by accident. It's about the same size as a cell phone. Easy to hide. You'll also carry a regular cell, and there are only three numbers programmed in it. Number one is the number of a colleague in Texas and number two another one in Louisiana. When you press the detonator, you also press one on the cell phone and then two. Nearly simultaneously. America will rock, as if it's hit by thunder in three locations. The panic will strike the rest of the country, expecting similar blasts in every state. Airlines will stop flying, planes will crash. Curfews will be announced, Armies will swarm all over, looking for additional blasts. Power plants will stop. Elevators loaded with people will hang in midair, and a state of war will exist over the whole continent. We'll just sit back and smile and wait for our Great Prophet Osama to air his demands: Evacuation of all Jews from Israel, release of all prisoners from Guantanamo and other jails. We will have control over the capitalist countries of the world, because they'll believe that we can deal a master stroke like this in every part of the globe. Which we can." He added with a smile.

Yousef was entranced. The black eyes of his countryman sparkled with hatred and enthusiasm. He felt his temperature rising as if he were getting a fever, and all he could say was, "*Allahu Akbar.*" (God is great.) "When will I do this and what is the third number for?"

"The what?"

"Omar, you said three numbers are programmed in the cell phone, but you only mentioned two . . ."

"Oh, yes. The third one you push is me, so I know that it happened although I should be able to see that on TV. Anyway, you push one, then the device, then two and then three. That way I know everything is going as planned."

"And when do I do this?"

"Two days from now. We still have a lot of work to do. So, be patient, young man. Good to have you on board. I also wanna learn more of your other adventures in the past few months. We hear you have a very checkered background."

"Well, nothing as exciting as this." He modestly lowered his gaze. "Nothing like this."

The Lincoln had eased its way out of Brooklyn onto the Long Island Expressway eastbound, and once it passed the massive Queens Cemetery, it slid down the next exit. After half a mile, the luxury car slowed and entered the construction gate of the huge burial ground. Moving at the posted speed of 15 mph, it took three minutes to get to the maintenance building that looked from the outside as if it had long been abandoned. Yet, the overhead door moved noiselessly as the maroon car slid underneath. The interior looked just as dilapidated as the outside, but once they opened an inner door, things looked different.

The room that they entered was beautifully lit and decorated, but had no windows.

Omar's pointed finger swung around the room. "This will be your home for the next few days. This is also the place you go back to, when your work is done. We have food for a week, but within the week, you will have been transported to a luxury yacht, off the coast of New Jersey. You will be well rewarded. Come over here." He walked into an adjacent room.

"This is our secret weapon."

"A wreath? A wreath is a weapon?"

"Yes, Sir! We'll attach a bomb to the back of it, and we'll place it at the monument..."

"Will they let us?"

"Will they let us? Boy, you have a lot to learn, Yousef. We're going to do it, as simple as that. Tomorrow night after most of the crowd is gone and the commuters have gone home, we're going to lay a wreath. The day after tomorrow, Obama and Netanyahu will carry a wreath to the same monument and then . . . you push the button . . . and both those infidels will enter hell together, which would seem very appropriate!" His voice has gone up by two decimals. The excitement was contagious.

"Wow! And I'll be the trigger man! Wow! Where's the bomb? Won't they see it?"

"Patience, young man. Pick up that wreath and follow me." Omar walked back into the garage, opened the door of a gleaming new Cadillac, reached in and popped the trunk.

"Here," he said as he opened the lid all the way, "is the bomb."

"That's it?"

"Small, isn't? One just like that blew the whole face off a luxury hotel in Bagdad, remember?"

"How do we attach it?"

"Put that thing down a minute. Stand here, directly behind the car, pick up the bomb and turn it over." He burst out laughing when he saw the look on Yousef's face. "It won't blow. We haven't armed it yet. Look at that little cover. Lift it. See the little toggle switch? That's what you turn on, after the wreath is in place. After that, the bomb is 'HOT.' Very simple. Then the next day, at the right moment, you will mash the little button on the detonator, and it's all over. You'll be on the garden roof of a building, right along the edge, so you can see the proceedings, and you'll push the bomb switch with one hand, the phone with the other hand, push it twice, and then a third time after the explosion, which will reach me here. I'll be watching the affair on TV, 'cause it will focus on the two infidels, so I won't see you, but I'll see the results. Now let's attach the two items." He lifted the wreath." See these two wires? These two clamps? The wires go through these little loops . . . now bend them and twist them . . . put the clamps on the wires for security reasons, so now when you and Ali pick up the wreath, the bomb automatically comes up with it. Each of you . . ."

"You're not coming?"

"I'm not needed. Besides, I look too much like an Arab with my beard and hair. Might arouse suspicion. You both grab it carefully, at the 10 o'clock and 2 o'clock positions and slowly, very dignified, carry the contraption to the Sphere and lay it against the other flower arrangements. Stand still for a moment and act like you're praying." He straightened up and asked, "Do you know how to make the Sign of the Cross?" He crossed himself. "Like this." He did it once more. "Then you bow your heads and walk back to the car, slowly." He caught himself "And, oh, before you walk away, or when you first put it down, lift the little cover and set the switch, okay?"

"Oops!"

"You're afraid it may blow up in your face. Don't worry. It's not supposed to blow till the next day, remember. A dead Yousef is of no value to Allah and Mohammed.

He laughed out loud. "Come on. Let me show you the clothes you'll be wearing and the pistol you'll be carrying. It's a beauty, just in case you'll have to shoot your way out of there." He laughed again. He sounded sinister, and Yousef shivered involuntarily.

42

FBI, NEW JERSEY.

"Foster, Bongers here."
"Oh, hi, Bruce, we had the boys trailed to the carpet merchant in Corpus and all the way into Galveston and . . ."
"I know, I know. That's not why I called you. You're in the Central Time Zone, right?"
"Yes, we are."
"Okay. Do you have helicopters available?"
"Sure, we can depend on them when we need them."
"You'll need them two days from today. Do you have sharpshooters or access to them somehow?"
"Yes."
"Guys that can take out somebody from a chopper?"
"Vietnam era veterans. Why do you ask?"
'Foster, prepare for the following. We have the final itinerary for our president on September eleven. He'll be landing by helicopter, Marine One, in New York City to lay a wreath at 3 PM, your time. We fully expect that at the same time, extremists with the rockets that are stored in Port Arthur as yet, will fire at explosive targets in the Galveston and Lake Charles areas. We still have no clue what the targets could possibly be, but be prepared to follow the missiles from the Port Arthur warehouse to their destination. When they stop

at three o'clock, have your sharpshooters take them out. Don't take chances! Don't let them pick up a rocket. Bullets through the heads, as far as I'm concerned."

"I'm writing as fast as I can."

"Good man. At the same time, have a team in Corpus invade the carpet store, arrest everyone in sight and confiscate all moneys and records. Coordinate the timing. Have someone on the copter call Corpus, as the shots go off. Precise time, so they won't have any forewarning, whatsoever. Any questions?"

"Clear as a bell. I'll call you when all teams are organized and in place."

"Thanks, Foster, and good hunting."

"Bryan? Bongers here, New Jersey . . ."

"Yes, Bruce, what's up?"

"You're on Central Time, right?"

"Why do you ask?"

"Two days from today, 9/11, at three o'clock, watch TV with your phone or phones in hand. When you see a disturbance or explosion taking place at the 9/11 monument, probably when Obama is speaking or laying a wreath, have your men invade Kaliff's office in Chicago and his home in Lake Forest. Have them arrest everyone in sight and confiscate all records and money. Seal off the places, okay? Timing is important. Okay, Brian?"

"Will do. Count on us."

"Great."

"Andy? Bruce. Anything new on our boy Yousef?"

"Not a hint. Disappeared in thin air. How do we find one man amongst ten million others?"

"Damn. I'm still at a loss about a possible explosion on Saturday. Are you aware that it happens to coincide with Rosh Hashanah? "

"Didn't think of it."

"What a great time to knock off Israeli's president, isn't it?'

"If you're a Moslem, it is."

"Anyway, Andy. Watch TV on Saturday, on or about four, Obama will be laying a wreath at the Sphere, along with Netanyahu. The moment you see any disturbance . . ."

"Like what?"

"Like Secret Service men hustling him into a car, or out of the way, or at worst, when there is an explosion, give the signal immediately and have your men invade the safe house in Canarsie and grab all records, equipment, money and people . . ."

"Everybody, including women and . . ."

"Everybody! Let the CIA sort all of it out later. They love to do that. So timing is everything, okay?"

"Okay, Bruce, you're the boss."

Bruce hung up. "What boss?" He said to himself. "I'm just an errand boy."

• • •

Herbert Hoover Building, Washington D.C.

"Lester, Jeb here."

"Oh yeah, anything new here? Like more info on the attack method?"

"No, I was going to ask you. Are you aware that Bongers has been giving orders all over the country, including to my men?"

"All over the country? Is this thing bigger than I thought?"

"Well, in a manner of speaking. He seems to know that something will go off at four on Saturday."

"He may be right. I'm still guessing."

"Are you aware of what he's doing and . . ."

"I would say, leave him alone. Just inspect what you expect, but don't interfere. I have confidence in that boy."

"But they lost that Lebanese in Brooklyn . . ."

"Our CIA and FBI agents lost them, Jeb. Not Bruce. We have two days. We'll get him."

Ritz-Carlton Hotel, Battery Park, N.Y.C.

"The reason why we're not staying at our Embassy is because we want to be close to the action. Walking distance, if at all possible. When it's all over, we can always check if we can enjoy a bit of their extravagant luxury one day, but for now, we're staying here." Meir Dagan was addressing his agents in his suite atop the hotel. "Besides, the hotel will provide kosher food and the prescribed dinnerware and utensils. Our rabbi is working with them in the kitchen. We will dine up here. We will spend our time, exploring the area. We have less than forty-eight hours before disaster might strike, so we'll go in pairs. As tourists, lovers, whatever is most inconspicuous and we'll take pictures of everything in sight. After dinner, we'll analyze what you've seen, and you'll be going out for an evening stroll and reconnoiter the area again. Especially check how they could possibly get a car or a truck close enough to do severe damage." He looked around the room.

"We've played these games often enough to where we should be the most experienced team in the world. Photograph every vehicle that's in the vicinity of the *Sphere*, and then we'll verify again, if they haven't moved by morning. We'll have NYPD tow them away, if anything even smells suspicious. We're going to be ready for these bastards, and we're not relying on American Security. There's this monument that proves that their intelligence isn't good enough. We'll take care of our own." Scanning the faces again, "Any questions? No? We'll meet here again at 6:30. I trust all of you had a chance to take a nap, so we won't suffer too severely from jetlag. Okay, till six."

FBI offices, Secaucus, N.J.

"We've dotted all the I's and crossed all the T's and we still have no clue what our targets are out west or the means of assassination in New York. I'm starting to wonder if we should have been torturing our handsome Lebanese into revealing all he knew about . . ."

"Who would have done the torturing, Bruce?"

"Oh, I remember a few tricks that we learned from the Chinese in Korea and the V. C. in Vietnam. They were brutal." He sat down. "Anything that someone might contribute?"

Nothing but silence.

"Let's call it a day. The next few days may be exceedingly long."

That didn't take much encouragement. The agents got up from their seats, retreated to their own desks to retrieve jackets and pocketbooks, ready to get into their cars and beat the traffic home.

On the way out, Bongers stopped by the receptionist. "Julie, didn't anyone from Mossad call back? I know it's twelve o'clock at night in Jerusalem, but they usually return calls, no matter what time of day."

"Sir, do you suppose that all of them are in Hollywood with their president?"

"All of them? Even receptionists?" He turned to go home. Stepping through the front door on his way to the underground garage, Bruno caught up with him.

"Nervous, Boss?"

"How'd you figure that?"

"When all the pieces don't fall in place like they should, I know you go home to think or watch your boys play soccer, and somehow a light comes on."

"Sure hope so. Not knowing what they're up to drives me up the wall. I wish someone had a crystal ball . . ."

"Boss, you could always try an empty Dewars bottle. You hold it up to the light a certain way and who knows . . ."

"Don't hit anybody on the way home, Bruno."

43

QUEENSBOROUGH CEMETERY. SEPTEMBER 10.

"Today, you'll be all in black, both of you. You'll have to look like a couple of undertakers. Let's see which of these hats fits you." Omar was doing the dressing. "The jacket looks a little wide, but it'll hide your pistol without a problem." He stepped back and looked at Yousef in his new outfit.

"You look fine. That Clark Gable mustache goes well with the outfit. Too bad, we don't have a black Cadillac, but that can't be helped. Now remember, everything has to be slow and dignified. Park as close as you can. Even double park if necessary. If a cop interferes, tell 'em you're just laying a wreath for the Funeral Home. We don't wanna draw any attention, okay?"

Omar moved over to the other "undertaker" and repeated the whole ceremony. Satisfied that everything was in order, he sat down.

"Now, Yousef, we don't want you to use that gun, but let's go over it once more anyway. Maybe tomorrow, after the blast, you may have to shoot your way out, but definitely, not today. Show me again how you take off the safety. Make sure there's a round in the chamber, aim and squeeze. Don't yank! It'll make the gun jerk and you'll miss your target. Just squeeze, while holding your hand as still as possible. Okay, take out the clip, slide the action open, and get the bullet out of the chamber. Now dry fire a few times."

He watched Yousef go through the motions.

"See what I mean? You pull the trigger and your hand jerks up. Wrong! Hold your hand still. That's it. Practice some more today and tomorrow. Didn't they put you through military training in Lebanon? Oh, well. Let's eat and by six o'clock, you start rolling."

• • •

Secaucus, FBI Headquarters, New Jersey.

Bruce had been on the phone all morning. CIA officials wanted to verify every detail, and the more they talked and the more they asked, the more worried Bongers became that too many people were involved and that some loose tongues might start slipping information to the wrong parties.

Andrews in the New York office seemed to have everything under control, although everyone was still uptight about the fact that Yousef had evaporated into thin air.

Jarvis in D.C. was actually the most calm of them all. He had everything and everybody marked on the huge operations board, and he saw no fault with anything, except, how was the attack going to take place in the city the next day, and what were the targets way out west?

"Snipers?" He asked his adjutant. "Impossible." He answered himself. "We have every rooftop, every balcony, every window, every office and every apartment covered. Impossible."

A click on the remote changed the picture on the TV screen to a close-up of the infamous square. "Impossible."

The next frame showed the whole Manhattan Island and part of New Jersey, the Bronx, Queens and Brooklyn. "Air corridors where a little plane can slip through?"

"Possible." His assistant answered, "but not likely."

"NYPD is going to have every access road blocked, right? All the dignitaries and guests will be bused in and will be in the bleachers when the chopper comes in, right?"

"Right."

"Let's hope that Bongers is wrong and that his information and hunches are all false and that nothing is going to happen"

"Yes, and the moon is made of cream cheese."

•••

By four o'clock, Bongers couldn't stand it any more. "Bruno, let's go into Manhattan."

Turning to the receptionist, he said, "Julie, we'll be on our cell. Ask anyone who calls how urgent it is and then relay the message to me. Get their numbers. I'll call them back when it suits me. Give Nancy the same instructions when she comes in."

"Do you want me to stay longer, Sir?"

"No, no, that's okay. Go home and cook. Those kids will be starving."

"You got that right."

In the garage he approached Garcia. "We're taking both cars. I may stay the night, and I may run home at an ungodly hour."

"Okay. Where will we park?"

"We'll see. Meet me at McGuire's on Washington square. We'll go on foot from there."

The two of them stood and stared at the Sphere and the bleachers that were being set up.

"The speaker's podium will be at the end of the bleachers, so they'll walk over here from the spot where Marine One will touch down, pick up the flowers, carry them over together, lay them right up against the other displays, and one of them will sit there," he pointed to the first seat of the grandstand, "while the other one gives his spiel." He walked into the direction in which he had pointed and stopped where he figured the president would stand the next day.

"If I were the man giving the talk, I would look straight at the building over there. The one on Vesey Street. The one with the roof garden on the twelfth floor, and the other roof, way on top. Let's go take a look."

The elevator ride was brief, but they were stopped twice before they got there. Once by a New York City Policeman in uniform and once by an undercover man from Homeland Security. They weren't searched or asked to check their guns. "A fake ID would get anyone up here, wouldn't it?" Bongers was not too impressed.

At the garden restaurant, a happy group of people was enjoying the shade of the beach umbrellas that kept the sun at bay. "Wall Street vendors," Bruno observed.

"Wonder what they did to your 401K today?"

"Do they look trustworthy to you, Boss?"

"Don't call me Boss in public. We wanna appear like we're money hustlers, not Feds. They don't like our types."

At the wall, overlooking the Sphere below, Bongers scanned up and down the structure. "Stone wall, four feet high, copper and brass fencing on top, an additional four feet, spaced six inches. Easy to fire through, but hard if you wanted to commit suicide."

"Can I help you gentlemen?" A tall bearded man approached them..

"It depends on who you are."

"I'm Brad Johnson, building security."

"I'm Bruce Bongers. This is Bruno Garcia, FBI. May I see your ID?"

"But of course. All I've been doing today is checking up on other security people." He grinned as he produced a wallet and showed his pictured card. "Now may I see yours?"

Bruce chuckled. "Of course, Brad." He reached into his breast pocket. "How many different forces are represented here?"

"I've seen four other FBI people, two City Detectives, two CIA agents and three strange ones. They had a foreign IDs as well as an NYPD clearance."

Bongers' ears perked up. "Foreign? Which country?"

"Israel. Funny looking scribbles, but the faces matched. I understand that their president will also be here tomorrow."

"The Israelis? And they haven't even contacted me? The nerve. How much longer will you be up here, Brad?"

"I'll be here until nine."

"Great. We're gonna grab something to eat and we'll be back. Keep up the good work. Bruno, take a picture from up here while we have favorable light. We'll see you, Brad."

"The food is excellent up here, gentlemen."

"That's okay. Bruno doesn't like their company."

An hour and a half later, the two G-men returned to the garden roof and found that the crowds had grown substantially. "Do you suppose that all of these people have been stopped three times on the way up?" Bruno shook his head.

"They'd better. That's the whole idea. I don't think anyone with a rifle could sneak up here, even if it were in a case and had to be assembled. There's Brad. Let's see if he has some news about this crowd."

"Brad, good to see you again. Anybody out of hand yet?"

"No, this is a great bunch. They have a snack and a few drinks and hit the train for home. Some will go out for dinner, some others try to get in bed with their secretaries or someone else's, but by seven, the crowd changes and couples drift in, settling down for dinner before a show or . . ."

"Anything unusual that caught your eye?"

No. Just one thing. Come over here." He took them over to the wall of the terrace and pointed down. "See that wreath? The big one."

"What about it?"

"It was put there half an hour ago by two men in black. They took it out of the trunk of a Cadillac and . . ."

"Is that so unusual?"

"No, what's unusual, there was no group of people, holding hands and praying, and there were no speeches . . ."

"That's it!" Bonger shouted. "The wreath, Bruno! THAT'S IT!" and he sprinted away.

44

LOWER MANHATTAN, SEPTEMBER 10, 2010

Bruce dashed to the farthest corner of the roof garden, where a wooden fence blocked the view of the garbage containers, next to the kitchen exit. Bruno, right on his heels.

"Bruno, get Andrews on the phone." He punched a number on his own cell. "Chief Geralds? Not in? Where can I get him?"

"Who's this?"

"This is Special Agent Bongers, This is a national emergency. What's his cell number?"

"Oh, can't give you that, Sir."

"What's your name? This will be your last day on the job, do you hear? This is a national emergency. Now connect me. NOW!"

A few minutes passed. "Who are you, threatening my . . ."

"Chief, this is Bongers, FBI. I need your permission to contact and direct your bomb squad. Who's in charge?"

"Bomb squad? What's going on? What do you want with the bomb squad?"

"Mr. Geralds, either you answer my question, or I'll call the White House on the other line, and then you can explain deaths and destruction to them."

"Hold it, I just want to know what's going on."

"I'll update you when everyone is safe. Who do I call and what's his number?"

"His name is Captain MacLeroy and . . ."

"And I have your permission to direct his operations tonight, right? I'll have Homeland Security confirm my status and authority. His number please . . . 248 . . . 4444. Thanks."

"Bruno, do you have Andrews?"

"Yes, he's on my phone." Bruno handed over the instrument.

"Andy. Who makes wreaths in this town?"

"What?"

"Wreaths. Like in funerals. Have your men take a picture of a brand-new one at the *Sphere* and have it duplicated. Don't arouse any suspicion and don't take it anywhere yet. Call me when you have it ready."

He disconnected and handed the cell back to his assistant. On his own phone he dialed the bomb-squad commander. "Captain MacLeroy? I'm Bruce Bongers, FBI. I just spoke with Chief Geralds, and I'm following his orders and the orders of Homeland Security. Are you on the job or are you off?"

"I'm home right now."

"Can you direct operations from your home or do you have to . . ."

"Depends. What do you want?"

"Listen carefully. Tomorrow at four o'clock approximately, our president and the Israeli president will lay a wreath at the 9/11 monument . . ."

"I'm aware of that. So what has . . ."

"At that moment, a bomb will explode and they'll be killed and a lot of people around them."

"Come on? I can't believe that."

"Well, believe it, unless you start acting instead of asking questions."

"Holy Patricia, what are you saying?"

"Are you ready to listen?"

"Where are you?"

"I'm at the site. When I stop talking, get into action. A bomb was deposited at the *Sphere,* ready to be detonated at the precise moment that the dignitaries walk up to lay the wreath."

"Good God."

"Yes, God help us, but I think He's on our side. Here's what you do. When I give the signal, you pull your bomb-disposal truck in front of the monument. You'll be shielded by City cleanup trucks, so no one will see what you're doing. You will pick up a wreath with a bomb attached and deposit it in your bomb-proof container on your department's truck. In its place, you will place an identical wreath that we will provide, and then you take the bomb to your disposal site. Okay, so far? How much time will you need?"

"A few hours, maybe more."

"Okay. Let's do this at one in the morning. Okay by you?"

"What's your name again?"

"Bongers, FBI. I'll talk to you again in an hour."

"Andy? Did you find a copy?"

"They're getting it now. The florist in Queens even remembers the man who bought it four days ago."

"Good, get those details. By midnight, we'll arrange to get it on a bomb-disposal truck. I'll call you back with the particulars. Who heads up the night shift of the sanitation department?"

"How would I know?"

"Call me back with that info. Call on Bruno's cell."

"Bruno, let's get a drink."

"A 'drink' drink?"

In spite of everything, Bruce had to laugh. "No, I'll have to have a soda for the moment and the next four hours."

They walked inside the restaurant and found a quiet corner at the end of the bar. Bongers took a deep breath. He nearly slumped on the bar.

"Bruno, Bruno! It finally fell into place. We looked at every angle, and nobody guessed it right. Those bastards nearly had us by the balls, but now the shoe is on the other foot. We'll have them by the short hairs within twenty hours."

He nodded when the bartender asked, "Ginger ale, Sir?"

"Yes," Bruno answered. "Ulcers, you understand?"

"I'm torn between calling Jarvis and updating him or waiting till the actual bomb has been removed and we know for sure we did the right thing."

While they were peacefully sipping their soft drinks and rehashing what they did and didn't do, Bongers' phone rang.

"Oh? Your name please? You're the night manager of the street-cleaning detachment for lower Manhattan?" He listened for a minute. "Great, you may earn a medal tonight . . .! Listen, first of all, none of your people will be in any kind of danger, but your job is of the utmost importance. Listen carefully. The bomb-removal truck will pick up a suspicious package and it's going to be harmless, because it has to be detonated by remote control or a timer. We're convinced that the timer is set for four o'clock tomorrow afternoon, so it is safe at this moment . .

Huh? . . . Yeah . . . yeah . . . they're trying to kill a lot of people, our president included. Anyway, just in case they're watching, we don't want them to know we're on to them, so when the bomb truck pulls up, they'll only be there for a minute, but your cleaning vehicles will be blocking the view, so it'll look like you're doing your regular street cleaning. Are you with me?" Bruce listened for a while.

"Right on! You're with me. We're planning on doing this at one o'clock . . . Yes, yes, at the Sphere monument. You feel five sweepers and a big dump truck will do it? . . . Isn't that a little overkill? . . . Yes, I know that you know what you're doing . . . Sorry . . . You can understand that I'm a bit excited . . . Well, I am, but it's good to hear you're confident . . . We'll talk again in an hour."

"Bruno? How many people do we now have in this circuit who can screw up?'

"Boss, you're doing beautifully."

"Get that barman, would you?"

"Mr. Barman, I may have to stay nearby for the night, rather than rush back and forth to Jersey. Can you make a call or two?"

"Because of tomorrow's events, the area is pretty well booked up, but I'll see what I can do."

"Good man. Thanks."

"Why don't you check in with our FBI facilities, Boss?"

"I want no distractions, no distractions. I want to be able to think."

"Like I said . . ."

"Sir, I can get you a small room at the Ritz down at Battery Park"

"Book it. The name is Bongers. Bruno, leave him a twenty."

At the Ritz, after a fitful hour-long sleep, Bruce was back on the phone, and at midnight, his Latin assistant hailed a cab back to Vesey Street, and they rode the elevator back up to the twelfth floor, this time after only two identity checks.

There was no sign of Brad, the bearded security guard, and the crowd had thinned out to a very few.

"What time does a place like this close, Bruno?"

"I don't know. This is the city that never sleeps, remember? Do you want me to ask?"

"No, that's alright. How can people drink this stuff all the time? If it weren't wet, I would never drink it at all."

Leaning on the wall, their eyes scanning the world below them, Bruno whispered, "There they go!"

Indeed, yellow mechanical street cleaners, there brushes swirling, started along the sidewalks below, scooping up cups and straws and all other junk that the visitors had left behind. Two other ones came in from the far end and a big dump truck stopped smack in front of the monument and one by one, the yellow brush machines, pulled up and deposited their collection in the voluminous cavity of the dump truck.

Nearly unnoticed, a black city truck moved behind all that activity and after thirty seconds, pulled out as if it had never been there.

"Bruno! " Bongers grabbed his hand. "Bruno! We did it!" We did it!" He thought about embracing his right-hand man, but pumped his hand instead.

"You did it, Boss. The hell with the rest of the world. You did it!"

"Let's see if they serve scotch in here."

45

RITZ-CARLTON HOTEL. BATTERY PARK, N.Y.C.

The insistent ringing of his cell phone woke Bongers, but he had a bit of a problem locating the source. For one, he was in a strange bed, second, the cobwebs in his brain interfered with his normal thinking, and third, it was pitch dark in the room.

When he located the light on the nightstand and finally his pants, the ringing had stopped and all he could do was open up the heavy curtains and orientate himself. He was looking across the courtyard at other windows of the hotel. He consulted his watch. Seven o'clock in the morning! Normally, that would not be an unusual hour to be called, but they hadn't hit the sack until about four, and his head was a little slow getting into gear.

The incoming number on his cell was unfamiliar, but he hit the return button anyway.

"Dagan!" was the response.
"Meir! You cheat! Where are you?
"I'm in New York. How about you?"
"Where in New York?"
"I'm in lower Manhattan in the Ritz-Carlton."
"In the Ritz-Carlton? What room?"
"22-21. Why?"
"I'm gonna look you up." He clicked his phone shut and then

realized they had not asked the front desk for shaving tools or a toothbrush. "What the hell? He said to himself and started putting his clothes on.

In the other bed, Bruno never stirred. On the nightstand was a pad with the hotel logo, and Bruce wrote on it, "I'm upstairs with Dagan in 2221. Go back to sleep." He deposited it on the toilet seat, figuring that was a sure place for his assistant to find it.

Making sure that he had his magnetic door key with him, he quietly opened and closed the door and walked to the EXIT sign. He was only two floors below Dagan, but the Israeli was on the opposite side of the structure, and it seemed like it was a long mile to 2221.

When he knocked, the door opened so suddenly, that it startled him, and two men grabbed him immediately and searched him. They took his GLOCK out of his holster and only then asked him who he was.

From inside the suite a voice called out, "Who is it?" and when Bruce shouted the answer, "Bongers!" Meir Dagan appeared in the doorway in seconds and told his men, "Give him back his gun. This is my friend."

"How the hell did you get here so fast?" Meir shouted as they stepped in.

"I slept two floors below you, that's how."

"What are you doing here?"

"Get me some coffee and I'll tell you."

"Sure, sure. Get the man some coffee. Let's sit here at the table. Did you have breakfast?"

"No, I . . ."

"How about some lox and bagels?"

"That sounds great. Let me tell you what happened." Between bites, Bruce told all about the past night's experiences and was hardly interrupted until he got to the part where the bomb disposal unit pulled out with the new wreath in place.

"So the place is secure? How big was the device?"

"Yes, the danger has been removed for your and my president, but out west we still have to track down the bastards and secure their targets. But how big a bomb? Let me find out. Excuse me a minute." He whipped out his cell, scrolled through some numbers and said, "Captain MacLeroy? Did I wake you up? This is Bruce Bongers."

"No, as a matter of fact, I just walked in the door. We were out at Floyd Bennett Field all night with your bomb."

"MY bomb? Any problems?"

"No, but as you suspected, it was to be detonated by remote control, so it never was a real danger, and then when we got to the site, we found a switch that disarmed it, so that made it easier to work with. The device was attached to the wreath with coat hangers, so that part was simple."

"How big a bomb is it? How much damage would it do?"

"Our real experts are coming in right now to work on that angle, but based on my experience, I would say, it would have destroyed everything and everybody within 300 feet."

"Good God!"

"You can say that again, it must be the same composition and size that blew up the hotel in Bagdad a while ago and the Marine Barracks in Lebanon, years ago, remember?"

"Boy, oh boy! Do I remember? Hey, Captain, thank you so much for your speedy cooperation, and I'll see to it that you and your department receive a commendation for it."

"Sir, that won't be necessary. To us, this is . . ."

"At one o'clock in the morning? That's beyond the call of duty. Thanks again and get some sleep."

Turning back to the Israeli Director, "It was a big one alright. Now, all you have to do is watch the proceedings and capture someone who's walking around with a detonator when the presidents walk up to the monument. I'll leave that to you. I'm heading back to Jersey, shave and showers and get into some clean clothes. I . . ."

"Clean clothes? Do you remember in the Sinai, we didn't get out of our clothes for nine days?"

"Yeah, but I'm not in the desert anymore. Besides, I can monitor all the action from my office, better than from a hotel room. That reminds me, I better call Jarvis. He doesn't know what happened last night. They're still chasing a bomb and a bomber. Let's put his mind at ease. Do you want to talk to him, Meir?"

"No, they know we're here."

"Okay! Two days from today, at the Paramus golf course. T-time 8 AM. Okay?"

"Where the hell is Paramus?"

"You'll figure it out. Shalom."

Bruno was still sleeping when Bongers walked back in.

"Come on, sleeping beauty, we're going home."

"Just a minute! I feel like shit."

"That should be a familiar feeling. Come on, we'll take a cab to our cars and you go straight home and sleep and come back to the office at noon. Not later than one."

While Bruno was in the bathroom, trying to make himself presentable, Bongers clued in Jarvis in D.C. and urged him not to spread the word about the disarmed bomb, so everyone would remain vigilant, and grab or kill as many terrorists as possible.

Their cars had several warnings on them from NYPD, that in spite of being government vehicles, they were considered suspicious under the circumstances and might be towed.

"Well, at least they're on the ball." Bongers commented as he mashed the papers into a ball and ditched them into a trashcan.

"Now get some sleep, Amigo. Sleep."

His phone rang three more times before he got to the office, but he wasn't about to answer them, while fighting traffic into and through the Lincoln Tunnel.

Once, sitting at his desk, he instructed his secretary, "Let me sleep till twelve, okay. I have clean clothes here, so I'll be fine. Just get detailed messages from everyone, and then I'll determine who I call first."

The Jersey chief pulled out his cot, unplugged the phone lines, put his cell on 'Buzzer', rolled himself in a blanket and zonked out.

By one-thirty, he was ready for the onslaught of messages. The most urgent one was from Andrews, because he had not been informed of the actions of the early morning.

"Jarvis didn't call you?"

"No."

"Well the bomb scare is off. Just look to arrest suspicious-looking characters with detonators in their pocket. Keep your people on the ball, that's all. The danger is over."

The New York Police Chief. "Thanks, Chief. Excuse me for getting back at you so late, but your department did an excellent job, especially the bomb squad, and please convey my thanks to the Sanitation Department. I'll get around to doing that myself after today. I'm sure they'll understand. And thanks again. Real professional."

To his secretary, he quoted his preferences;

"No, I don't want to talk to Taylor. No, not today. I'll call him back. No, just tell'em there's no threat. Get on with the show."

Next call?

"Who? Kopolosi? That idiot? Tell'em I'm tied up with foreign dignitaries."

"Next? No! Who? Brian in Chicago? Yes, I'll talk with him." He pushed a button. "Brian? There will be no explosion, but there will be some consternation at the Sphere Monument. Watch it on TV. That's your 'GO' signal. No you don't need another signal from me or anybody else."

"Next? Foster in Port Arthur? Okay."

"Foster? . . . They're moving? . . . Two SUV's? . . . Are your choppers up? . . . Great! . . . Watch TV . . . At the commotion at the ceremony, go into action. You will not need any further instructions. Pass the word to your boys. Just don't let the bastards get a shot off with those Stingers."

"Trust in us, Bruce. We're on it."

"Trust? Bruno? Trust? What has ever become of that word?" He addressed his assistant, as they were getting settled in the ready-room. They established themselves in front of the big white board, full of names and numbers in three different colors, and a huge TV screen on one wall and a dozen phones on the long table in front of them. Bottles of water and pitchers of coffee were dispersed along the whole row of chairs and the tables behind them.

"That's one thing about you, Bruno. I trust you're feeling better?"

"Bring'em on, Boss. Bring'em on!"

46

QUEENS BOROUGH CEMETERY.

Yousef had never been so nervous in his life. Everything had gone so smoothly, everything was so well organized, that there really was no reason for him to be uptight about anything. Yet, as the time approached for him to get on the subway and make his trek downtown, he broke into a cold sweat. Omar noticed his discomfort and tried to reassure him.

"You push the buttons as we rehearsed it. Once on the detonator, and three times on the phone. Then, after you duck for the explosion, you stay with the onlookers and only move away and down in the building, when everyone else moves as well. Don't become conspicuous. Right now, you look elegant enough to be an Italian movie star. Just remain calm. Allah will support you and reward you."

He indeed looked handsome with grey shoes and slacks, a light-yellow open shirt and a navy-blue blazer. The little blue hat, with a tiny red feather, topped it all off. The jacket was loose and didn't reveal slight bulges in the pants pockets where his instruments were, nor did it show the Glock under his arm. He shook hands with his partners and bowed to Omar as he whispered, "Salaam Aleichem." He stepped out the door into the garage to be driven to the subway station.

Beirut. Twelve midnight.

Gathered in the penthouse, hash and sleep had overcome most of the gathering, but Ahmed remained alert. He had turned the volume down on the giant TV, so his brethren could get some rest as he watched the ABC anchor describe where the helicopter would land and showed clips of Netanyahu's visit to Hollywood ("All rich Jews," he murmured) and of the banquet at the White House on the previous night.

The commentator was a pretty blond, and he said to himself, "I wouldn't mind wrestling in bed with that woman."

The Hezbollah leader had received word that immediately after the killing of the presidents and the explosions along the Gulf Coast, Osama bin Laden would appear on Pakistani and Egyptian television with a speech full of plaudits for the Islam cause and stringent demands from the capitalist infidels. It would be seen worldwide, and Ahmed glowed with pride at the thought that he was instrumental in that glorious victory. All he had to do was stand by for two more hours. He couldn't wait. He hoped that the Prophet would not refer to the incident coinciding with the start of Rosh Hashanah, like he did the last time, because that had already passed two days ago. Sometimes Ahmed wondered who Osama's advisors were and if they were really inspired by Allah.

"Better grab some more coffee."

CIA Headquarters, Langley AFB, Langley, Virginia.

"According to Lester Jarvis, there is no more bomb threat in New York, and our president won't be in any danger. Do we still maintain all the standby-alert procedures?"

"Yes, Mr. Taylor. We don't know how many extremists may be floating around the Twin Tower monument and what desperate action any of them may take."

"Alright. Alright. Are any of the networks covering the arrival already?"

"All three, Sir, and Fox will start within the hour."

"Aggravating as hell. Have some sandwiches and coffee brought up. We'll watch the proceedings in the ops room."

Lake Charles, Louisiana.

"The two Filipinos have left the hotel in a pickup truck. A white Nissan. They're heading toward the bridge."
"Which direction is that?"
"That's west."
"What is out there?"
"Well, mostly the refinery, but not many big storage tanks."
"Keep me posted."
"Oh, Sir, they turned off to the harbor."
"What's out there?" Brian's breath was giving away his anxiety.
"Ships, boats, large and small. Freighters mainly. From that side, you look back at the casino boat that is just shoving off for its trip around the lake."
"How many people does that gambling ship hold?"
"A few hundred. Maybe three hundred."
"Then that's not it. That target isn't worth all this effort, all this preparation. What else do you see?"
The agent aboard the helicopter responded, "They parked. They backed into a parking space at the harbor."
"They don't have any missiles, do they?"
"Not that we're aware of."
"What are they doing now?"
"Nothing. They're just sitting there."
"Call some cars to go over there and shadow them. You stay out of sight. Don't startle them."
"Wilco."

Galveston Harbor Patrol.

"Foster? We're on a harbor patrol-boat. Very inconspicuous. What's the status?"

"The SUV with the rockets is about an hour away at this point. We have cars and a chopper covering. Is there anything that you can see that could cause a huge explosion, if it were hit with a missile?"

"No, and the storage tanks are too far from here, so I may be in the wrong location."

"No, you stay right there. The Marine chopper will keep them in sight, and our own helicopter is on top of that building to your west, complete with sharp shooters, so stand by. You're doing good."

FBI headquarters, Secaucus, N.J.

"Lester, everything is looking good. Bring on the bandits! We're ready for them and by the way, set aside Monday, September 13, at the Paramus golf course. Meir will be there too. "

"You have a weird mind, Bruce. How can you think of golf with all that's going on?"

"Easy, I haven't played for so long, my palms are itching."

"Are your eyes glued to the tube?"

"We're watching ABC. We like Diane Sawyer."

"Okay."

Washington Square, NYC

The subway ride wasn't all that bad, because it was Saturday and the working crowd was not bulging out of every car. He did attract some attention with his good looks and dressy outfit, but he didn't mind that, as long as they didn't ask for IDs.

From the Square to Vesey Street took about fifteen minutes, but the heat was so oppressive, that he wished he could take off his jacket. In the lobby, he went to the bar first and ordered a coke, feeling that it would take some of the spying eyes off him, rather than rushing to the elevators immediately.

With a tall glass in hand, he meandered over to the battery of elevators and wasn't even stopped once for identification. Well, neither was anybody else. It seemed like a group of happy sightseers on a sunny Saturday afternoon. He started to relax as he walked onto the terrace and decided to go into the air-conditioned restaurant for the time being. It was only three-thirty. In order not to be too conspicuous, he had taken off his hat and sat at the end of the bar, looking at the crowd. He wondered how many of them were undercover-agents and secret-service men? Intermixed were a dozen New York City policemen, and every so often, he felt that someone was staring at him, but he concentrated on his coke. He could wait until he heard the sound of the helicopter and he was sure everyone would race to the railing to glimpse at the V.I.P'.s. That's when he would follow and find a favorable spot.

FBI Headquarters, Secaucus, N.J.

"Bruce? Meir. He's been spotted. He looks sharp, Italian playboy. Even has a thin mustache."
"You're kidding?"
"No, I'm telling you, he's looking good."
"Anyone with him?"
"No, he seems to be alone. What's the latest on the chopper?"
"Crossing over the Bayonne Bridge right now, two Cobras escorting him and four F-16s overhead. TV will start picking them up momentarily."
"Great. Talk to you soon. Shalom."
"Shalom, brother. Shalom."

47

TWIN TOWERS MEMORIAL

Yousef left his hat on the bar, but carried his drink in his left hand, the moment he heard the whop-whop-whop of the helicopter. Everyone else moved in the same direction, so that was easy. What was not so easy was pushing his way right up to the wall, but by moving away from the center, he gained better access. Little by little, he moved closer to the edge, and he wished he had brought a camera. People with recorders of any sort were given more leeway, but it was too late to worry about it. Finally, he was right up against the brass fence and deposited his glass on the wall, put his hands firmly on his instruments, detonator in his right, phone in his left.

The helicopter settled down gracefully, and a Marine guard lowered the steps and saluted sharply. The first one off was Obama, second his wife, followed by Mrs. Netanyahu and finally, the Israeli Prime Minister.

The ladies were escorted to the bleachers across a red carpet, and the two world leaders walked forward to the Sphere. Ten paces from the monument, two Marine Officers handed the gentlemen a beautiful wreath, and while holding it between them, they walked to the *Sphere*, Obama on the left, Netanyahu to the right.

When they bent over slightly to lower the flowered ensemble, Yousef pushed the button in his right pocket once and in his left pocket, three times. Nothing happened. The politicians bowed, and the Israeli leader moved to the bleachers while Barack Obama stepped behind the podium.

With a swift move, he moved some papers from his right breast pocket and started speaking.

Yousef panicked! What happened? Maybe the wall blocked the signal? He took the detonator out and on top of the stones, pushed again . . . and again . . . and again.

"Mr. Prime Minister, Mrs. Netanyahu, distinguished guests. We stand here today, to commemorate the many valiant victims of the 9/11 attack, just nine years ago, but also to honor all the men and women, who have died since then, protecting our land from terrorism.

As we speak, thousands of courageous Soldiers, Marines, Sailors and Airmen are protecting us on far away soil, so we can stand here in peace and safety . . ."

"WHAT THE HELL IS THAT?" He shouted as Secret Service men swarmed all over him and his entourage and hustled them into nearby cars with bulletproof walls and glass.

On the roof, a frustrated Yousef considered trying to shoot him from up there, but a soft voice behind interrupted him, *"Josef Saban, Il y a-t-il des problemes?"*

He swung around . . . *"LAVANA?"* and instinctively reached for his pistol. He was too late. She shot him through his hand, into his chest.

"THROW HIM OFF THE ROOF!" She ordered. "Grab that table, stand it against the wall. Up, up, two of you. Here we go."

Five Israeli agents, including Lavana, lifted Yousef onto the table and pitched him over the fence.

"Grab a table inside. Far corner, order wine! *Chateau Neuf du Pape* for me. I've got to find a television set." She rushed inside the building

THE WHOLE WORLD GASPED! Someone had screamed as a body came flying off the roof and landed on top of a TV broadcast truck, his head dangling off the side, blood trickling down his face.

In Forest Park, Illinois, four agents stormed in the front door of Kaliff's house while two more stormed in the back.

"On the floor, NOW! On the floor." The TV watchers, barely budged. " What's going on?" The middle-aged Kaliff hollered.

"On the floor, now!" Agents pushed them down unceremoniously and handcuffed them behind their backs.

"What the hell do you think you're doing?"

"Shut up! You have the right . . ."

"Watch out! He's got a gun!" One of the agents pointed at a teenage boy who appeared in a doorway, holding a shotgun. Another agent didn't hesitate. He shot him right between the eyes with his pistol.

"My son! You just killed my son!" The crooked lawyer screamed.

"Now you know how it feels, you bastard! How many have you ordered killed? Let's go. Let's get them in the wagon."

In Chicago, very few people were in the Kaliff Law Offices as a half-dozen agents swept in, handcuffing the two women and a man. While they were taken out, other CIA officials ransacked the place for files, documents, records and money. There was lots of it. At least half a million in cash.

Canarsie was a cinch. Four men were sitting, glued to the television, when FBI agents stormed in and arrested them without much resistance, just a lot of cursing and screaming, but no violence.

From the copter over Lake Charles, the observer with the binoculars shouted. "They're moving out. The white pickup is moving. Wait a minute. They're making room for a black SUV that's backing in."

"That's them. Get them in your scope and take them out. Someone else follow the pickup. Take them out if necessary."

"What's on the other side of the street from the SUV?"
"Water and a ship on the far side."
"What kinda ship?"
"Looks like a tanker, like an oil tanker, lots of pipes and . . ."
"That's gotta be it. Do you have them in sight?"
"Yep, our shooter just got one in the head as he opened his door, and now he's got the driver. He's lying in the street."
"Good going. Everybody! Move in. I wonder what's in that boat?"

Galveston.

"Foster? That you on that building?"
"Yes, we're ready to swoop down. What's your twenty?"
"I'm at tree-top level at your eight o'clock. They turned north along the canal. You should see them momentarily."
"Got them in sight. They're stopping. There's nothing here but ships tied against the docks. We can shoot them from up here. Get ready, guys."

Two sharpshooters laid their rifles on the edge of the roof and chambered a bullet.

Below them, the black SUV pulled to a stop and the driver got out, but immediately fell on his face. His brain scattered on the concrete. The second one walked around the front of the vehicle to check on his buddy, when a bullet in his forehead smacked him backwards against the hood.

"Nice going, guys. What the hell is so important around here. Just ships, some small, some big. What do you suppose that big one is?" Foster was pointing down from the roof at a thousand foot monstrosity.

"That's a tanker. Oil, I think."

"Wow, that's bigger than two football fields, maybe three. Let's go clean up that mess."

In the living quarters of the carpet store in Corpus Christi, in back of the store, the inhabitants stared at the TV in absolute wonder.

"What went wrong?"

The owner got up when he heard the front doorbell go off. He got up and started to stroll to the front when his back door opened and several men in black windbreakers ran in and shouted, "On the floor! All of you! On the floor. Hands in front of you."

"What do you think you're doing?" The bearded owner screamed.

"We're sent by Allah and he wants you in hell. Now shut up!"

FBI Headquarters, N.J.

"Did you see that close-up? That was Yousef, wasn't it?"

Bruno was glued to the TV. "It sure looked like him. Do you suppose he committed suicide?"

"Suicide? With a bullet hole in his shoulder? No way. He sure as hell interrupted the ceremony, didn't he?"

"Do you suppose he'll survive?"

"Doubt it, Bruno. He didn't act too lively, lying there, spread-eagled with his head hanging over the side."

"Well, what do we do now, Boss?"

"The phone calls will start coming in from all those people asking questions, so since it's Saturday, I'm going to take my boys out for the juiciest spare ribs you've ever tasted. A new place opened up on 46, and they have the best ribs east of Texas!"

"What's it called?"

"West Of Texas." He laughed at his own joke. "How about you, Bruno? Whatsyergonna do?"

"There's this little redhead who will need consoling after learning that her boyfriend died."

"You're not talking about that little girl in the hardware store?"

"Yes, she'll need a shoulder to cry on . . ."

"Bruno! She's too young for you!"

"She's twenty-one and someone needs to dry her tears."

"You're incorrigible."

48

BEIRUT, HEZBOLLAH HEADQUARTERS.

The whole team was sitting on their pillows in front of the large TV screen, watching live coverage from the Twin Tower. The reception was outstanding, and the attractive blonde who was presenting the program certainly had their attention.

"I wouldn't mind wrestling that woman in a big bed." Ahmed commented again. It was two in the morning, and the majority of the group were bleary eyed and sleepy, partially because of the hash they'd been smoking all evening and partially because of the late hour.

They were anticipating a huge explosion at the monument, the moment the two presidents were to lay a wreath. The Marine helicopter had not yet arrived, but according to the gorgeous blond reporter, it was only five minutes out.

The recently liberated Emir, decked out in his most beautiful robes, readjusted the volume on another TV set, tuned to Cairo, Egypt.

"Our esteemed Prophet Osama will deliver his victory declaration shortly after the blast and we're all set to record it for posterity. This is a great day for Islam."

When the chopper appeared in between the office buildings of

Lower Manhattan, the tension in the room was starting to build. Shouts were heard all around the room. "There they are, the Heathens!" "Look at them waving! They don't know they'll be in hell soon." "There they go, picking up the wreath. Just a few more minutes!"

The shouts of jubilation started to change, as Netanyahu sat down and Barack Obama took his spot behind the podium.

"Where's the blast?" " Where the hell is Yousef?" What's going on?" "Obama's talking as if nothing is supposed to happen." "What's going on?"

The Emir hollered across the room, "Ahmed! Get me Omar on the phone!"

As they waited for Omar to come on the line, the American President stopped talking, security men rushed him away from the podium into waiting automobiles, and the camera switched to a scene on top of an ABC television truck.

"That's Yousef! He committed suicide. He did not detonate the bomb, but instead . . ."

"No, no! See that blood? See the bullet hole in his shoulder? He was killed. What went wrong?" Everyone was screaming something, but very few were listening.

"I have Omar on the line!"

"Give it to me." The Emir grabbed the phone and shouted, "Omar? What is going on? Why didn't the bomb explode? You don't know? You don't know? What happened? What did you do wrong?" He looked into the instrument as if he could see Omar on the other end. "And what about the explosions along the Gulf? The TV reports nothing about that . . . They don't answer?"

He hung up. "Ahmed, get me Kaliff in Chicago. He may know something." The frustrated Muslim turned back to the TV, but other than close-ups of Yousef's face and the winding blades of the president's helicopter that started to windmill slowly, there was nothing new to be seen.

"Kaliff isn't there. Someone answered, but he spoke no Arabic."

"Did you try his house? It's Saturday. He should be home." He started to pace back and forth.

"No Kaliff! Another man who speaks no Arabic? What's going on?" Nobody in the room had answers for him.

"Here comes the Prophet!" Someone shouted and everyone turned to the other TV set, while somebody raised the volume.

An old version of the former bin Laden appeared in a studio setting. His hair and beard were nearly totally white. His dark eyes were deep-set and dull. He began reading from a sheet in his right hand without the use of glasses.

"Allah be praised. Today is a glorious day for the State of Islam. Today Allah has eliminated two of our greatest enemies, the presidents of the United States and Israel.

They are now in the presence of Satan, where they belong. Hundreds of thousands of infidels had a taste of hell while the City of Houston burned and the town of Lake Charles turned into a fireball.

But we want the whole world to know that we are not a group of murdering fanatics! No, we offer the teachings and the blessings of Islam to everyone who wants to convert and embrace the writings of Mohammed in our Quran.

As you have learned today, we can reach every corner of the world, and we are now in control, with the help of Allah, of the entire universe.

We have two immediate demands: First, all Jews must immediately leave Palestine, now known as Israel, and all detainees must be released from that devil's island Guantanamo.

If these demands are not met, other big cities in England and America will feel the same wrath of Allah as those cities in Texas and Louisiana.

Let us now give thanks and praise to the Benefactor of us all, Allah.

Brothers, Salaam."

His face disappeared from the screen and a hush came over the group.

"He must have pre-recorded it," The Emir offered. "He must not be aware that the whole thing fizzled out." He gathered his robes around him and got up. "I must go. This disgrace will require a lot of explaining." He stood up and turned toward the door, but a bullet shattered his glasses and his brains splattered on the carpet, along with back of his skull.

"Is there anyone else who feels he should leave in a hurry?" Ahmed slowly pointed the pistol at everyone in the room.

Nobody moved.

• • •

Herbert Hoover Building, Washington, D.C.

The FBI Director, Lester Jarvis, was checking off the events on his list as the reports came in, one after the other. "We got them all, it looks like." He was talking to his assistant, who kept handing him faxes.

"A couple of prime catches. I'm sure Dagan is going to want the two Filipinos that were caught in Louisiana, because they mustered on that Dutch freighter all the way back in Lebanon. They're gonna want to pump them for all the details of the Hezbollah operation in Beirut. I guess we can work that out. Check with Mossad and the CIA."

After scanning through another few pages, he commented, "They're gonna have a ball with this guy Kaliff. They're going to brag about the capture and all the info they've obtained, while washing the egg off their faces, for letting the guy operate a terrorist operation right under their noses and with their approval, for years on end." He snickered. "It was like having a direct line from Guantanamo to Beirut. How convenient!"

"Call from Mr. Taylor." The overhead speaker sounded off.

"I'll take it here." He pushed the blinking button. "Jarvis here."

"Hey Lester . . ."

"Great job, Jeb. I'm going through the reports right now . . ."

"That's not why I'm calling."

"Oh?"

"The president is furious! He . . ."

"Because we saved his life?"

"No because he feels like we used him for bait and unnecessarily exposed him to danger, just to stroke our own egos."

"In other words, he doesn't know what was going on and how much we've accomplished."

"He has no clue, other than that we knew in advance that he was going to be the target of an assassination attempt and that we let him go through with it, without his knowledge or consent."

"Jeez, doesn't he pay his Secret Service enough? Isn't it their job to protect him?"

"The Secret Service told him they weren't aware of the scope of the operation, and Napolitano of the Homeland Security joined him in his protests."

"Oh, well. Can we get someone in that White House to prepare a note of thanks?"

"You're kidding, and now they want to know all about Osama's speech and what is going on in Texas. Is Houston really burning? Their mayor has already called Homeland, and they started evacuation procedures."

"Oh, my God. What has the media done so far?"

"CNN has helicopters in the sky over Galveston and Lake Charles, but they find nothing to report, so all they're doing is scaring the hell out of the viewers."

"I better switch channels and catch up a little."

"But Lester, the reason why I called: Do you want to handle the briefing of the president tomorrow morning?"

"On Sunday? Not on my life. Besides that, you're the overall organizer of this multi-pronged operation, and you can tell them how successful every phase of the sting was."

"Sure! Except a body flying off a roof in the middle of a presidential address. How do you expect me to explain that? Do you know yet what happened? Who threw him over the wall and who shot him?"

"I haven't gone through all of the reports yet, but I'm not sure that anyone reported the event."

"In other words, things are still happening right under our noses without us having a single clue."

"It's a rough business, Jeb."

"Oh, don't give me that! I need real answers before I meet up with those clowns. They'll do anything to discredit us, I'm sure."

"Jeb, do just what Bongers did. He said that the president's Chief of Staff was well aware of what was going on and . . ."

"Kopelosi?"

"Yes, and then let him squirm his way out of the predicament. Every denial on his part will come across as a lie, and the media will eat him alive."

"Could be fun."

49

QUEENSBOROUGH CEMETERY.

Omar was bewildered, to say the least. The phone calls from Beirut shattered his confidence, and when Osama bin Laden's message was played back again and again on American TV, he made up his mind.

"Brother, I don't know and you don't know what went wrong, but one thing is for sure, everything has become a disaster. I'm not even going to try to talk to Canarsie or Chicago, because if they haven't been raided yet, I'm sure they'll be captured or killed within a few hours.

We need to get the hell out of here. I don't know what you plan to do, but I'm going to retire to the Caribbean. I have some money saved, and I know that our lives are not worth two cents, here or back home." He pointed to the garage. "You can have the Cadillac. I'll take the old Lincoln and I suggest that we get as far away from this place as possible before . . ."

"You will let me have the Cadillac? How nice! Is it maybe, because it may show up on some surveillance tapes when we were planting the bomb and they'll be looking for it? Well, brother Omar, it was very generous of you, but I'll take the Lincoln. You can drive the Caddy."

"Okay, okay! I wasn't thinking. I'll drive off after dark. I'm going to cut off my hair and my beard. What are you going to do? The yacht is supposed to be off the Jersey Shore in three days. Do you think you'll try that route? Or . . . "

"You think that after this disaster any yacht would be coming for us? You're crazy! All they want from us now is to kill ourselves, or otherwise they'll do it for us. I have a brother in Corpus Christi, and he'll put me up, I'm sure. I can work in his store, or I can slip back to the Middle East and . . ."

"You really think that you'd be safe there? Where would you hide?"

"I have two wives in Cairo. They'll be glad to see me."

"Good luck. I'm gonna shave and change clothes. Do what you want." Omar retreated to the bathroom, while his partner Ruban stared at the TV image of Osama bin Laden for the fifth time. "Allah help us," he finally sighed and lit a hash pipe.

Cutting off all his hair and beard was not as easy as Omar had anticipated. In a moment of sentimentality, he took a leather money pouch and stuffed his black curls in it for future reference. He didn't really know what he'd do with it. All he knew was that he couldn't part with it. Yousef had left some razors, and after an hour, Omar reappeared totally bald and clean shaven. He looked so different that Ruban thought for a moment that a stranger had walked into the room, and he whipped out his gun, but started laughing instead.

"That good? Do I look that different?" Omar didn't quite see the humor. "Would anyone recognize me?"

"Do you have a passport with your new image? How will you get on a plane or a boat?"

The hash was having an effect on the Arab, and he laughed uproariously.

Omar didn't share his sense of humor and turned to get dressed. "It'll be dark in two hours. You better do something!"

"I'm staying till after midnight. I'll be nice and sober by then."

"Suit yourself."

Dressed like a tourist, but with a hat that was too small for his round head, Omar reappeared with a small suitcase in his hand, "Allah be with you, brother." and headed toward the garage.

"Don't take the Lincoln." Ruban slurred.

"Well, I am. Rest in peace!" Omar twisted around and fired once. Blood spouted out of Ruban's face.

• • •

The florist was most helpful.

"Yeah, he was an Arab of sorts. He told me what he wanted and it was strange, 'cause he didn't want real flowers. 'Wilt too fast in this heat.' Made me wonder how long he was gonna keep it. Most people put them in the church or the grave on the same day, but . . ."

"What did he drive?"

"A white Cadillac. Brand new I guess. It . . ."

"Did he give an address for a receipt or say where..."

"No, but when I put the wreath in his trunk, I noticed it had Jersey plates and the first three letters were H E H and those are my wife's initials. Ain't that funny?"

"Did you notice which way he was going?"

"Yeah, he turned around toward the cemetery . . ."

"Thank you very much." The two FBI men got back in their car, and while one of them drove, the other called the Motor Vehicle Computer, which taught them little, except that the car belonged to a University professor in East Orange.

"We better have Jersey jump on it. I'm gonna drive to that cemetery. I don't know what I'm looking for or what I hope to find, but as long as we're this close, we might as well take a peek."

He passed the construction entrance, but decided to back up and enter the graveyard from that angle. Fifteen miles an hour seemed slow, but the road was barely a path, so that speed made sense. Within the first twenty seconds on the gravel surface, a maroon Lincoln headed toward them, and the agent behind the wheel started to pull to his right in order to let the car pass on his left. Instead, the big luxury car in front of him came to an abrupt stop and turned 90 degrees. He stepped on the gas and shot in between a row of crosses, laying rubber, spraying dirt and sod in its wake.

"What the hell?" The G-man yelled as he mashed down the gas pedal and chased after the disappearing car. "What do you suppose possesses him?" He yelled at his partner, who rolled down his window and prepared to fire at the speeding Lincoln.

Omar panicked when he saw the plain white Ford coming at him. "Cops!" Flashed through his mind and he made a run for it. He didn't get far. Twice he was at a dead end and when the Feds shot out his rear tire, he spun into a mausoleum that collapsed on top of him, while an old rusted crucifix smashed through his windshield into his left eye. He was dead instantly.

After the spooks, the white-coated investigators, were finished fingerprinting and photographing in the old maintenance building with a white Caddy and a dying terrorist, the agent in charge called Andy Andrews at home. "Do you know what's most peculiar about this whole thing?"

"Go ahead."

"The bag with dollars and Euros was smaller than his bag of hair."

"They have a weird sense of values, I guess."

50

CALDWELL, N.J., BONGERS RESIDENCE. SATURDAY NIGHT.

After happily stuffing themselves with baby-back ribs, the Bongers family relaxed. Two boys borrowed the old station wagon, because there were some heavy dates on the horizon, and the other one retreated to his room to study. Study video games, Bruce assumed.

They didn't have many quiet nights together and Bruce even thought back to the days, when times like that deserved a good Havana cigar and a brandy. Now it was just a scotch on the rocks, some Gouda cheese and a good TV show. He had not checked his messages and had no intention to do so that evening. He and his wife would watch *A Bridge Too Far,* a movie that he had seen ten times before, but the scenery of Holland and the memories of his father being involved in that action, were enough reasons to see it again. In '44 his dad had joined the American Forces in southern Holland as an interpreter at age 17 and ended up making the U.S. Army a career.

By nine o'clock, halfway through the movie, his cell phone rang, and the display told him it was Bruno. Even though he had made up his mind he wouldn't talk to anybody that night, he made an exception for his number-one assistant.

"Yes, my man. What's happening?"
"Have you seen the TV since we left the office?"
"No, why? The restaurant had no TV, thank God, and at home we turned on a movie on TCM. What happened?"
"Finish the movie and then watch the news. Osama bin Laden recorded a victory speech. Catch it!"
"I will, thanks."
"What was that?" His wife Helen wanted to know.
"After the film, we're going to watch bin Laden's victory speech."
"The what?"
"Later, Honey, later. Here comes the good part."

Secaucus FBI Headquarters, Sunday noon.

Between the messages left at his home, his cell and the office, he had to decide whom to call first.

His boss in D.C. seemed like a logical choice. He wasn't in, but he answered his cell phone immediately. "Well, Bruce, did you finally get some sleep?"

"You said it, finally. The night before was a doozy, but a good one. What's urgent today?"

"Well, did you read the papers and watch the news?"
"Both."
"The president is furious!"
"Did Netanyahu forget to thank him?"
"That's not funny. He's mad because he was really and totally in the dark about the whole affair."
"He wouldn't have shown up."
"That's true."
"Does he have any idea what a tremendous dent we put into the Taliban, al-Qaeda, Hezbollah and Hamas operations?"
"He probably doesn't realize that yet. They're threatening to chop some heads?"
"For what, Lester? For what? For everyone doing an outstanding job?"

"Are you going to write a report, detailing everything?"

"If I can keep my name out of it."

"By the way, have you heard what their targets were out west?"

"Not exactly. Bin Laden talked about half of Houston being on fire? With what?"

"With millions gallons of liquid LPG gas."

"Whoa! Millions of gallons? How big are those tankers?"

"Big enough to carry a million gallons or more, that's for sure. A rocket into the hull of that ship would throw a ball of liquid fire thousands of feet into the air and engulf an area of many square miles."

"Great Scott! And these boats just lie there unprotected?"

"Isn't that unbelievable? Nobody ever thought of them as a danger to the public."

"But the Muslims did."

"Isn't that terrible? Just like the Twin Towers, it seems their engineers are a step ahead of us at all times."

"And we keep educating them at our colleges? Are we, as a nation, really that stupid?"

"Seems that way."

"We need to change that slogan, *'God bless America'* to *'God help America'*."

"By the way, did you hear what your boy Yousef was carrying as an ID?"

"No, I haven't caught up on all my messages yet."

"He had an Israeli ID."

"He did? Hahaha!" Bruce laughed uproariously. "He did? That is funny. That is really funny."

"What's so funny about that?"

"The Israelis always rib us about our gaps in security and the lack of communication between the agencies. And here is a definite sign that Hezbollah can directly invade their security system and even cut ID passes at will. That is funny. Dagan is gonna blow his cork. That's funny. Wait till I meet him." He again laughed out loud. "That reminds me. He'll be there at eight at Paramus. You'll join us, right?"

"I'll see if I can get away." Jarvis didn't sound too convincing.

"Do like me. Work on Sunday, clear your desk and sneak out on Monday to play golf."

"Good thinking."

Bongers went through the stack of message slips and shoved some aside, turned some of them over and finally shuffled four of them, trying to decide which to return first.

Before he even dialed the first number, the intercom buzzed. "Diane Sawyer on line three."

"Diane Sawyer? Well, she's about the only reporter I will talk to." He pushed the blinking button. "Miss Sawyer? I miss you!"

"Sir?"

"I used to catch you in the morning when you worked with Charley on Good Morning America, but I haven't seen you in years."

"Don't you watch the evening news?"

"Miss Sawyer . . ."

"Call me Diane."

"Okay, Diane. At that hour of the day, I'm still working, or at best I'm stuck in traffic on the way home. What gives me the honor of this call?"

"I'm calling you on Sunday, because you don't return calls on Saturday, but anyway, I want to do an interview with you . . ."

"With me? I'm flattered. About what?"

"About the events at the Twin Towers yesterday . . ."

"You're calling the wrong office. Andy Andrews is in charge of the New York office and . . ."

"I know that, but your name keeps popping up when I ask questions about . . ."

"Are you recording this conversation?"

"Well . . . uh, yes."

"So am I, so let's terminate this altogether. Nice of you to call." He hung up.

Bruce walked out to the break room, which was deserted, since there was only a skeleton staff on duty on Sunday. He hadn't even finished pouring his coffee when the receptionist walked in. "It's Barbara Walters on the phone. She apologized and said that they were not recording their conversations anymore and she does want to talk to you."

"Now it's Walters? Okay. I'll pick it up in my office. Which line?"

Coffee in hand, Bruce pushed the button again. "Ms. Walters?"

"Barbara."

"Okay, Barbara. Let's get this straight. I don't think you're a good reporter, and because of the network policies, concerning truth in reporting, I don't trust any of you, so I won't come in for an interview. Okay?"

"You sound bitter."

"I'm not bitter as long as I don't deal with the media, government or elected officials. So how can I help?"

"We would like more, or maybe all, of the details about yesterday's successful prevention of an assassination attempt and complete interruption of bin Laden's attack on America."

"Call Mr. Kopolosi or Koloposi, or whatever his name is. He knows everything."

"He does?"

"Oh, yes. He convinced me last week. So he may be your prime source."

"I would still like to set up a taped interview with you in our studios. You seem to have been a center figure in the whole operation..."

"Ms Walters, lil' ol' me? I'm just in charge of the New Jersey office I'm just one of the underpaid peons. Besides, you're not honest with your audience."

"What do you mean, I'm not honest?"

"You don't report the whole truth, just your warped interpretation."

"I resent that, give me a for instance."

"Right after the first Gulf War, you interviewed Colonel and

Cindy Acree about his capture and torture by Saddam Husain . . ."

"I did, so . . ."

"She had written a book, 'The Gulf Between Us' about her husband's capture and her torment by the media. You never mentioned her plight with you inconsiderate bums, who created a hell on earth for her here in America. She was kept a prisoner in her own home by all the media trucks that blocked her street. You left three hours of taping on the cutting room floor and never gave your viewers the truth about her book. No, you shamelessly kept endorsing some silly book about a sad father, whose boy joined the service. Totally unrelated to your subject at hand, which was; 'torture by Saddam and the American media.' And then you endorsed that 'Quisling' Jane Fonda. You ought to be ashamed of yourself." He hung up and laughed out loud. He grabbed his jacket and stopped by the front desk. "I've had enough laughs for one day, Marci, I'll see you Tuesday."

She shook her head and sighed, "What a guy!"

EPILOGUE

ARCOLA COUNTRY CLUB, PARAMUS, NEW JERSEY

Bruce Bongers and his wife Helen pulled up to the clubhouse and found Bruno Garcia waiting for them.

"We're the first ones here. I reserved four carts and scheduled tee-offs for eight of us. That should do it, right?"

"Should as of last count. I don't know how many Dagan is bringing, and Jarvis may show up alone, not at all or with a lot of company."

"We're plenty early, so let's grab some coffee." Bruno needed to get a bit of a hangover under control. Last night's celebration had been a doozy.

They were barely seated when Meir Dagan walked in with quite an entourage, including Lavana. Bruno's eyes nearly popped. She wore short yellow shorts that accentuated her long tan legs, white sneakers and a loose fitting white T-shirt, displaying a blue Star of David.

The Mossad chief did the introductions and when he introduced "Lani", Bruno repeated, "Lonnie?"

"No, "Lani", pronounced "Lahni", I guess, one of our most efficient agents."

"Wow! Most efficient agent?" Bruno couldn't take his eyes of her. "Can I go on some of our overseas assignments, Mr. Bongers?"

"Not with that attitude." The whole group laughed out loud.

Before they were settled around two tables, Lester Jarvis walked in with his wife.

"That makes a total of ten," Bruno observed. "Any more coming?" He looked around the group.

"Not that we know of." Was the general response.

"Either I arrange for another Tee-time, or Lonnie, would you rather see the beautiful green countryside of Northern New Jersey?"

"Well . . ." She fluttered her eyes ever so attractively, as if she were shy. "I don't care that much for golf."

"Okay, me neither. No additional Tee-times needed." Garcia grinned from ear to ear.

Dagan interrupted, "Bruce, you won't believe what a pleasure it is to be on a green golf course, with green surroundings, compared to our ever brown desert land."

"Well, Meir, I'm glad we could arrange all that for you. As a matter of fact, we can even bring on some green beer."

"Hoorah for America! What's our T-time?"

"You have fifteen minutes. Do any of you have to rent equipment?"

"What do think? That we go on terrorists' missions with our golf clubs in tow? Where do we go?"

4:30 PM. Bongers' back yard.

The four sons of the FBI couple had a barbeque grill going, plenty of beer on ice, and a complete bar set up in the lanai. Lounge chairs were lined up all around the pool, with dozens of towels and bathrobes spread among them.

About half of the guests took advantage of a quick dip, because the temperature on the golf course had hovered around 90 degrees all day.

The mood was highly spirited, and it was hard to believe in that relaxed atmosphere, that two days ago, these same people had diverted an international crisis and a national catastrophe.

Bruno took Bongers aside for a moment. "Do you know what Lonnie's job was when she was in the Army?"
"No telling."
"A tank commander!"
"Somehow, I wouldn't doubt it."

The End

THE FOLLOWING ARE SOME EXCERPTS FROM FRITS FORRER'S OTHER BOOKS

Excerpt from:

Five Years Under The Swastika

Pappa has preceded him down and is warming milk on the electric stove. Mama and Jopie file into the kitchen too and Mama begins again: "You should..."

"HUSH!" Pappa interrupts softly, but sternly. Mamma gets cups down from the cupboard and puts cocoa mix in them, waiting for the milk to get warm.

"Why Pappa? Why? What have they done? And that little girl, what's her name? The granddaughter? They hurt her Pappa! Why Pappy, why? What did SHE do?"

Pappa stirs the chocolate milk. "Come sit at the table."

Frits turns, Joop and Mama are deadly quiet.

"Drink your cocoa! Watch it, it's hot. Hold it.... let me add some cold... here you go. Stir it! Okay, okay."

"Why Pappa, why? I know what you're gonna say: They're JEWISH right? But what did they do? They're not rich Jews that ruin the world and all that garbage. They're poor working people. He's been working for the County-Water-Department for as long as we've known him. He goes to work on his bike at four in the morning, every morning, I know Pappa, he's not rich, I know! Why then Pappa, why? They'll never come back, I know it. They're gonna kill'em!"

Tears are running down his cheeks, Mama is not doing much better and Jopie is staring in his chocolate milk as if there's something fascinating in it.

Mama hands Frits a handkerchief: "Here, dry your tears. Drink your cocoa."

"There's nothing I can say, Frits… nothing! Goddamnit!"

Pappa's last word shoots out with such vengeance that all three of them look up at him, startled.

"Sit down, Herman, drink your cocoa too!"

She's worried that his ulcer will flare up. "Why don't we all drink up-up-up and go to bed. It's too cold in here. Take your cocoa if it's too hot and let's go. Come boys."

Frits is still crying uncontrollably.

"Come in bed with us."

For the first time in years, he's in bed between his father and his mother, his skinny body shaking with the sobs that won't stop.

Finally, with his head against his father's chest, he falls asleep, blissfully.

The WOHLSTEINS were the first.

Excerpt from:

Smack Between The Eyes

"Now comes the hard part!" Frank walked away from Joey, who looked like a businessman on his way home. Nice suit, white shirt and a very conservative tie. His brown briefcase and a laptop bag swung over his shoulder completed his disguise.

Several detectives, including a cleaning lady, were posted near the arrival spot and two were at the end of the ramp, in case anyone wanted to escape from the rear door.

The large bus slowly rolled to a stop. The door opened and Frank stepped up to give the folks a hand, exiting the bus. Some refused his hand, some gratefully grabbed it.

Frank looked at each face as they unloaded and tried to match it with the pictures he had received on the fax and the e-mail.

The only one who bore the least bit of resemblance was an elegant gentleman in a light suit, blue shirt and white tie. His white fedora and his goatee gave him the look of a Caribbean planter.

After the last passenger descended, Frank boarded the bus, scanned it quickly and jumped off.

"Joey! That's the one! The guy with the white hat!" He mouthed it, rather than holler it, but Joey got the message. He ran after the disappearing figure in the crowd. Frank followed. Luck was with them. The elegant planter stopped to look around.

"Probably looking for Nita." Frank thought.

The man reached into his coat pocket and Frank as well as Joey pulled out there guns. The man's hand came out with a cell phone that he flipped open in order to dial, so he never saw the two officers rushing toward him until he heard: "Hands up! You're under arrest!"

His reaction was swift. With his left hand, he threw the cell phone at Frank and with his right hand he reached in his pocket and fired a shot at Joey, hitting him in the hip.

Frank ducked and the phone hit him in his bus driver's hat. In that very second, Hotta Hotta fired off one more shot, turned and disappeared in the crowd.

PANDEMONIUM!

People falling to the floor, officers shouting orders, women screaming and Frank jumping over bodies, trying to get to the fleeing man. An off-duty policeman tackled Frank, thinking he was the culprit and the gunman escaped.

All the police ended up with was a white hat and a cell phone.

Frank was sooooooo mad, he could have spit bullets.

ISBN 0-9714490-6-6

Excerpt from:

The Fun Of Flying

Pieter drove around, looking for a quiet spot and settled for a corner lot, surrounded by trees. From the debris on the lot, they built a campfire and concentrated on the task of opening up their beer bottles without the benefit of a bottle opener. That was an interesting challenge!

Two guys would take a bottle each, hook the 'crown-caps' together and pulled till one of them came off, while the other guy got sprayed with beer. Harm was soaked in no time flat and took off his beautiful jacket and threw it someplace. Soon, his shirt was soaked as well and inasmuch as he couldn't handle the buttons in his inebriate state, he tore the shirt to threads.

Meanwhile, some 'serious' singing was being done by the campfire and everybody was in 'excellent' voice that night.

Somewhere during the evening, it was decided that throwing beer bottles all over the place was not very civilized, so they improved the situation by organizing a 'trapshoot'! One guy would throw his bottle in the air, while others threw theirs after it, trying to hit it in mid-air.

Their 'hit' averages stunk, but it felt like a refined kinda way to discard the empties.

Just as the averages were improving by the light of a bigger and improved campfire, sirens started screaming in their direction and soon two police cars ran onto the sidewalk, spitting out four bulky policemen.

"Hands up over your heads!" They meant business!

The boys didn't.

"So nice of you to come! Find a seat and we'll see if we can find you a beer."

"Shut up and raise those hands!"

"In our country, we are more polite than that!"

"We don't give a shit about your country! UP! Up! Now! Put your hands on top of the cars! Now!"

"That won't be necessary, Mr. Policeman. We believe that they're your cars."

"Shut up, I said. Put those hands on the cars!" They were getting mad and rough and started pushing.

"After you, sir!"

"Like hell! Up! Up!"

"Officer, all we were doing was singing a few songs. Is that so bad?"

"You're all under arrest for 'Disturbance of the peace'"

"Officers, if you ever came to visit in our country, we would treat you a lot nicer, I'm sure."

Meanwhile the cops felt them down, but other than 'hiccups' they had nothing on them.

"Get in the cars!"

"After you, sir. After you!"

"Negative. Get the hell in!"

On the way to the station they asked the cops if they had any special requests and they would gladly perform them for 'em.

The total ride took only five minutes and they were put in a big cage with just one more occupant; a dead-down drunk who stared at them with wide eyes and a dumb look on his face. He had probably never seen a spectacle like that before in his entire life.

Seven guys, profusely thanking the cops for the ride and offering to pay the cab fare.

Once left alone, the songs started up again and at the stroke of midnight, they stood at attention and sang the American and Dutch National Anthems.

The policeman on duty thought it was very funny and kept supplying them with ice water. Nice touch.

ISBN 0-9714490-3-1

Excerpt from:

Tampa Justice
No Money, No Justice.

Your Honor, I was not informed of all the things that are involved in probation and I want to change my plea to Not Guilty, so I can have a trial and that will clear me for sure."

Well 'Fisheyes' objected vehemently. He had his 'conviction' and he was not about to take a chance on losing it.

"Mr. Fernon?"

"Your Honor, I do not want to represent Mr. Forrer in a trial, because I told Mr. Forrer that I don't do criminal work."

"Then why the hell did you take my case?"

"Mr. Forrer, you will maintain order!"

"Yeah, but Judge, I hired him to...."

"Mr. Fernon, raise your right hand. Is the testimony you're about to give, the truth, the whole truth and nothing but the truth, so help you God?"

"I do."

"Go ahead Mr. Fernon, state your case."

"Your Honor, I told Mr. Forrer, I don't do criminal work and I can not represent him in a trial."

THAT LYING BASTARD! I presented him with two CRIMINAL summonses and he took my thousand dollars to represent me.

"Very well, the motion to change plea is denied and we'll schedule a restitution hearing. Case dismissed."

The bastards! Just like that, in a matter of seconds I'm stuck with a verdict and there's not a damn thing I can do about it. I'm on a five year probation and I'm stuck with it.

To make matters worse, I received a notice from the Department of Professional Regulation that because of my "Nolo Contendere" plea, my Contractors License was revoked.

Apparently, when someone pleads "No Contest" in a construction case, it is assumed by the Department that the person is Guilty and it calls for an automatic revocation.

In other words: I was put out of business.

ISBN 0-9714490-5-8

Excerpt from:

To Judge Or Not To Judge

Pandemonium

J.F.K.
1:30 PM

Three people down! Two shot and one knocked unconscious. Two on the outside of the X-Ray check-in, one on the inside. For a minute or two there was so much confusion, that undercover security police nearly tangled with undercover FBI agents. The problem was everyone was incognito. Nobody was in uniform, not even a jacket with FBI on it or an I.D. card around their necks or pinned to their chests. Bongers' loud voice finally restored order and had the law enforcement officers holster their pistols again without any more friendly casualties.

Peter was the only one so far and Bruce wanted to make sure it stayed that way. It took a little while to convince the locals that Peter was NOT with the FBI and NOT a suspect, but he DID work with them and shouldn't have been shot in the first place. Ambulances roared up to the entrance, EMS personnel raced in with stretchers, I.V. bottles and medicine bags. City police officers tried to take control, than backed off and offered help and cooperation and ten minutes later, all there was left to do was clean the blood off the floors and get the passenger lines moving again.

The Feds had cuffed the captives and moved them into the Rembrandt room temporarily, much to the frustration of the KLM personnel, who had to transfer their cherished first class customers to other, less luxurious quarters. Bruce had everything under control again except; *what to do with the two terrorists?* If the CIA snatched them from his possession, which was certainly within their rights, he might be limited in his access to them. If the New York City police took over, defense lawyers would immediately be informed according to the law and of course, they would tell their clients to zip their mouths.

He called his New York counterpart and got some good advice. The City police would just hold them in *protective* custody in their maximum security prison at Rikers Island and that way, the FBI and CIA could interrogate them while awaiting transportation to Guantanamo Bay where all the Taliban and al-Qaida prisoners were being held. Federal laws provided them with that loophole and Bongers would have at least a few days to put their noses to the grindstone and find out what that whole plot was all about.

A police paddy wagon was provided and while the city cops transported the culprits, Bruce had a chance to track his shooting victims, Peter and Sahira, to the Queens Hospital where emergency surgery was scheduled to take place any minute.

In Washington, Travis washed his hands of the transactions, 'cause he would have to inform the CIA immediately and Bongers had begged him for patience.

"I gotta have some time with them, Lester. If the CIA big shots get involved, the Arabs may clam up altogether and I need to find out what this is all about. I'll get it out of them. I know these clowns, I've worked in the Middle East long enough to know how to deal with them. I'll play one against the other. Just buy me some time

Lester. Stall them by saying ; *'There is an operation in progress, details will be released as soon as they become available.'"*

"Okay, Bruce. I have to trust you on that, but keep me posted immediately, okay?"

"Will do. Thanks."

The New Jersey Bureau Chief knew he was walking a thin line, but he had seen it too often, that when too many different agencies or individuals get involved, the suspects tend to draw into a shell and that wouldn't really help anybody.

"Bruno," he asked his sidekick, "get me a ride to Queens Hospital and hold it for a trip to Rikers Island. Preferably a local cop who knows the territory. Thanks."

He reached for the coffee pot that was ready to serve some first class customers and filled a tall mug. "Good God, I'm hungry. Forgot to eat. Well, it'll have to wait a little longer." He finished the hot tasty liquid. "Good stuff. Must be Dutch."

Rikers Island was originally purchased by the Rykers family in 1683. It's located in the East River between the Bronx and Queens and had many different uses over the years. Most memorable was the training of African-American soldiers during the civil war and the conversion to a prison in the 1930's. The facility houses over 15,000 inmates and is now connected to Queens by a bridge. With the cooperation of the Warden, Bongers should be able to keep his culprits secluded and hidden from the press and over-ambitious lawyers.

"So far, so good!" He said to himself as he climbed into a patrol car for the trip to Queens Hospitals and his innocent victims. "Let's hope they're alright."

ISBN 0-9714490-7-4

Excerpt from:

The Golden Pig
(El Cochino de Oro)

The sharpshooters unpacked their rifles, mounted their scopes and loaded the magazines. One shot with a Remington 30 odd 06 and the other had an H&H 222. Bongers admired the weapons and after putting on the safety, the shooter handed him the H&H and Bruce balanced the weapon in his hand as if he were guessing the weight, He shouldered it, pointing out the window and said: "Nice weapon, very light."

"Love it. Very flat trajectory. I bag groundhogs at three hundred yards.'

"Really? That's great." He handed back the rifle. Ten more minutes and they should be there. The silver snake in the distance grew larger by the minute and soon became a brownish band of muddy water.

"Target to our right at one o'clock." the pilot announced on the intercom, turning about ten degrees. He was looking directly at the mansion, but his passengers couldn't see it from the passenger compartment. Bongers undid his safety belt and got up in order to look over the pilot's shoulder. The captain in the left seat pointed straight ahead with his left hand while keeping his right on the joystick.

"Got it" He stared at the beautiful layout of an antebellum plantation with a massive lawn in front of the two-story colonial. "The plane's moving!" he shouted suddenly and indeed, although it was barely as big as a flea from this far out, they could detect movement. The yellow and black flea was drifting away from the dock.

"Get'em," Bongers ordered.

"Sir, please sit down and buckle in." The pilot spoke without looking up, both hands busy on his throttle and his control stick.

"Right." But he didn't budge. "They're gonna take off down river." He turned around and hollered: "Get ready. Secure that window. Hand me the hailer." That last order was directed to the co-pilot who handed him a mike that was connected to a bullhorn. The chopper nosed down and the throttle had the engine screaming. Their speed went up by forty knots.

Below and ahead, the yellow and black bug had turned with the bend of the river and after it passed two tugs with multiple barges in front of them, its wake became longer and wider, leaving two silver streaks in the water behind it.

"Get next to them." Bongers remained upright, holding on for dear life.

At that point the chopper was doing at least one hundred and thirty knots, while the little seaplane was struggling to pick up a take-off speed of sixty, so they closed fast. The helicopter pilot had to bank steeply to the left in order to end up in the same direction of the seaplane and Bongers was thrown into the side of the craft.

"Told you to buckle." The pilot said calmly as the G-man struggled to get back up. It didn't take long. "Fly alongside him, same speed."

The copter lurched back, its nose pitching up fast, but this time Bongers held on. Their speed bled off from 140 to 70 in no time, but Bruce lost sight of the plane. Thank God, the pilot didn't because all of a sudden, the little seaplane and the helicopter were flying formation, just fifty feet apart.

The man in the little bug wasn't aware of anything except his rate of climb and his speed. He was doing a good job. The plane was climbing at 400 feet a minute and his speed was slowly creeping up to ninety. Then, all of a sudden, he had the shock of his life. Over the noise of his engine, he could hear the drone of another motor, much bigger and louder than his. He looked to his left and there was a copter, fifty feet back and a loudspeaker bellowed: "Throttle back and land. This is the FBI."

His reaction was instinctive. In a second, he turned the plane on its right wing, dove to the ground and gave it full throttle. It was a case of desperation of the worst kind. There was no way he could outrun a helicopter that size, but his nerves were shot by the events of the last twenty four hours. He realized that his maneuver didn't work very well. Within minutes the helicopter was back in position off his left wing. By now, he was skimming the sea grass and flying between the cypress trees. He figured if he could stay on this heading and at this altitude, he'd be over the swamps of Texas and before long he'd be over the Gulf of Mexico, where he would have an advantage. He'd have more fuel than the chopper and they would have to land somewhere and he could possibly make Mexico without refueling. He concentrated on staying as low as he dared and he even throttled back a little in order to conserve gas. He was cruising at 110 and that was not bad. The annoying load speaker came on again: "Throttle back and land or we'll shoot you down."

Henry was gaining more confidence. He said to his wife, who was crying: "Shoot me down with what? They don't have rockets or a Gatlin gun. Who are they kidding? Mow me down with a pea-shooter?"

At that same moment, his side window shattered. "What the hell was that?"

Inside the copter, the window of the passenger compartment was lowered and two rifles were sticking out in the slipstream.

"Can you hit the gas tank or the engine?" Bongers was still very much in control, but also buckled in. Flying formation on the left of the plane gave him a front row view. Both guns fired. Both gunners aimed again. "Go.!"

This time, fuel streamed from the left wing and the cockpit disappeared in a fog of vapor. Henry banked sharp right, but he didn't have a chance of losing the chopper. It was nearly too easy. When the plane leveled without any attempt to slow down or land, the Jersey director ordered: "Take him out."

The shooters aimed for his head, but the buffeting of the chopper as well as the aircraft made them miss, still the 30-06 hit Robinson in the left shoulder and he inadvertently pulled on the stick with his right hand and the plane went straight up.

"Watch it!" Bruce hollered, because for a moment it seemed that the seaplane would land on top of the helicopter. The captain banked sharply and threw the coal to the engine and in seconds they were at three hundred feet, making a steep right turn and looking down on a spectacular sight. The seaplane had been yanked up so steeply, that it stalled and slid back momentarily, then it nosed over and glided down toward the swamp below it as if it were going to dive into the murky waters. The plane behaved as if someone was still at the controls, but Henry's body was slumped backwards and against the door, so the plane handled itself and just before hitting the water and sea grass, it nosed up again while the floats hit the surface and the plane glided along.

Up in the helicopter, they wondered if Mrs. Robinson was an accomplished pilot, but Bongers wasn't taking any chances. "Hit the pontoons. Shatter them if you can." Below them the throttle was still wide open and it looked as if it could take off again. Four shots apiece rang out and the floats started to settle a little deeper in the water, while the gas from the left wing still made for an impressive spray. From up above they watched a scene, reminiscent of a movie. With the motor running full blast, the plane sank deeper into the water until the propeller hit and at first just churned, but then seemed to be grabbed by a magic hand that pulled it under water and the plane dove, rolled on it's back, went under momentarily and floated back to the surface, upside down, the floats sticking up out of the water.

ISBN 0-9714490-8-2

Excerpt from:

Brothers, FOREVER!

His chance came the following day. They were introduced to remote-control explosives. Each one learned to attach a bomb to a tree or a car, run for safety and detonate the device by pushing a button on the remote-control.

In a flash, Yousef switched controls with Amwar and watched as the older man ran downfield and tied his bomb to the rear wheel of an old truck and Yousef quickly pressed the button. Nobody noticed his thumb on the control, but everyone did see the Egyptian explode into a dozen fragments of human flesh. Screams of agony roared from a dozen mouths as they ran toward the victim, and Yousef ran right with them, dropping the remote in the dirt.

All bombs were inspected and reset, making sure there would not be any more accidental deaths. Training was suspended for the rest of the day and a proper funeral was arranged for the bits and pieces that had once been the Ugly Egyptian.

In bed, the young undercover man tried to feel remorse or any other emotion about the fact that he had killed a human being, but all he felt was satisfaction that he had done it so cleverly and aroused no suspicion. Everyone felt that it was the grey bearded Egyptian's own fault or maybe faulty equipment.

Joe slept like a baby. No nightmares.

ISBN 0-9714490-9-0

Excerpt from

The Curse Of The Black Mamba

For a moment she considered putting the diamonds back in the safe, "What could be a safer place?" but she quickly changed her mind. Slowly she walked out of the den, through the spacious living room and into her 'green room'. Burying them with the orchids seemed like a good idea at first, but when she spotted the Water Buffalo on her workbench, she hesitated. The trophy was nearly ready for mounting. It was the biggest buffalo her son Eric had ever bagged and she had single-handedly cleaned it, prepped it and all she had to do was mount it. She had become an expert taxidermist over the years.

"Brilliant!"

Quickly, she unscrewed the wooden back plate and it immediately exposed the hollow of the animal's head and the unusual horns. In seconds, the treasures disappeared into that vacuum and just as she was about to screw the plate back on, a vicious thought hit her, "If they find it, I'll make sure it'll kill'em."

Off the side of the greenhouse was the shed with her trophy snakes. She caught them, she bred them and she milked them. Mieke had a knack for getting venom out of the fangs of vipers and the Black Mamba was her favorite.

She put on her rubber gloves, grabbed a bottle of Mamba venom and in seconds she was back in the other room, ready to pour poison on the box with the golden coins and to soak the leather pouch holding the diamonds. A thought interrupted her, "How long will the poison last when it dries out and how effective will it be a year from now?"

From her desk in the 'snake room', she extracted a pamphlet and quickly scanned to the Black Mamba. The instructions about poison preservation used a lot of expensive and confusing words, like localized necrosis, enzymes, toxins, envenomation, etc., but she got the drift of it. All she had to do was mix the contents of a small bottle, showing a skull and bones on the label, with the poison and that would perpetuate the life of the potion through the development of protein. She didn't understand all of it, only that the venom would remain potent for a long time.

Careful not to spill any of the liquids, she poured them in a larger bottle over the sink and returned to the water buffalo in the next room. She poured the mixture over the cigar box holding the gold coins and into the leather pouch until the Eland skin was soaked, through and through.

Next, the board was screwed back on and the real task began.

The buffalo head weighed a ton, or so it seemed. She had planned to hang it in the den, but there was no way to get it over there by herself. In desperation she decided to hang it in the greenhouse right where it was, even though it would be terribly out of place.

"What the heck!"

A rope around a rafter helped her get it up and a chair on top of her workbench held it in place until she got some big screws through the board and into the wall. She stood back and looked at her handy work with satisfaction.

"Wait till I tell Eric."

She never got to tell him.
She was brutally murdered that night.

ISBN # 978-0-9822207-0-2

Excerpt from

Golden Nuggets

Flying east at 90mph, they soon were again over a desolate stretch of desert. Furmann figured this was his chance. He would have loved to throw the old sex freak out of the chopper alive from 1,000 feet and hear him scream all the way down. Wrestling with the door against the wind and heaving the sheik at the same time, might be dangerous for his own health, so instead he shot him through his forehead. The soft *plop* of the silencer couldn't even be heard above the engine noise, so nobody noticed. After undoing his own buckle, he freed up the old man, strapped his left leg against the rear seat and pulled the body down on the floor. Pushing the door as hard as he could with his shoulder, he slowly got the head through the crevice and little by little shoved the whole body out. He latched the door again and sat down, exhausted.

The pilot heard the commotion, but couldn't see what was happening, because he couldn't really look behind him. Jeff leaned forward and lifted the man's headset and hollered, "How's the gas?"

"We can't make it to Dubai. There's an Air Force base not far from here, I think I can reach that."

"How far is Dubai?" Furmann had to shout to be heard.

"About forty miles."

"I'll tell you what. See that abandoned house up ahead? That ruin out there along the road? Land there and we'll get out and hitchhike and you can fly back. Land behind the building so they can't see us from the road."

The pilot was not entirely stupid. "But sir, the land may not be suitable…"

"Don't worry about it. Put it down. Retard the throttle. *NOW!*" For emphasis, he shoved his pistol against the aviator's temple. "I said *NOW!* If you want to live, do it now, very carefully."

The aircraft slowed down and descended slowly toward a sandy spot behind a dilapidated building. There was no sign of life, only a lot of dust created by the rotor blades. He nearly had to land on instruments, his visibility became nearly nil. The chopper landed a bit hard, but safely.

"Turn the key off." The pilot obeyed, the engine stopped and so did his breathing as a bullet exploded in the back of his neck.

ISBN 978-0-9822207-1-9

ABOUT THE AUTHOR

Born in Belgium of Dutch parentage, Frits grew up along the German Border in Eastern Holland, enduring five years of German occupation and relentless bombing by the Allies.

This led to his first book, *Five Years Under The Swastika.*

At age twenty, the Royal Netherlands Air Force shipped him to the U.S. for training with the U.S.A.F., earning his wings in October of '53. After completing 'gunnery' in Arizona, the young pilots returned to their home country flying the F-84 Thunderjet. Result; *The Fun Of Flying*.

Upon completion of his military duty, Frits came back to America, this time as an Immigrant. After twenty years in the New York Metropolitan Area, Frits and his young family, (one girl, one boy,) moved to Tampa, Florida, where he became a General Contractor, which was the basis for; *Tampa Justice, No Money, No Justice*.

He stayed active in the flying business, maintaining a Commercial and Instructors' rating, flying with many Flying Clubs and the Civil Air Patrol.

On a trip to Arizona, he met his present wife Katy whom he married in 2000.

During Hurricane Ivan, they lost their home and most of their possessions and decided to spend the rest of their lives on a boat. They now live on a 51 foot Cruiser, where Frits hammers out his novels and they sing their hearts out with several choirs and entertainment groups. He visits his old Squadron and his many relatives in Holland on a yearly basis and lives a happy and active life, speaking, singing, boating and writing.